Emily H. Watson

Child-Life in Italy

A Story of Six Years Abroad

Emily H. Watson

Child-Life in Italy
A Story of Six Years Abroad

ISBN/EAN: 9783337420062

Printed in Europe, USA, Canada, Australia, Japan

Cover: Foto ©Andreas Hilbeck / pixelio.de

More available books at **www.hansebooks.com**

CHILD-LIFE IN ITALY;

A STORY

OF

SIX YEARS ABROAD.

BOSTON:

J. E. TILTON AND COMPANY.

1866.

TO ANNA,

FOR WHOSE ENTERTAINMENT MANY OF THE FOLLOWING PAGES
WERE ORIGINALLY WRITTEN,

AND

TO HER YOUNG BROTHERS AND COUSINS,

THIS VOLUME

IS

AFFECTIONATELY DEDICATED;

AND

TO ALL BETWEEN THE AGES OF FIVE AND FIFTEEN

WHO MAY BE

INTERESTED IN ITS CONTENTS.

To those whose early travels, pleasures, and pursuits are here recorded, this surprise — for so Christmas presents always are — of their published record will, at this interval, come as pleasantly and happily, it is trusted, as the recollection of those scenes has been happy and pleasant to their former teacher and affectionate friend,

THE AUTHOR.

Boston, U. S. A., 1865.

INTRODUCTORY.

THE value and interest of this little work, consist in its being a true record of events and incidents connected with the earliest days of the children of one of our most distinguished and lamented artists.

Residing always abroad, happily and favorably situated, with much that was pleasant and instructive to remember, we know not why they might not be entitled to the pleasure of possessing those early reminiscences in such a form, or why a volume of a child's travels might not be as useful and acceptable to the younger portion of the public as volumes of travels usually are to older persons.

Had there been, originally, any intention of publishing, much of a more dramatic nature might have been collected. But the volume has been composed principally of extracts from familiar letters written on the spot, in which little incidents relating to the children were casually recorded, with the dates, at the time of their occurrence; thus making a running journal of events. And, however simple these may be, it is hoped and believed that they will afford some interest and amusement to those for whom the work has been prepared.

From the variety of the reading, — some portions being adapted to the youngest reader, or even listener, and other parts requiring a maturer mind, — the author has ventured to include in the dedication both little ones and " children of a larger growth." She would not have desired to obtrude herself in a narrative almost exclusively of children; but being, besides their instructor, the very frequent companion of their walks and diversions, it would have been impossible, in general, to avoid frequently using the first personal pronoun, without rewriting much, or rendering the style more constrained and artificial.

Liberty, of course, has been taken in changing the names of the characters; and it is but proper to state that the work was prepared for publication, entirely without their knowledge; but it is believed that it will not be by them less agreeably received.

A companion volume of fairy stories and others, written also, in part, while the writer was abroad, will follow this.

The present volume commences with the return of the family to Italy after a visit of more than a year in America, the author going with them as private teacher to the children.

We left New York about the middle of July, but did not arrive in Rome until three months afterwards; the interval being passed principally in France and Germany.

TABLE OF CONTENTS.

SECOND YEAR.

THIRD YEAR.

FOURTH YEAR.

APPENDIX.

CHILD-LIFE IN ITALY.

FIRST YEAR.

CHAPTER I.

DESCRIPTION OF THE VILLA.

It was evening when we arrived in Rome; and on awaking in the morning, and looking out of the window, we found that we were in a beautiful villa,* which, although it was the middle of October, was still looking as green and fresh as at midsummer. A part of it near the house was a pretty flower-garden, where roses were still blooming, and dahlias, and other flowers. In the centre of the garden was an old mosaic pavement, with a beautiful fountain in the middle, the water dripping prettily over the edges; and around, on the garden-wall, were some great stone lions. Along by the house was a row of ancient marble statues, which

---

* A villa comprises, in general, the house and grounds of an estate. It may be of larger or smaller dimensions. This one was very extensive; and, besides the flower-garden, it was laid out principally in a vineyard and vegetable-gardens.

had been dug up from this very ground, where they had been buried under the earth for centuries; for, in all parts of Rome, statues have often been found so. Some of these had broken noses or broken limbs: still they looked fine and handsome, mounted on their tall pedestals.

In the villa, which extended to a great distance, were long avenues, affording delightful places in which to run, or roll hoop, or play ball; and along the avenue which led out to the street there was a row of orange-trees, with bright oranges upon them; and there were smaller paths, and walks bordered by pretty hedges,— all these making it a beautiful place for the children to stroll and play in every day.

And inside the house — but what a flight of stairs for going up to our parlor!— to our rooms, which were mostly on one floor, — eighty-seven solid stone steps! It was a grand old stairway if it *was* fatiguing to ascend it (but that was only at first; we soon became used to it); for this was once a palace, built by a pope, and was older than any town in the United States. It was about three hundred years old, and was built in fine style in those former times.

Our rooms were on one floor, or story; for such is the way most families live in Rome. They seldom occupy a whole house. The houses are generally so large, and contain so many apartments, they take but one suite of them, or one story. We had this house, however, mostly to ourselves; for no one else occupied it excepting the porter's family, who lived in the basement. But, for a few weeks in the spring and autumn, the gentleman who owned the house (and who was a prince *) came with his family, and took the suite of rooms on the first floor. Among these was a large and splendid hall with a solid stone floor, and hung all around with tall family portraits, where the children were allowed, when the prince's family was not there, to go and play on rainy days, when they could not go into the garden.

And *our* room — Nannine's and mine — was a nice cosey place (although a large room), with a warm, bright carpet on the stone floor, and the ceiling sweetly painted with lovely birds and flowers. There were two beautiful little wrought iron bedsteads, two large bureaus, a pretty walnut-wood dressing-table, with marble slab and mirror, and a large desk-table in the centre. Here Nannine had her lessons every day. It was the only room in the house, excepting the parlor, and the kitchen, of course, where there was a fireplace; for, in that mild climate, one does not need

* Prince M., distinguished as belonging to one of the oldest families in Italy. His oldest son (by a former wife), then a boy of twelve years, was cousin to the late King Charles Albert of Sardinia, father of Victor Emanuel.

fires all over the house in winter as one does in New England. But, in our room, we could have a bright wood-fire whenever we wished it; and how often, as Nannine sat warming her feet before she went to bed, did she ask me to tell her stories of "*home*"! Not *her* home, for she was born in Italy, and her sisters were born there; but my home in America, and of what I used to do when I was a child. No sooner was the door shut, and we were quiet by ourselves, than she would say, "Now tell me about home! tell me about Millo's!"

Millo's! the group of trees in the field where a thousand times we went, my sisters and I, and gathered leaves, and called them "people," and seated them all round for a dinner (a stone for a table, and leaves again for the plates and dishes), and pretended that they were eating; and the walnut-grove and grape-vine, and the bower at the end of the orchard, where we lay on the grass with a book, but watching the sky and the birds overhead, and taking in all the sunny enjoyment, — this was *my* happy home when a child; and Nannine liked to hear all about those things, as children in America like to hear about Italy and other foreign places.

Before going on with our daily pursuits, I will tell you a little more of our in-door life, and give a few other descriptions; and then you will see afterwards, from the journal which follows, what occurred from time to time.

During those short mornings of the autumn and winter, it was as much as one could do to get ready for breakfast at about eight o'clock. The children, Nannine, Gianina, and their little cousin Lulu, took breakfast with all the family. Little Lulu, with her papa and mamma, was with them that winter: but she and Gianina were but little more than three years old; so they were too young to have any lessons then. At ten, Nannine went with me to our room for her lessons, which she learned extremely well; for she was very fond of books, and liked to learn. At the end of a year, when she was between five and six years old, she had learned to read English so well, that she began Italian also. She already spoke it, so that in one more year she had learned to read that too. And then she began French; but, as she knew nothing about it before, it took two years to read and speak that well: at least, it was two years before she commenced another language.

At half-past one, the little girls had their dinner, and the rest of the family, if they wished it, took a lunch with them; and then all went out in one direction or another. Sometimes the children would go with the others, or with their nurse; but often they preferred to play in the villa instead.

2

At half-past five, we dined; and afterwards the children, they having had their supper at the same time, all came into the parlor, and their mamma would play for them on the piano, while they danced around in a ring; or they would have a great frolic with their papa until bed-time.

CHAPTER II.

THE MOUNTAINS AND CAMPAGNA.

I MUST describe the Campagna, and the mountains which we saw from our windows, — the beautiful, beautiful mountains, the Sabine and Alban Hills, so famous in ancient history. They are twelve and twenty miles distant; but you would not think they were more than three or four, they appear so near in the clear soft atmosphere. Sometimes, in the winter, their tops are covered with snow, which is beautiful in the distance, contrasting with the lovely blue of the hillsides lower down; but the snow lasts only a few days, when it melts and disappears, flowing down to fill the Tiber and other rivers. To this day, the Tiber, at certain times, overflows its banks, as it did in those days when the twins Romulus and Remus were placed in a basket, and thrown upon the water to drift along the stream; but, when the river sank again, they were left high and dry upon the bank.*

* See the companion volume,—Fairies of our Garden: Roman Stories.

These mountains I have described stand around the Campagna, on its borders, like a beautiful frame to a handsome picture.

And the Campagna? It is a great plain a hundred miles long, and thirty or forty wide, covered with green fields and gentle hills and pretty slopes. On this Campagna stands Rome, the old, old city, with its walls and streets, and many houses, spreading far and wide; and towering above them all is the splendid dome of St. Peter's. Very fine and beautiful the city looks, seen in the distance, with its many tall churches and towers, and the green Campagna near, and the beautiful blue mountains around.

From the mountains, the peasants come to plant and cultivate the fields on the Campagna. In many parts, this is very unhealthy; and they often become sick, and die. This is the reason that there are but few houses on the Campagna: only once in a while you see a farm-house, besides little shepherds' huts. Great flocks of sheep, however, are numerous; and it is delightful to see them roaming about. There are also great herds of splendid-looking cows and oxen. They are of a beautiful gray color, and are immensely large, with long, spreading horns, making them look most grand and stately. But the horses, the mules, and the donkeys that are used in carts, are often miserable little animals; so sorry and neglected, — being never washed, and never combed or brushed, — but appearing all the more picturesque and interesting just because they are so wretched-looking.

On all the roads coming into the city, there are many small, meek-looking donkeys; and you meet them everywhere in the streets with their loads on their backs. Sometimes the loads are immense: a large pack of wood, or fagots, strapped all around them, or a great bundle of hay covering them up, leaving but the head and fore-feet peeping out, — so funnily! And sometimes there is a huge bag, as large as the donkey, hanging over each side of him; while on the top may be mounted a man or a boy as sorry-looking as the little creature itself, as dirty and ragged, but appearing as contented as possible. They often go singing along, and frequently have a bright flower in their button-hole or on their hat; and sometimes there are flowers around the donkey's head.

When we were travelling through parts of France, Germany, and Switzerland, we saw all sorts of little animals used: any thing that had *four legs* and a *back* seemed to be put to some service. Even dogs were going around in little milk-carts. In Geneva, the little market-carts, with such little donkeys drawing them; the woman, with a great broad-brimmed hat, sitting in the cart, and half filling it, it was so small, — looked like children's play. At Lyons, the market-women·usually rode upon the little animal, which was sometimes not larger than a Newfoundland dog, with their panniers slung across; sometimes they walked by their side: in either case, it seemed like sport. Certainly our children at *home* would be delighted with such small equipages to drive around all by themselves; with real milk, eggs, and vegetables; and going from house to house, in play, as if they were real market-people!

There are many beautiful drives on the Campagna, and we often went to visit the ruins which are everywhere scattered about; ruins of old temples or tombs, which were made, many of them, more than a thousand years ago. One was a tower built by the first Roman emperor, the Emperor Augustus, more than eighteen hundred years since, or about the time our Saviour lived. It was of a round form, and built of brick; and the bricks are still strongly cemented together as if they would never fall to pieces. It is said that the emperor afterwards gave the slaves who built that tower their freedom. In those times, in Rome, all the great and wealthy citizens, and any who could afford it, had slaves; not black, but white men. A large portion of the common people were slaves. Sometimes, from affection, or for reward, the master would free a slave; and sometimes slaves would purchase their own freedom.

When St. Paul was seized upon, and made prisoner at Jerusalem, the captain of the soldiers who guarded him, being a Roman, — for they were Roman troops that were stationed in that city, as the French are now stationed in Rome, — was much surprised when St. Paul called himself a Roman citizen, and said that he himself had obtained that freedom only "by paying a great sum;" which shows that he had once been a slave.* St. Paul replied, that he was "born free." He belonged to one of the Roman provinces: therefore he had a right to call himself a "Roman," although he did not live in the city of Rome.

The slaves who obtained their freedom were called "freedmen," and could then live as respectably as any one, and often became the intimate and affectionate friends of their former masters. There is no such system of slavery now in Rome: it was done away with a long time ago.

On the great square in front of our house, a regiment of French troops was stationed. There were buildings or barracks in which they lived, and they drilled on the square. The French soldiers are re-

---

* This is thought to be the most probable meaning; for, although citizenship was sometimes purchased by foreigners, this was against the laws of Rome, and could usually be done only by bribery, or in a covert manner; and would not then have been likely to have been so readily acknowledged as in this case.

quired to be very industrious: they make their own clothing, mattresses, and such things. Sometimes there was a day for inspecting their equipments, to see if every thing was in a proper condition. The companies were arranged in order on the ground; and each soldier laid his knapsack down before him, and took every thing out of it, even to his comb and brush, placing them in the most orderly manner in front of him, to be looked at by the officers. They are obliged to keep every thing as orderly and neat as possible. Every day, their guns and accoutrements must be rubbed and polished like shining gold and silver. But the hardest work of all, one would think, must be the drumming, which the drummers have to practice,—not a thorough, hearty drumming, which there might be some pleasure or satisfaction in, but a little quick tap, tap, tap, one after another, as steady and precise as the strokes of a clock. It was so like machinery, regular and monotonous, that, before we knew what it was, we used to think it was a machine. And this low, steady, tap, tap, tap, the poor drummers had to practise two hours every day: we often thought they must be *so* tired! But it helped to make fine music when the whole band played together, each one having practised so thoroughly.

The soldiers exercised every day on the square or

piazza,* as they call it in Rome. The children were often entertained in standing at the window, and seeing them go through all their various manœuvres. Sometimes they would kneel, as if hiding behind a fence or barricade; and then cautiously raise their head as if peeping~over it. Then they would half rise, and move slowly and stealthily along like a cat creeping after a mouse. Often they ran in a line, one after another; or ran all together, dodging this way and that. It was very odd and amusing; and often, when they were drilling in squads, I was reminded of a story I had recently read in the "Life of Cyrus the Great" † (the same Cyrus who is mentioned in the Bible as restoring the Jews to their country).

This king had given a dinner-party one day to some of his officers, and they were relating to him their various experiences. One of them said that his soldiers were so stupid, he could not make them do as they should when they were drilling. At last, one morning, he told them very emphatically, that they must all "*follow the leader*," and do precisely as they *saw him do.* After they had been drilling a while, unfortunately he took a letter from his pocket, and gave it to the leader to carry to the post; desiring

* Pe-at-sa, pronounced.
† Abbott's History of Cyrus the Great.

him to "run with it" quickly. He did so; and immediately every soldier started after him, running with
all his might, to the great discomfiture and despair
of the captain!

CHAPTER III.

ANCIENT BATHS. — ST. PETER'S.

On the piazza stood a fine, noble church, very near us, where we liked often to go with the children; and their nurse took them there very frequently to walk about, and to see the pictures and the statues. You would not suppose it to be a fine church, seeing it only from the outside; for it is very plain, and looks quite as much like a barn as any thing. But when you had opened the door, and entered a few steps, it was like a grand and beautiful hall all before you, where you could walk up and down; for there was not a pew or a seat to fill up the space.

The light came in so softly through the windows, and it was so still and spacious there, it was a lovely place to visit. It was almost like a picture-gallery; for there were large pictures on the walls. There was seldom any one else there. But one morning, when we were in, there came a very beautiful boy of ten or twelve years of age, who went very quietly, and kneeled down a long time, saying his prayers softly to himself... At this moment, I remember an anecdote of two little children whom I know very well. The little girl, who was about six years old, was kneeling by the bedside to say her morning prayers. When she arose, her little brother, who happened to be in the room, and who was only four years old, exclaimed, " Why, Mamie ! you didn't say any thing."—" Oh, yes, Frankie ! I prayed to myself," was the answer. " Oh, how naughty that was, to pray to yourself! " said the little brother. " Mamma told me that we must pray only to God." And so the little sister had to explain to him that she did pray to God, but said the words softly, in her mind, " to herself." *

I was going to tell about this great church on the Square, and how it came there. It was designed by one of the great sculptors of former times, — Michael Angelo, who was also an architect. It was built among some ancient ruins, which he did not wish to destroy more than was necessary: so he took a large hall, which was a portion of the ruins, for the body of the church, and built the rest about it. Some of the great stone columns remain standing in the church, just as they were placed originally in the ancient building. These ruins were once baths, and covered the whole

---

* In the Bible, it is said of Hannah, the mother of Samuel, when she was praying in the temple, " She *spake in her heart: only her lips moved ; but her voice was not heard.*" — 1 Sam. i. 13.

piazza; for, in ancient times, the public baths, or bathing establishments, were on a very large scale, containing oftentimes libraries or reading-rooms, places of amusement, and so forth. The great hall, which now forms the body of the church, was a portion of one of these bathing establishments.

These baths were built fifteen hundred years ago by the Emperor Diocletian; and it is said that many thousand slaves, who had become Christians, were employed upon the work; and that afterwards, during a terrible persecution which arose, many of these slaves were put to death on that account: for the Emperor was not a Christian, although his wife and daughter are supposed to have become so, and also many who attended him in his palace, and some of the best and noblest persons in Rome. But the religion of the public was still the same system of heathen gods and goddesses that it had ever been. The Christian faith had not then been acknowledged by any of the emperors, although this was about three hundred years after our Saviour was born. Would not those Christian slaves or workmen, who had to suffer so much on account of their religion, have been happy, could they have looked forward, and seen that those very halls, which they were building for so different a purpose, would one day be turned into Christian churches?

The great church of the city of Rome, as is well known, is St. Peter's, which always appears beautiful, with its paintings on the walls, and its marble statues, and the pretty though big angels holding the fonts of " holy water." These angels are, in reality, as large as a man, although they do not appear so until you are very near them: the church being so large, they look small in the distance. Then there is the row of a hundred lights always burning day and night around the high altar, and the great bronze statue which is thought to have once represented a heathen emperor, but is now called St. Peter; and there are the many persons, young and old, rich and poor, monks, beggars, and all classes, who, as they pass, stop, and *kiss its toe.* There this statue has sat on its lofty chair for hundreds of years, I suppose, and received this homage, until the toe that has been kissed is half worn away.

There are vespers at the church two or three times a week, at four o'clock in the afternoon. On one of those afternoons, soon after we arrived in Rome, we went to hear them. The music is in one of the chapels, of which there are many in the church (a chapel, in one of these large churches, is a sort of apartment, or a smaller church, each with an altar in it). The singers are within this chapel, and many of the priests and high officers of the church are seated around, which leaves very little room for other persons; but the music is very fine, and crowds collect around the entrance of the chapel to hear it. St. Peter's will hold forty thousand people. What an immense church! But you would not suppose it to be so large until you have been in it many times, and discovered all the chapels and out-of-the-way places. Before coming in, we had seen hundreds, almost, entering: but when we ourselves had entered, there seemed to be scarcely any one there; for they directly disappeared among the different parts of the church; and, unless one is very careful, he might become separated from his friends, and be quite lost, and not able to find them again.

When you go up into the great dome overhead, you discover how very large the church is; for there are immense letters, printed in mosaic, around the walls of the dome, each as tall as a man, but which, while you were standing on the floor below, looking up, you could scarcely see, they were so small in the distance. And when you stand in the gallery that runs around the dome, seeing those letters larger than yourself close by you, and look down upon the people who are walking about beneath, they appear like small animals moving around, or like mere children. It is delightful going up into the dome of St. Peter's. One can ride upon a donkey, if one pleases; for the stairs are so gradual, each step so low, that a donkey can easily go up and down: and, if one is not very strong, it will save the trouble and fatigue of the long, long, winding way. Probably many persons go up and down on donkeys.

And when you go out upon the roof, how wonderful it is again! so spacious and extensive, — almost like a little village. You can imagine that the smooth places on the roof are paved streets, and that the smaller domes here and there are churches. There are enormous stone statues, too, on the parapets, which look like grand ornaments for the little town. And there are also rooms to live in quite like cottages, where some of the workmen stay; for there are always workmen attending to the repairing of the church. And there is a great reservoir of water always standing, with a long-handled dipper tied to it, where you can stop to drink.

And from the roof you can have a magnificent view, — the city with its houses, towers, and domes; the green country, and beautiful mountains at a distance; for the Church of St. Peter is the highest in the world excepting one, — the Strasburg Cathedral.

But, at this particular time, we did not go to ascend into the dome, nor to the roof of the church: we only went to hear the vespers, — the music. So we will return now to the entrance of the chapel, where crowds of persons were waiting, and we found it impossible to enter. It is very fatiguing to stand all the while for an hour or more outside the chapel; for, although one can hear the music there,. there are no seats: therefore what should we do?

The young gentleman who was with us happened to be acquainted with one of the priests, of whom there are always several about the church; and he went and asked him if he would be so kind as to allow us to go into a little gallery that was inside of the chapel, and where we could sit and see as well as hear. The priest very politely conducted us in, where we had a fine place opposite the choir, and could observe all the choristers, each with his white lace or linen surplice over his shoulders; and seated all along below were rows of little boys who officiate in the church, each with the crown of his head shaved, as all the priests have theirs, and wearing a little white, short, loose surplice,* with a black robe underneath. And there were dignitaries with handsome lace capes over black or purple gowns, and cardinals with a little scarlet cap on the top of the head.

When the singing commences, all is as still as possible; for it is a sacred service, and the music is beautiful, — different from any other that is heard, excepting in these Roman churches. Many persons are so fasci-

---

* This surplice is a loose white garment of lace or linen, reaching down to the waist, and gathered around the neck: it is made with sleeves.

8

nated with the music, that they consider it their greatest pleasure to go and hear the vespers at St. Peter's.
We also enjoyed it very much, and went whenever we
had an opportunity.

CHAPTER IV.

CHRISTMAS FESTIVITIES.

About a month before Christmas, the festival season begins, and then continues all winter. In the afternoons, the streets are full of animation, thronged with carriages and people. We, too, went about shopping, and looking for things for a Christmas-tree, which the children's mamma was going to have at her house. The shops were filled with the most beautiful toys of every description. Great tables and counters were set out in the middle of the floor, on which the things were spread as if all ready for a festival.

And, at this season, peasants come from the mountains with their bagpipes, and go about the city, and stand before the shrines * of the Madonna, which are often at the corners of the streets, playing their wild ditties or some sacred hymn.† They are dressed in curious style, in their country costume, with sugar-loaf hat, and an old brown cloak over the shoulders,

---

* Pictures of the Virgin Mary, set up in a little box, or frame.

† These peasants are called " Pifferari."

They have usually a little boy with them, with long curling locks, dressed in small-clothes, with little gaiters buttoned up to the knee, and a little pointed-crowned hat, adorned with a feather, on his head. Artists and painters often seize upon this little boy while he remains in the city, taking him for a model: he looks so like a picture, with his long fair hair and rosy cheeks. Many a time, when we went into a studio, we have met him with his sparkling black eyes, looking so roguish, yet taking hold of his good old gray-headed grandfather's hand, walking quietly by his side; and you could not but toss him a penny, he looked so pretty and good-natured.

On those evenings before Christmas, we often had entertaining times at home. Sometimes an Italian friend would come in, and, playing on his violin, would accompany the children's mamma on the piano, making beautiful music; and once a German gentleman, an artist, brought in some puppets, which he had made on purpose to amuse us. They were the funniest little creatures, made out of potatoes! A potato was painted for the head and face, and then a little body was dressed, and joined to it. They were arranged on a table, with a screen placed behind them; and behind the screen the gentleman stood, that he might not be seen: then, putting his hands through to manage them, he made them act a little comedy, going through all sorts of tricks and funny speeches. They were comical enough!

The Italians are very fond of plays and farces, and sometimes one was extemporized for our amusement; such as imitating a *foreigner* buying pictures and statues in Rome, making mistakes so very ludicrous in the language and all, that it made one laugh very heartily.

We were also very busy at this time making various little things for the Christmas-tree; such as pen-wipers, needle-books, pin-cushions, &c. There was to be quite a large party, and every one was to have a present. At length the evening came; and I wish you could have seen the beautiful tree! It was filled with presents; and all the American children were invited to come and receive them. There was something for each and for every guest. There were about twenty children, besides their parents and friends. It was in the evening, and every thing looked *so* beautiful!

The tall tree was a laurel, taken from the garden, and hung all over with oranges, also from the garden; large yellow oranges, some of them gilded (the laurel itself is not very unlike an orange-tree, with its deep-green, polished leaves). It was lighted with forty or fifty candles, placed in among the green leaves; and from it were suspended all the bright and gay things that were to be distributed. There were dolls and lovely baskets, and numerous pretty things.

When the company were assembled, and had looked at all the pretty gifts, there was then a dance in a ring, of a child and a gentleman or lady alternately. It was exceedingly pretty and delightful; and both great ones and little ones enjoyed it much.

When any of the artists came in, the children's papa led them up to the tree, and gave them some of the laurel-leaves. It is the same laurel of which the ancient Romans used to make wreaths and crowns. After a while, the presents were distributed; and such beautiful things to the children!—splendid toys, baby-houses, tea-sets, dolls, and bonbons of every description, in all sorts of fanciful styles. And shall I tell you what *somebody* received? A beautiful mosaic bracelet with a pin to match, and a little cross of green malachite, and a pretty china muff lined with silk, &c.

Then came refreshments; and afterwards every one departed, delighted with the evening's entertainment. Nannine went to bed fairly tired out with delight and pleasure, never having sat up so late before. Little Lulu and Gianina* had long been fast asleep.

I should have told you of Christmas Eve first of all, since that came before; for our tree was on Christmas *evening.* There was, on that eve, a beautiful ceremony, which is held every year in a church near us, the Santa

---

* G has the soft sound before the diphthong, as in the syllable *jah:* the second *i* has the sound of *e,* as if Gia-nee-na.

Maria Maggiore. The church was splendidly illuminated by thousands of candles. The Pope was there,
in a handsome dress; but we were too late to see him,
as there was a great crowd, and we only went in for a
short time after he had entered, and soon came away.
We saw the procession, however, up and down the
long nave, carrying the cradle, or piece of the cradle,
in which the infant Saviour was laid (as the Roman
Catholics believe). This is carried back and forth
through the church several times, that every one may
have an opportunity of seeing it. It is enclosed in a
pretty glass case; and the people in gay dresses,
and a guard of soldiers with their bright uniform,
stand around, making all look very handsome and
beautiful.

.   .   .   .   .   .

The ceremonies at St. Peter's, on Christmas Day,
are too long and magnificent to be described here: we
must leave such for larger books, and only say that the
Pope is carried through the church, in a chair raised on
poles, across the shoulders of four men, all dressed in
scarlet gowns; and on each side of him is carried an
immense fan of elegant ostrich-feathers. As he passes
along, he extends his hands, and blesses the people,
who kneel a little at his approach. He is a pleasant,
kind-looking old gentleman. The procession of cardinals and bishops and priests and monks, and the long

files of soldiers between which the procession passes, make a splendid show.

Nannine and her sister were too young to go to such scenes then; but they went when they were older. There was, however, a pretty festival of the Church, to which their good Italian maid Pina* liked to take the children every year: it is described in the next chapter.

* Pronounced Pē-na; a contraction of Giuseppina, — Josephine.

CHAPTER V.

FESTIVAL AT THE ARA CIELI.

TWELFTH DAY, the Epiphany, or Befani, as the Italians call it, is the grand day of the Christmas festivities; the day on which they make their presents, and not on Christmas Eve, or Christmas Day, as we do in America. There is a great fair then held in one of the public squares, where all kinds of things are to be bought, — little carts and horses, trumpets, drums, and dolls.

How noisy the square is with the many screeching trumpets! — almost every child buying one, and thinking he is making delightful music.

But the great festival of the day is that of the "Santissimo Bambino."* The Bambino is a carved wooden figure of the infant Jesus. It is richly dressed in silk and jewels, and is carried upright, in a procession which goes up and down the church. It is a great occasion; and crowds of people, who come in from the country around, fill the church. As the Bambino

* " Holy Child."

passes, they fall on their knees; for they think that this image performs miraculous cures : and, in time of great sickness in the city, it is carried around from house to house, and money is paid just as it would be for a physician. In a part of the church, the Ara Cieli, where the festival is held, a small stage is fitted up, with several figures in wax as large as life; namely, the three wise men and Joseph, with the Virgin mother, showily dressed in silks and laces, sitting in the centre. By her side is the manger with the infant Jesus; and a great ox or cow stands behind it.

And, besides, there is sometimes a sweet little *real* girl or boy of five, six, seven, or eight years, who stands before the Virgin and Child, reciting a pretty piece; his own, if the child be large enough, otherwise a piece learned by rote. Hans Andersen gives a very pretty account of one of these.* He says, —

"I was waked every morning by the bagpipes of the pifferari; and my first occupation then was to read over my lesson; for I was one of the children selected, 'boys and girls,' who ... were to preach in the church Ara Cieli, before the image of Jesus.

"I ... the boy of nine ... had had a rehearsal, standing upon a table. It would be upon such a one, only that a carpet would be laid over it, that we children should be placed in the church, where we, before

* In the Improvisatore.

the assembled multitudes, must repeat the speech, which we had learned by rote, about the bleeding heart of the Madonna, and the beauty of the child Jesus.

" I knew nothing of fear: it was only with joy that my heart beat so violently, as I stepped forward, and saw all eyes directed to me. That I, of all the children, gave most delight, seemed decided; but now there was lifted up a little girl, who was of so exquisitely delicate a form, and who had, at the same time, so wonderfully bright a countenance, and such a melodious voice, that all exclaimed aloud that she was a little angelic child. Even my mother, who would gladly have awarded to me the palm, declared aloud that she was just like one of the angels in the great altar-piece. The wonderfully dark eyes, the raven-black hair, the childlike and yet so wise expression of countenance, the exquisitely small hands, — nay, it seemed to me that my mother said too much of all these, although she added that I was also an angel of God.

" There is a song about the nightingale, which, when it was quite young, sat in the nest, and pricked the green leaves of the rose, without being aware of the buds which were just beginning to form. Months afterwards, the rose unfolded itself: the nightingale sang only of it, flew among the thorns, and wounded itself. The song often occurred to me when I became older:

but, in the church Ara Cieli, I knew it not; neither my ears nor my heart knew it!"

To such a pretty scene the children often went with their good nurse Pina.

It is.true that these ceremonies in the churches are fine shows; and often they are very beautiful, from the many bright-colored dresses, and gay soldiers all around, and picturesque appearances of every kind; and they are interesting also, from the enjoyment of the people, and the great earnestness and seriousness they manifest in what they are engaged in; as when the Bambino is carried up and down the church.

But it seems strange to us Protestants that they should believe that this can perform miraculous cures; for we never have been accustomed to think that an *image* is capable of such things. There is no doubt, however, that most of these persons really believe it; for it has been the faith of the country for very many years. And it is very possible that cures may sometimes be effected in this manner, — carrying it around from house to house; as often a little new excitement, or change of ideas, and a *hope* and *encouragement* of getting well, work wonders in sick persons; and, if they only have *faith* that they are going to be cured, this of itself puts them in the very best condition for being so, even if it were but *medicine* that they believed in.

And the "cradle" also, that was carried on Christmas Eve, the Roman Catholics believe to be a piece of the real manger in which the child Jesus was laid. We do not think so; for we do not suppose it to have been sufficiently thought of at the time to have been preserved. Besides, being of wood, it could not, probably, in the numerous changes that were occurring, have been kept and handed down for so many centuries, — almost two thousand years.

. . . . . .

It was now January, and the following extracts from letters, after the mention of the children, show the beautiful winter we were having. . . . "Yesterday was Nannine's fifth birthday. She has already made a good deal of progress in her lessons; is a bright, amusing little creature, and very capable; and, occupying the same room with me, is a great deal of company morning and night. She has been with the others in the garden, and has just brought me up a large purple anemone, 'because,' she says, I 'had not the pleasure of being there too.' . . . Every morning, after breakfast, we go into the garden, and stay an hour, and play about. Nannine's mamma and little sister and cousin go too. We sometimes pick up oranges that have fallen from the trees in the walk, and play ball with them. The children play horse, and have a hoop, which they are learning to roll; and they jump and

run, and gather flowers; for many flowers are blooming all winter, such as the violets, pansies, gillyflowers,
and some kinds of roses. The wall-flower and narcis-
sus and laurustinus began to blossom by the first of
January. The weather is very sunny and pleasant.
The green vegetables are growing all the time, and
make the garden look quite beautiful. There are
many, many birds among the bushes and hedges: they
are building their nests, and are beginning to sing very
pleasantly. The pretty little lizards too, which have
been hidden away for some time, are creeping out of
their little holes, and running about in the bright sun."

.   .   .   .   .   .

In February, the Carnival came; and what a merry
time it was! Day after day, the grown-up people
played and frolicked in the streets just like children.

Every day, about one o'clock, the sport begins. The
Corso, the long street of the city, was hung all along,
out of the windows, with gay-colored mats and carpet-
ing and drapery; and the sidewalks and doors below,
and the windows and balconies above, were filled with
people ready to look on, or take a part in the public frolic.
There were ladies in bright costumes, and gentlemen
in any fanciful dress that they pleased, and all sorts of
clowns and harlequins going through the street, the boys
following after them, and everybody laughing, and play-

ing funny tricks, and throwing *confetti* at each other (little balls of lime, white and small, like sugar-plums). Great baskets of *confetti* are for sale at all the corners of the streets, and are brought up into your balcony if you wish for them; and baskets filled with little bunches of flowers. What quantities of flowers! hundreds and hundreds of basketfuls are thrown about from one to another.

The gentlemen in the balcony above showered the *confetti* upon us; and, when that was gone, they poured upon us quantities of sugar-almonds, many of which fell into the street, as well as many bouquets which were thrown, to the great delight of the little ragged boys, who scrambled for them, and who were especially delighted when coppers were thrown down to them.

All, of course, are good-natured, let happen what will, — even with a whole quart of the white, flowery lime-pease, thrown right into their faces, and on their heads, and all over their coats. They only look up, and shrug their shoulders, and turn away and laugh, and try to do the same to some one else.

Then, after everybody has had a great deal of sport all the afternoon, about sunset comes the great excitement of seeing horses race through the street. The carriages are all cleared away, and every one is made to stand close upon the sidewalks, that they may not

be run over; and then from one end of the Corso, when
the signal is given, nine or ten horses start to run.
They have gay trimmings about them; and, having no
rider on their back, they dart by almost with the swift-
ness of lightning; and the horse which arrives first at
the other end of the Corso is the victor. The race is
a mile long, and the horses really look quite handsome;
and it is very exciting to see them pass by so swiftly.
Every night, while Carnival lasts, the same horses run
in the same manner.

On Sundays and Fridays there is no Carnival, but
all the rest of the time it grows merrier and merrier
every day, — it seems as if people were wild with sport,
— until the last day, which is more merry than all;
for, after the horse-race, the "Moccoli" begin. These
are little lighted torches, which every one takes in
their hand, and tries to keep burning, while everybody
else tries to put them out. So, when you have taken
great care, and think you are quite secure, and that
nobody can touch your light, all at once, before you
know it, comes a great handkerchief flapping over it,
putting it out in a moment! Then you try to get it
lighted again, and you have such a time! Some one
blows it on one side, and somebody else blows it on
another; or, when you have succeeded in getting it
safely lighted, you think you will slyly blow out some
one else's; and lo and behold! when you turn round,

some one has thrown a huge wet towel perhaps over yours, and put it all out again! Then you get a long pole, and fasten your torch to the end of that, thinking you will keep it far out of anybody's reach; but again, before you know it, some one has got a pole longer still, and has dashed yours all down!

Still every one is as good-natured as can be; and, when his light is extinguished, he calls out, "Senza moccolo, senza moccolo!"—"No light, no light!"

It is so beautiful a sight to see these lights all dancing about, the whole street filled with them, and all the carriages and windows and balconies! After an hour or more, the people, tired out, begin to drop away, calling out, "The Carnival is dead, the Carnival is dead!" and soon the street is cleared. Those who wish go to the opera or the masquerade-ball,—when there is one,—and this is the end of the week of frolicsome sports in the street; and then come on the forty quiet days of Lent.

From the next chapter, we follow the journal, or diary.

4

CHAPTER VI.

SPRING AND SUMMER.

MARCH 13. — All winter, the children were in the habit of going into the garden to play directly after breakfast; but they have long given it up, as it is too sunny and warm there now in the mornings. Instead, we go into the street, and walk an hour on the shady side of it. The hyacinths with many other flowers have been in full bloom in the garden. The perfume from them is very strong. Nannine brought up a bouquet of them the other day, and we had to put them outside of the window; and even then, when we went towards them, the scent was quite strong enough to be pleasant.

We have had a box of earth placed in our window, and planted with morning-glories and sweet-pease and mignonette and china-asters. The seeds all came from America, although they have all those plants here too. The vines and flowers will look so sweet about the windows when they are grown! Far down below our window, in a little yard near the basement, is a family of hens, which we often pet by throwing them something to eat. We like to hear them cackling and crowing, it sounds so like the country; and sometimes the good porter's wife, who takes care of them, brings us in some fresh eggs for breakfast.

One of the favorite calls of the children often, when we are walking out in the morning, is at a yard of hens and ducks, geese, turkeys, and peacocks, which all live very lovingly together apparently. We have never seen any trouble among them; and so they are quite entitled, we think, to the name of the "Happy Family." The great door of their yard is always open into a passage-way, also with *its* door always wide open, and which leads directly into the street; and yet we have never seen them straying out. We think them a remarkably contented, well-behaved set of fowls. They have a good space to move about in, plenty to eat, I suppose, and a fountain of water always trickling for them; all which, perhaps, tends to keep them in such good heart and spirits. The peacock is a handsome creature, with his long, splendid, trailing feathers. Three pea-hens, *without* the showy tail, accompany his lordship; but he does not seem to be a very gallant bird: he appears not to take any notice of them at all; which is not treating them quite civilly, in our opinion.

.   .   .   .

April. — The children have a new, sweet little baby-sister; a lovely little thing!

In the afternoon, Nannine, Gianina, and Lulu, all three went with me to walk down town. On our return, when we came into the villa, we found the prince and princess (who own the house) there with their three children. They had been walking in the garden, as they often do; and when their little daughter, who is four years old, saw our little girls, she came running down the avenue to meet them, and give them a bunch of flowers she had been picking. Then the prince came up, and inquired about the baby, and asked what was her name (she was almost a little "May" flower; and in this book, when she becomes old enough, we shall call her "Memie"). . . .

Although it is now only April, the weather is like June in America; and the country is looking very rich and beautiful. Every thing is full of life. Numerous little lizards are running about the garden walls; and the fountains and reservoirs are full of frogs, which croak from very happiness day and night, joining the chorus of the birds which fill every tree.

Some nightingales have made their nests in a hedge of laurel-trees near the house, and sing all night very sweetly near our window.

The following letter tells more about the nightingales:—

Rome, April 15, 185-.

My dear M., — It is about nine o'clock in the evening; and the nightingales, as usual, have begun their singing for the night. They sing during the day, but stop about sunset, — I suppose, to rest themselves, — and then begin again about this hour. Their song is very sweet, and I hear it almost as plainly in my room (certainly I should quite if the windows were open) as if I were out of doors. They sing all the time they are sitting upon their eggs, day and night. Their note is nearly or quite as loud as the robin's; not long, but very sweet and liquid and musical. Part of it is a sort of whistle. I presume they enjoy the bright moonlight nights; for their song does not seem to me mournful as we have usually heard that it is. Indeed, it seems rather cheerful, — especially in the evening, when almost every thing else is still, — and as if their little souls were full of joy. It is delightful to hear them.

I believe the nightingale is not very common in the city, but they have them in the country; and our large villa back of the house is just like the country. I dare say the birds deceive themselves, and think they are far away from many people; for there are thousands of them, thrushes and sky-larks, in the trees and hedges. The poor little thrushes get shot sometimes. We often have them for dinner (not *our own;* at least, not to our knowledge) : they are bought in the market, and cost very little, — about three cents a piece.

The little larks too — they are such mites of birds when dressed for the table! they look very pretty; but I think they are too small to be eaten.

Perhaps you would like the little innocent-looking lizards that run about in the grass and on the walls. They are pretty little creatures: some are cunning little ones, all green; and others are brown and striped. The children often try to catch them; but they are too swift. They dart into their holes the moment you put out your hand to touch them; but, by whistling, you can make them stop perfectly still. It seems to be a sort of charm for them, and they turn and look at you with their little bright eyes; and their little heart, which you always see panting quickly when they are suddenly startled, goes quieter and quieter, as if they enjoyed the sounds.

. . . .

April 23. — This morning, we gathered wild-flowers in the villa, — daisies, buttercups, &c., like those in America.

The orange-trees are now covered with their beautiful buds and blossoms, and the whole avenue is fragrant with them. The sun is very hot, and we avoid walking in it almost as we would in a pond of water.

But a fresh wind springing up frequently makes the shade comfortable.

May 9. — We have had strawberries for a fortnight, and now have cherries.

May 31. — This morning, Nannine went with me to the Gesù, one of the great churches in Rome, where there was some grand music, and a beautiful illumination too; for every day during this month they have candles lighted around the high altar, — beginning with a few, and increasing the number every day, — until, at the last day, it becomes a splendid illumination.

Before the candles were lighted, there was some magnificent music on the organ. Then there was quite a long sermon; and, while the congregation were turned towards the preacher, the candles were being lighted behind them; and when the sermon was over, and they turned round again towards the altar, it was all sparkling with light, — just like a magic scene. Then there was more beautiful music for half an hour, and all the time the people were kneeling.

While we sat listening to the music, we thought two or three times that we heard thunder, but concluded it was a sound of the organ. When we came out of the church, sure enough, it was no make-believe. The sky was darkened; a few drops began to fall; and we had just time to take the last carriage on the square, when the rain came down in a perfect sheet of water, and there were hail-stones as big as large peas! In five minutes' time, the streets were like running rivers, and our poor horse looked drenched through and through; but we could not help it. All we could do was to keep the boot close around us (for it happened to be a little, one-horse cariole, which was all we could get), that we might not get thoroughly drenched also. In a quarter of an hour we were landed safe at home, although quite wet. I think I never saw so heavy a shower, and it was the first we have had this season.

How obliging the driver was through all that hard rain! He might almost have refused to take us home until it was over; but we did not know that the shower was going to be so heavy when we started, or we might have waited somewhere.

June. — The children have had to part with their dear little cousin Lulu, whose society they have enjoyed so much all winter. She has gone home to America with her papa and mamma. She learned to understand and speak Italian very nicely while she was here, almost as readily as she spoke English, — and French too; for she speaks both, although she is only four years old. Her own nurse was an English woman: but little Lulu picked up Italian playing in the nursery with the children, who frequently used it in their play; and their Italian maid was almost always there, who spoke no English, excepting a few words that she picked up when she went with the family on a visit to America the year before, and which she would use sometimes *so* funnily! This good nurse Pina was very lively with the children. She generally took them out to walk in the afternoon; and in the nursery she would play with them, and amuse them by singing, and telling stories. This was a very good school, too, for little Lulu, in learning the language; and although it was some time before she was willing to speak Italian out of the nursery, in presence of the rest of the family, before she went away she had learned to speak it very well.

How sorry were the children — and we all were — to have their dear uncle, and sweet aunt, and little cousin, go away, we had had such a delightful winter with them all!

Lulu had a fine baby-house at home, filled with all sorts of dolls; and, just before she went away, I made her a little doll's cradle to put into it, to remind her of us. It was really quite pretty, made of pasteboard, about six inches long, stuffed with cotton to make it soft and to give it a handsome shape, covered with pink *de laine*, and lined with silk; and it had little rockers to rock like a real cradle. It was thought to be quite a "triumph of *genius*."

It is now summer; and the dining-hour has been changed from five to two o'clock, and the two little girls dine with the whole family.

The sun is so hot, that we cannot go out excepting very early, and towards sunset: so, to get a little more exercise in the open air, Nannine goes out with me before breakfast; and we walk an hour or more, and find it very healthful. And then between five and six in the afternoon we go into the garden, and the children play; their mamma and I strolling about, and reading or working, and talking or playing with them: and their papa, after his work, often comes and joins us; and then the children have a fine time walking and playing with him, if he is not busy walking and talking with their mamma.

Often we drive out on the Campagna, and ramble about among the green fields, picking daisies, which Gianina and Nannine are very fond of doing.

And the dear baby!—I remember me, I have said nothing of late of the little one, now three months old; a good, bright, pretty little thing; indeed, an "uncommonly fine" child! She begins to laugh, and to take notice of things.

On the *Fourth of July*, we were all to go into the country, to Albano, to spend the day. But poor baby had been vaccinated, and was so sick and feverish that day, that she could not be taken; and mamma could not leave her to go: so none of us went. The baby is quite well now.

July 20.—Just as I was writing, the children's mamma called me to go down street with her to buy a hat for the baby. We walked down, and found a lovely one of white and pink silk; and then we took a carriage on the square to come home.

We had not driven far, when we were stopped in one of the streets by the *cortége* of the Pope, which was approaching. One of the escort, an officer on horseback, rode forward, with a drawn sword in his hand, to clear the way; for the Pope's carriage was just behind. He was returning from the country, where he had been spending a month. There were about twenty or twenty-four gentlemen of the "Guardia Nobile" for escort,—who always accompany the Pope when he drives out,—mounted on horses, and looking very handsome in their riding-suit, which is dark-blue, with gold trimmings and long boots. They came first; and then the Pope's carriage, with four elegant black horses. We had a fine chance to see him, as he sat by the window of the carriage, looking very cheerful and happy.

We had to wait on the side of the street while the *cortége* passed. They drove quickly by; and, though it was soon over, it was a beautiful show,—the many horses were so spirited, and the gentlemen, all of whom belong to the nobility, were so elegant in their appearance!

While the Pope was in the country (at Castel Gandolfo), the King of Naples brought his baby to him there to be christened.

.   .   .   .

The following letter to a little girl mentions among other things a visit that we were then thinking of making into the country: —

JULY 18.

DEAR LIZZY, — ... I have not written before that we are having fresh figs, which, I dare say, you would think very delicious, and like better than I do, as you have such a sweet tooth. I like them better, however, than I did; and probably I shall soon be as fond of them as every one here is. The natives of warm climates, I believe, are always fond of them. The apricots and peaches are very good.

Next week we are going to Albano for a few days, a town twelve miles from Rome. Then we shall spend the time in making excursions to the neighboring towns, and to Lake Nemi, which is very beautiful. All the rides are taken on donkey-back, and we are anticipating great pleasure. . . .

The model for one of the great statues of the Richmond Monument has just been finished by the children's papa. It is now to be cast in bronze, and must be sent for that purpose to Munich, which has the greatest bronze foundery in Europe. There are to be six statues of some of our celebrated men, besides an equestrian statue of Washington. They are all twice as large as life, and will look very grand indeed. When it is completed, this will be the most splendid monument in our country. I hope you will one day see it; for those great and good men who so faithfully served their country deserve to have a memorial that every one can see, and through which one may learn to admire them.

. . . .

Rome is the city of artists; and very often we go into the studios of the sculptors and painters to see their many beautiful works, — marble statues and paintings. The children like very much to get clay, and model it into little figures, as they see their papa do.* They will sit almost a whole afternoon with an

---

* A model of his work in clay is the first thing that a sculptor makes. He forms it completely, just as he wishes to have the finished statue. A mould or cast of this clay figure is then taken in plaster of Paris; and finally a *fac-simile* of the plaster cast is made in marble, if that is to be the material of the finished work. The marble figure might have been copied immediately from the clay, only that the clay cannot be preserved long enough: it dries and cracks. It is necessary, therefore, to put it into the more enduring material of plaster.

apron on, and a little table before them, making all sorts of things; not minding at all their clayey, blackened fingers. And the little Italian boys in the streets will take a piece of clay, and model it into a little animal — a dog or a cow — very nicely indeed, and so readily! We have sometimes seen them working or playing thus out doors on the sidewalks.

•　　•　　•　　•　　•　　•　　•　　•　　•　　•

CHAPTER VII.

EXCURSIONS IN THE COUNTRY.

IMAGINE us on a bright Monday morning, a week ago, all packed into a vettura (a common carriage or carryall), driving along the Via Appia, across the green Campagna, twelve miles, to the town of Albano.

How fresh and pleasant the air became as we arrived near the hills, the Alban Hills, — those very hills where the "long, white city" was! * And we were going to the very town that stands near the site of the old Alba, where were born the twins that were thrown into the Tiber; and who, after they were grown to be large boys, were taken back to live in Alba again with the king their grandfather. And there were other interesting events connected with Alba; for here lived the *triplets*, the Curatii, who contended hand to hand with the Roman *triplets*, three brothers at a birth, the Horatii. In this contest, the Romans were victors; and, after a while, the city of Alba itself was

* See the companion volume, — Fairies of our Garden: Roman Stories.

conquered and destroyed by the Romans, and the people were made to leave their homes, and wander — whole families, fathers and mothers and children — across this very Campagna that we were travelling over, to go and live in Rome. This helped to make Rome so large a city as it was in ancient times.

Well, we came to this old town, Albano, among the mountains, or near the mountains; for it is on the slope of a hill, and so old a town! It looks dark and dingy with age. The streets are narrow, and the houses built close together; so close, it is almost like one long house.

It seemed as if everybody was in the street; not only men, but women and children, — without any bonnets on their heads, — as if they were all living together, one family: they looked so sociable and unceremonious! And the houses — they appeared to have no windows; or the lower stories, at least. There was only the door to let in the light; and you did not wonder that the people should like to be out in the bright open air, instead of in those dark rooms. And the streets — they seemed full of every description of litter; but sometimes, in the mornings for instance, they were swept up a little.

But it was all delightfully interesting, every thing was so wonderfully different from the life we see " at home;" that is, in America, where almost every thing has a fresh, new look. This town is as many as two thousand years old; and probably it looks almost exactly as it did in those old days when Pompey, Cæsar, and Cicero, and all those celebrated men, were living, and came into the country often to pass some time in their beautiful villas : for Pompey the Great had an elegant villa in this place, which is now the Doria Villa. It is at present a sort of wild grove, but a beautiful place to walk and play in among the shady trees; and we often went there, for it was near the hotel where we stopped. There are some brick walls remaining, which are the ruins of Pompey's house, and the cellar, as the boys* told us, where he used to keep his *wine*, with a rough-carved stone lion on the side of the steps that go down to it. On the roadside, before we come to Albano, is a large stone tomb like a tall tower, where Pompey is supposed to have been buried. It is very near; and, when you are in the villa, you can see it through an opening in the trees.

How interested Nannine was in hearing the story of Pompey the Great!—how he cleared the Mediterranean Sea of the pirates that infested it in those days, troubling all the vessels that came along. In three months he had conquered them (and there were thousands), and compelled them to give up their ships; and then he

* Our friends the C.'s, who were spending the summer at Albano.

5

transported them to towns upon the land, where they might live respectably, or, at least, not trouble the seas any more.

Pompey married the daughter of the great Julius Cæsar, which kept those two distinguished men in harmony while she lived: but, after she died, they remained friends no longer; for each wished to be master of Rome. After a long conflict, Pompey was defeated at the battle of Pharsalia, and afterwards sailed in a vessel to take refuge with the King of Egypt. After bidding adieu to his affectionate wife Cornelia (who was his last wife, and was on board the vessel with him), he entered a little boat which was to carry him from the vessel to the shore; but upon reaching it, and being all ready to step upon the land, he was cruelly betrayed and murdered. Although surprised as he was, he remained calm and dignified; just drawing his cloak about him, and making no resistance. There was no one to take care of his remains but a faithful freedman, who had been his slave, but whom he had made free. He took them to his master's loving wife Cornelia, who laid them in the tomb we have mentioned, and which *she* built for them, near the villa, in Albano, which Pompey had loved so well.

.   .   .   .

During the week, we made several excursions to the towns and places in the vicinity. We spent a day at

Gensano; and there was the lovely Lake Nemi! a beautiful little lake; so deep in the crater of a volcano (as it was once), that it looks like a little nest of water. The ancients called it the " Mirror of Diana," it was so pretty and sparkling; and all the region round about was sacred to Diana. On the border of another lake (Albano) are the ruins of some baths called the "Baths of Diana." Some of the small stones of the old mosaic pavement are still preserved; and, when we visited there, we picked up some to bring home with us : also pretty green maiden-hair grows all about the floor of the baths.

The day we passed at Gensano we spent in a lovely villa on the very banks of this pretty lake, Diana's Looking-glass; so that we could go through the garden walks, and stand right over its polished surface; and, had we been as beautiful as Diana, we might have been pleased to look at ourselves in it as she did.* As it was, we could think of nothing but the beautiful villa. How lovely it was with its garden, — an English garden, full of flowers, — and its beautiful white swans sailing in the pond! These swans came and ate out of our hands. Then there was a pigeon-house filled with pigeons and doves, and a pretty English cottage, which seemed so like *home*, with its nice carpeted floors and furniture. The secret of it is, the place be-

* See Fairies of our Garden.

longs to a duke who married an English lady ; and I suppose she likes to have these things after the English style.

The duke and duchess live in the cottage in the winter; but in the summer they remove to the great stone palace close by, which is cooler, and let the cottage to any one who likes to take it. Some friends of ours are occupying it this summer, which is the reason why we were there to pass the day. They have a sweet little girl, two years old, with golden, fairy-like curls,— so like a little niece I left at home in America, that I thought she was the prettiest little ornament of the cottage; as indeed she was. They have a boy too, Thomas, eight or ten years of age; and, during the morning, the eldest son of the duke, a boy about the same age, with a sweet face, modest and pretty, came in to return a book, and get "Tom" to go and visit him a little while. The book he had been reading was Cooper's "Spy," in which he had been much interested; but he was to read "no more novels at present." The little duke has a younger brother, who is named George Washington ! . . .

At another time we went to Castel Gandolfo, where the Pope spends the summer; and saw his cool-looking summer palace, with the avenues of trees that lead up to it.

Another excursion was to a monastery, on the banks

of the Lake Albano, where the good fat monks came out to meet us, dressed in their brown gowns, with the hood hanging down behind. They showed us all around the garden, and pointed out the beautiful views; for the monastery stands high, and overlooks a great extent of country. And then they took us into the great hall of the monastery; and one went to a cupboard and brought out a flask of wine, and treated us with wine and water so politely! We thanked the monks for their kindness, and took our leave of them; and then, returning, what a pretty, pretty road it was on the border of the lake, with shrubs and bushes often meeting overhead! and there was a beautiful sunset over the water.

These excursions were made on donkeys,—the dear, good-for-nothing little fellows! Nannine's donkey proved to be rather vicious; for, in coming home, he threw her off. Then I changed with her; and what should he do, the first thing, but throw me off too, as if he had been determined that no one should ride on *his* back! I would not try it again, but suffered him to go along by himself; and I walked the rest of the way, and reached home almost as soon as the others did: for the little lazy things do not go much faster than one can walk; and they *will* be stopping to get a nibble of grass as they go along, and sometimes you can hardly make them go at all. How amused you would be to see us each mounted and setting off, with a man or boy to almost every donkey, following behind, to drive him and keep him going! for all that one can do with the reins and whip has but little effect. Then, if the donkey-boy should lag behind, your donkey will be sure to go off to the side of the road, and make quite a good meal of the mouthfuls of grass he snatches, as if it were the most proper thing in the world to be done. He never thinks that he has got to carry the rider on his back anywhere; that never enters his mind: but he just takes his comfort as he goes leisurely along, unless the boy with a big stick reminds him that he has something else to do.

But they are *so* trusty when you come to a steep, rocky place, and they put their steady little feet so exactly in the right spot, and take you so safely through a dangerous or difficult pathway, that you cannot help loving them, seeing how faithful they are. And then they are so intelligent; always seeming to know just which path you are to take out of several diverging ones! We never could understand how it was that they always chose precisely the right one, when *we* could see no difference between one and another; and, when we asked the driver for an explanation of it, all he could say was, shrugging his shoulders, "They know; they know!"

CHAPTER VIII.

AUTUMN.

WE all enjoyed our week in the country very much; yet it is pleasant to be in Rome again. There are so many interesting things to be seen, and we have had such a beautiful summer, with clear, bright, sunny weather, though exceedingly warm! We have kept ourselves comfortable by remaining in the house during the heat of the day, going out only very early in the morning, and towards sunset.

From many of our windows we have only a country view, with no sight or sound of the city excepting the bells (which are ringing a great portion of the time), and the drums of the French soldiers on the Square in front of the house. All day long, in the many trees, the birds are as merry as they can be.

None of us have been ill, — not even the children, with the exception of Gianina, who was very slightly so for a day or two. She took a little cold standing at the open window one morning, before she was dressed, to see the soldiers on the Square. All our friends in the country think they had better have staid in Rome too. The Americans who have remained in the city, the artists, &c., are going to have a picnic soon at Lake Nemi; but we do not go, as we have been there so recently.

We may expect the "rains" in two or three weeks; for in the latter part of summer, and beginning of autumn, there are usually a few weeks of rainy weather.

Aug. 31.—The "rains" have come on. They last about two or three weeks at this time of the year, and are the breaking-up of the hot season.

Sept. 10, Wednesday.—It is very clear, but cool enough, this morning and evening. We have had some very heavy rains of late. It never rains all day; but the rain comes in showers. We always get our walk morning or evening.

Last Monday was a grand festa of the Madonna, at which the Pope officiated, in the Church of Santa Maria del Popolo. So after breakfast, Nannine and I got ready, as usual, for our walk; intending to go down to see the procession. There was so much blue sky, and the clouds were so light, we had given up the idea of its raining; but we had not reached the *Capolecase* (street) when a heavy peal of thunder brought some sprinkles, and we had but just stepped into the nearest *portone* (doorway) when the whole shower came down. We were forced to stay there half an hour, the street running with rivers.

When the shower was over, we stepped out from the *portone* to go in pursuit of a carriage in which to return home; and at the same moment a hack stopped opposite the door, out of which jumped a priest and another gentleman; and, as they very politely offered it for our accommodation, we were glad to accept it, and turned in it homeward. Thus ended our walk, and sight of the festa, for that time; but, towards evening, the children's mamma and I got a good walk on the Quirinal,* meeting throngs of people in their gala-dresses.

This will give you an idea of the rainy season in Rome. Anywhere else I should not call it a rainy season, as there are intervals of two or three days, when there is no rain, not even showers.

Oct. 8. — Our baby is just six months old, and is sitting alone to-day for the first time. She is a dear little thing, — good, fat, pleasant, pretty, sweet. But we can scarcely ever get her even for a little play, there are so many who want her, — the nurse and the other women, mamma and papa, and all. We did, however, succeed, Nannine and I, in giving her her first little lesson in sitting alone this morning; but over she rolled once or twice upon the carpet!

We are going to make her *so* accomplished! differ-

* A street not far from our house, where the Pope has a palace, in which he lives a portion of the year.

ent from the Roman babies, who, I think, hardly ever sit alone; and they never creep. As soon as they are four or five months old, they have a string put round their waists, and are dangled along by it; the points of their little toes just touching the ground. And, when their mothers wish to go away and leave them, they hang them, by the string, over the pommel of a chair, letting their feet just reach the floor! When they are large enough to bear their weight, they are placed standing in a little wicker-work frame, with a shelf for playthings; so that the poor little things never know the pleasure there is in creeping about upon all-fours! Almost before they are large enough, they are made to walk by means of leading-strings; so that their feet and ankles often become weak and bowed. Of course, these are the children whom one sees at all tines in the streets and doorways; but even those better cared for are not allowed to creep as children do in America. *Our* baby is going to creep like an English or American child; and she is not going to be made to walk until she is strong enough, and takes to it all of herself!

You would be amused to see how funnily the young babies here are wrapped up. They are all bound round with bandages, feet and all, exactly in the shape of a mummy, or like the Indian pappoose, until they are large enough to have the leading-strings, which is at three or four months old. When they are two or three years old, they are put into school. Often do we pass some door where there is a school of these little children. It is just a room of the house, with small chairs placed around, where the children are seated, and kept quiet. As soon as they are able, they learn to knit and sew, and perhaps to read a little. The door of the room is always open, so that we can see the little things as we pass by; and they seem to be quietly kept there out of mischief, while their mothers are at work. . . .

We have attended lately an exhibition of a girls' school kept by some French ladies. A young Italian girl whom we know, Carlotta, a neighbor of ours, belongs to it. She and her family invited us to go: so Nannine, Gianina, and myself walked down with them, about three o'clock in the afternoon, and found ourselves the first visitors there; but this only gave us the better chance to inspect the various articles of workmanship on a table, with the names and ages attached of the pupils who wrought them. It was really surprising, the quantity and quality of the work done by little creatures five, six, and seven years of age. And the more remarkable it seemed, when we saw these little butterfly-looking children, all dressed in the highest style of theatrical taste; for the performance was scarcely any thing more or less than a little *theatre.*

In the mean time, *we* and the household (consisting of several lady-teachers, French and Italian) undertook to make ourselves very agreeable to each other; and they were all charming, polite, and friendly, as all the ladies here are. Presently the room was completely filled with spectators, sitting one before another; and the little fancifully-dressed actors had taken their stations behind a curtain, which was suspended across one end of the room, and was undrawn and drawn at the beginning and end of every performance.

They began with little dialogues and recitations, just as is common at such exhibitions in America; but these were generally of a more dramatic character, and the little performers gesticulated and attitudinized exactly like grown persons who have been trained upon the stage. Then there were several fancy-dances, the Cracovienne, Salterella, &c., by one or two at a time; two violinists being placed within the charmed circle.

In the midst of it all, one of the youngest and most interesting of the children was dancing alone; a little thing of four or five years. The audience were as still as mice, gazing intently; for the little girl was dancing in a sweet, child-like, graceful way: but, when the exercise was nearly finished, all at once her infantile but earnest little voice broke out with, "My shoe is coming off!" This, of course, brought her up suddenly *all standing!* Every one burst into laughter, it was so comical as well as sweet and pretty; but the poor little thing was quite abashed by it. She was so confused and distressed, that one of the teachers ran to her, kissed, and re-assured her; but, although she did not cry aloud, the tears were starting from her little eyes as she went on with the most serious air to finish the dance.

Then came more *acting;* but, as it was getting late, we were forced to leave. We heard that they had a grand dance of all the children together in the evening; and the bishop was there, and distributed presents to the best scholars.

SECOND YEAR.

CHAPTER I.

WINTER-TIME.

CHRISTMAS, this year, was as beautiful as the last. But how fatigued we were, working for the tree! and, although we made but a very few things, it took a good deal of time.   Almost all the presents were purchased, however; and only the children had them this year.   We really enjoyed going into the shops for them, just to see the beautiful things; for they were filled with elegant toys and knicknacks of every description.

The tree was very prettily improved by having underneath (on the top of the box in which it stood) a little landscape arranged. Small stones for rocks; green moss for grass and trees; pieces of looking-glass placed here and there for water; little lakes and ponds, a little rustic bridge spanning them; a little Swiss cottage, which, for size, was exactly in keeping; and some of the small Swiss animals carved so beautifully in wood, — all looked quite natural; and the whole thing was quite a success. (This was the work of a dear friend of the children's mamma.)

January. — Through December, the weather was cold. The ground froze at night, and ice remained on the sides of the streets for several hours in the day. Some of the fountains — among them ours in the garden — had long solid icicles hanging from them for a few days. But now, since January has come in, it is all spring-like, as balmy and exhilarating as possible, like the warm days of May in New England. The birds have been singing, too, for some days; and Gianina has just brought up from the garden a sweet bunch of violets, so fresh and beautiful! It is the children's delight to gather these: they are never tired of picking them, and making them up into lovely little bouquets.

One of the children's real pleasures all this winter, during their morning's walk, has been to drop a penny or two into the hand of an old woman who sits on the steps of a church (San Paolo), as we pass. She sits there with her knitting, and looks quite brightened up in her expression since we have commenced our daily pensions. She looks so pleased always to see the children coming along, and has a kind *grazie* * to give them with a pleasant smile. At first, she was their papa's pensioner. As he passed by every day, he always

* Thanks.

gave her some pennies; and, when Nannine and Gianina began their walks in that direction, he told them
they must not forget her. Near by is a lame old
man who limps up and down with his cane, holding
out his hat to the passers-by. He was so gentle and
respectable-looking, we could not resist taking him also
under our *penny-patronage*. About three weeks ago,
we missed him; and the old woman told us he had
been put into prison. How sorry we were for him!
But, day before yesterday, we met him again in his accustomed place; and his poor old face was touchingly
sad as he told us how they had put him in prison because he begged in the streets. " Ma," said he, " che si
può fare? non aveva niente da mangiare!" ("But
what can one do? I had nothing to eat!") Then with
his blue eyes he looked up into the deep-blue sky, and
in his earnest way begged the " blessings of Heaven "
upon us. We frequently give him a five-cent.piece (a
large copper coin), from which, mamma says, there is
no doubt that he takes us for "princesses of the blood-
royal," — it seems to him so much!

In another street, where we often pass, is a poor
blind old woman, who sits upon the sidewalk, holding
a little box, which she rattles when she hears the approach of footsteps, begging for charity "for the love
of the Madonna." She, too, is one of our pensioners.

But it almost frightens the children to give any

thing to old Beppo, who stays upon the Spanish steps; he moves about so queerly on his hands and knees, coming up to one with such a boisterous air as he says, "Bon giorno, signorina!" We are always very glad when we see him going off on his donkey before we get there; for he always rides to and from his house in that manner, as he is a cripple, and cannot walk. We think he hardly suffers very much from poverty, as he has laid up several hundred dollars for his old age.

How sad it makes one feel to see so many poor beggars about the streets! If it were not for the mild, pleasant climate, they would suffer a great deal more than they do. But they look wretched and miserable enough, notwithstanding; and yet a great deal is given in charity in Rome, and there are places where even the poorest can go and get a good bowl of soup every day without paying for it.

After the Carnival, — which the children enjoyed very much this year, — and the long, quiet Lent, came all the interesting ceremonies of Holy Week at St. Peter's, commemorating incidents in the last days of our Saviour. One was the washing of the feet of the twelve apostles by the Pope.

A place in the church was arranged for the priests, who were to represent the apostles; and they were all seated in a row. Before the Pope entered, two gentlemen in common dress went, untying the shoes of each, that they might be in readiness. Then came the Pope, wearing a handsome dress of white and gold brocade, and attended by several cardinals. I think one of these tied a white apron round the Pope.

One cardinal held a large silver basin of water, and another held the towel; each presenting them in turn to the Pope when he was ready for them. To each priest (or apostle), after his feet had been washed, and dried with the towel, a handsome bouquet of flowers was presented.

Afterwards the same twelve men went to another hall, where they were seated at a table, and were waited upon by the Pope, to represent the Last Supper of our Lord. A handsome table is spread; and upon it, before each priest, stands a pretty little gilt figure, about eighteen inches high, of the apostle he represents, with a large bouquet of flowers by the side of it. There was real food, and a roll of bread, at each plate; and the Pope went up and down the table, — *they* were all seated on one side, and *he* stood on the other, — passing to each of them, in turn, the different dishes and some wine.

"They really ate and drank!" exclaimed a young Roman girl near us, who was very much delighted at the show.

All the Romans standing around appeared very much interested; for the Pope is their *monarch* as a king is in other countries; and, of course, it was a great occasion, — his performing these ceremonies.

In the Sistine Chapel * is performed, two or three times during Holy Week, the celebrated music of the Misereres. A Miserere is music composed for such occasions, very affecting and sublime. It is the last piece which is sung on Good Friday (and the other days): before it, they have other music, — the psalms, &c.

During the singing of the psalms, several lighted candles are arranged on the altar, in the form of a pyramid; and, at the end of every psalm, one of them is put out, until they come to the last, which is only taken away, not extinguished, to signify, that, when our Saviour was crucified, the light which he brought into the world was not extinguished at his crucifixion, but only hidden away for a little time, to appear again.

One of the most interesting scenes during Holy Week is at the Hospital for the Pilgrims. The pilgrims are those who come on foot from a great distance to Rome to join in the services of Holy Week. They are received and taken care of at the hospital for three days; and, when they leave, they are presented with a bundle of provisions and a little money. But

* This chapel is in the palace of the Vatican, where the Pope resides.

our interest in the scene consisted in seeing the poor pilgrims come in and have their feet washed, and then have a good supper and beds provided for them.

From the long, long journey they had taken, — for, to be a pilgrim, one must come a distance of sixty miles, — they were weary, soiled, and dusty; and it was a delightful sight, when we entered the rooms, to see the long tables arranged for an excellent supper to refresh them. Young ladies and matrons, all with dark dresses and red aprons, — the uniform that they wear, and *so* pretty! — were busy in preparing the tables with bread and excellent salad, and getting things ready in general; great baskets of provisions being brought in, and placed upon the tables. With that completed, and the pilgrims assembled one after another, they were taken to a lower room, and seated on a long bench which went all round the walls. The ladies were there also. Then came a priest, and read prayers for a few minutes; and a little tub of warm water and soap was placed before each poor tired woman (for there were only women in the part we visited: in another hall were male pilgrims, waited upon in the same manner by gentlemen). The sandals and stockings were untied and taken off; and before each one a lady kneeled, and bathed and rubbed her feet, until, no doubt, they were very clean and nice, and "shone again!" I wondered if they had ever had

so good a bathing before! We were sure it must have
made them very comfortable and happy, for the time
at least; for what could have been so refreshing, after
their long weary day's journey?

After this ceremony was over, they were marshalled
back again into the great hall, and seated at the tables;
and then, in addition to the rest of the supper, was
brought a bowl of hot soup for each one; and the
same ladies waited on them as before, so graciously
and kindly!

The provisions that remained after they were satisfied they bundled up in their *handkerchiefs*, and took
away with them. Then came the going to bed; but
this seemed to us all hubbub and confusion. I dare
say that the most of them never slept in such good
beds and nice rooms before; for they appeared not to
know what to do. They would go into one room, and
turn, and come out and try another. We came away
in the midst of it, for it was growing late; and whether
they had a good night's sleep or not, we never knew.

At St. Peter's, the great splendid show is on Easter
Day, when the Pope enters the church, as at Christmas,
in a chair raised on men's shoulders, with the great fans
carried on each side of him; extending his hands, and
blessing the people, as he moves along. What a long
procession of cardinals and bishops and priests in their
red and white and purple dresses; and monks, chanting

as they pass along; and files of soldiers in handsome uniforms; and the Swiss guard with armor on, who stand firm and irresistible to keep the line open for the procession!.

The ladies have seats arranged expressly for them on each side of the church or of the high altar, where they can see well the elegant show. Many foreign ladies are there,—*forestiere* as the Italians call them, — English, French, Americans, &c.; but all of them have to wear a black dress, and a black veil instead of a bonnet on their head. This they always do whenever the Pope officiates.

The Pope himself at the altar, assisted by cardinals, performs high mass. The choir for the singers is near, and the music is beautiful. When all is over, the Pope is carried out again through the church, and goes to a balcony outside, over the front portico, that he may bless the people. Then the immense crowd that had entered the church comes pouring out to stand upon the steps, and on the great Square in front, to receive the benediction; and thousands of others perhaps come up who have not been in the church, and whole regiments of soldiers in their uniform,—some of them mounted on horses,—until the whole Place, or Square, is filled. Then the "Holy Father," as the Roman Catholics call his holiness the Pope, spreads his hands, and with a loud voice pronounces the benediction, with the people and soldiers kneeling while he speaks. It is a very imposing sight to see so many thousands of persons kneeling to receive a blessing.

When this is over, and the crowd has begun to disperse, there is still another great show, — that of the carriages drawn up to receive their occupants. These belong to the nobility and the distinguished persons about the court. They are so handsome with their showy colors, and the horses also with their gilt trimmings, and there are so many of them, that they make all together a beautiful array. When they have passed, the private carriages and hacks draw up to take in their people: and there are so many of them too, they become entangled and obstructed in the crowd, so that it is sometimes an hour or more before one can move on; and, when they get started at last, it is like an immense procession going through the streets.

You will think I am never coming to an end of the Easter festivities; but there is another, *so* beautiful, it would be like a fairy-scene were it not on so large and grand a scale. This is the illumination of St. Peter's, which takes place on the same evening of the benediction, after that ceremony.

This is almost too wonderful to be described; for the whole outside of the church, from the top of the dome to the ground, is all covered with light, soft, sparkling, golden light. But first it was a *silver* light, and that changed instantaneously to the golden.   It looks, as you draw near, as if it were studded with jewels arranged in beautiful forms; and these sparkle there half the night, even after people have gone to bed, until they vanish of themselves one by one, as the oil in the little pans which hold the wicks becomes consumed.

To wind up all, on the next evening (Monday) there were magnificent fire-works; so magnificent, that I can scarcely begin to describe them to you.   There were splendid "serpents" and "pigeons," and "parachutes" and "bouquets," and a golden water-fall, and an illuminated temple, and a landscape all glowing with crimson light, and many other things; and, at the end, such an immense number of rockets went up all together, and came down in such showers of splendid-colored stars, that the whole heavens were covered with them.

These pieces all went off in so quick succession, with real cannon firing rapidly all the time, that it was almost terrific.   When little cousin Lulu was here the year before, and was taken to see the fire-works, or *girandole* as they are called in Rome, she was afraid to look at them, and hid her face away; but she was so very little a girl then.

CHAPTER II.

SUMMER EXCURSIONS.

In May, we spent a day at Tivoli among the Sabine Hills; those hills whence came Numa Pompilius, the wise, good king, who reigned in Rome when it was only an infant city, — the next king to Romulus, — who was loath to leave the country scenes where he dwelt to come and be the king of a busy city; and to whom the goddess Egeria showed herself so friendly and kind; for so the story is of those old times.*

The views among these hills are charming; nay, exceedingly beautiful. Elevated so high, you look over the Campagna, which is spread out like a plain, and see the "yellow Tiber" winding around; but it looks silvery from among these hills.

Going up the ascent to Tivoli, — for it is situated on the brow of a hill, — what groves of olive-trees we passed! — the strong, sturdy-looking olive-tree, homely enough, but is very useful, yielding from its fruit all the oil used here. Even the streets are lighted with

* See the companion volume, — Fairies of our Garden: Roman Stories.

the soft, pretty, mellow light of olive-oil. On the top
of the hill are the remains of a temple with graceful
pillars, which the ancients themselves built, and dedicated to one of their deities. And in this town, too,
in its best days, lived sometimes a Roman emperor in
a splendid villa; for Tivoli, even older than Rome
itself, was then a favorite place of resort. Yes, the
dark-looking houses as you passed them, with the doors
wide open, looked as if there were nothing but the
doors to light them; just, I suppose, as they were built
in those ancient times, when glass windows were not
known.

Our day was delightful. I do not know whether we
most enjoyed walking in a beautiful villa with grand
old cypress-trees, and where the children ran up and
down the avenues, — the villa where the celebrated
poet Tasso had often visited his "lady-love," to whom,
or to whose family, it belonged, — or seeing the falls,
one of the great sights of Tivoli. They are beautiful
cascades, falling so gently in such delicate white foam
over the rocks, that they are very graceful. The children enjoyed greatly the circuit of three or four miles
we made, on donkeys, to have all the views of them.

Even little Memie was with us, and was carried on
a donkey, in the nurse's lap. How afraid her mamma
was, at a certain steep place, that the nurse would let
her suddenly fall! The baby is now more than a year

old. She learned to creep all in due time, and was as cunning as a little kitten, going about on all-fours. Then she began to walk by chairs; and now goes tottling about, very much to her amusement and ours. . . .

The *great* excursion we made this summer was in June, — several days at Frescati, a town among the Alban Hills, not far from Albano.

What a pleasure it was, from one height after another, as we ascended the mountains, to see the splendid views all around; and the trees, the groves, the woods, all so richly green; and the many beautiful villas to which we made excursions, especially the Villa Conti, not far from the hotel, where we went every day with the children to enjoy the cool shade in the noble avenues! And the dear little donkeys we enjoyed more than ever. How true they were in going down a steep or rocky place! never making a misstep, or stumbling over a stone, or doing any such naughty thing. Where there was any danger, no *man* could be more mindful or careful. But indeed we must confess that they paid themselves for it, in a smooth, grassy pathway, by doing pretty much as they pleased; *never* trotting, or thinking of such a thing, but when they were made to: on the contrary, turning out on the side of the road, and comfortably snatching a mouthful of grass whenever they fancied! Nevertheless, we enjoyed it for all that; it is such a quiet, pleasant way of sauntering through the woods: you have plenty of time to see every thing that comes in the way as you go along, — the flowers, the nuts, the squirrels, or whatever else there may be.

One of the places which we visited was Tusculum, perched on the summit of a high hill, where the patriot Cicero had a favorite villa. There he spent much of his time in study, and in receiving visits from his friends. Here also, at Tusculum, was born another of the patriots of ancient times, the celebrated Cato the Censor, who, when he was a young man, was in the war against Hannibal. Afterwards, when he had been to Carthage, the city of Hannibal, and had brought some figs from there, he took them with him into the senate-house at Rome, under his cloak, to show to the other senators. He had been surprised to find the city of Carthage still prosperous after it had suffered very much from war; and, for fear that it might yet become a very powerful enemy, he ended all his speeches after that with this remark, "I am of the opinion that Carthage must be destroyed."

Cato was a stern old patriot. He could not bear that even the ladies should dress in any kind of luxury; and he had great influence in keeping the country from falling into extravagances and follies. He was born poor and unknown; but by his great honesty, and uprightness, and fine eloquence, — for he had improved his talents by study, — and by his ardent patriotism, he came to receive, one by one, the highest honors of the State. Rome was then a republic; and all who showed themselves capable and worthy could make their way as well as with us in America. It is now more than eighteen hundred years since Cato the Censor first wandered about in Tusculum, a poor boy, perhaps bare-footed; but his memory still remains in history. The hills, the rocks, the sky over all, are, of course, the same that they were then, and must, in general, look as they did at that time, when Carthage and Rome were great and prosperous cities, and Tusculum was a pleasant place of resort, and Cato, and afterwards Cicero, lived there. The town is now deserted, and there are scarcely any ruins even left to tell what it was. But there is a little theatre partly remaining, with the seats all around, where actually the ancients sat, and saw plays performed; and, on those very same seats, we also sat for a little while.

On one of our excursions, we passed over the plain, or field, where, it is said that Hannibal encamped when he came to besiege Rome with his African soldiers. Of course, it was very interesting to think he *might* have been there; but it is not quite certain if he was.

.   .   .   .

June 28. — We are back again in Rome. . . .

Our garden is lovely this year. It has been all re-made; at least new beds and flowers have been planted, and a gardener is constantly employed. It is in full bloom. The tall oleander-trees are very handsome with their rich red blossoms; and all the other flowers — particularly the larkspur, pink, white, and blue, all mingled together — are beautiful and in profusion.

Last spring, the children's mamma and I had great ideas of working ourselves in the garden, and having little beds of strawberries, &c., to take care of. But it never amounted to much: for it is warm in this climate to work out of doors; that is, for those who are not used to it. But the poor women who are obliged to labor do work in the gardens and vineyards almost all day. We frequently hear them singing at their work. The children, of course, are delighted always to have their little shovels and hoes, and to dig here and there. Many a hole in the ground do they make for a well, and pile up earth for little mounds, &c., when we go into the garden in the afternoons.

One of the pleasures of their nurse Pina is to take them into the villa to hunt for *snails;* for the Italians make a little dish of them to eat. But it does not re-quire much searching. At some seasons, the stems of some shrubs and plants are perfectly covered with them. Their shells are as large as a hickory-nut, and sometimes as a good large walnut. When we go into the avenues early in the morning, it is often quite an amusement to trace out on the ground the little pathways which they have made during the night, where they cross from one side of the avenue to the other. These have been made at least since the evening before: it may be that they creep out very early in the morning and make them. They are pretty little distinct tracks just grooved in the soft earth. They might be a winding road for a fairy, if the fairies ever deigned to walk upon the ground.

These little animals go along pretty slowly, snail-like, to be sure; and we often find them just on their way, with their big round house on their back.

July 5.— In our walk this morning, Nannine had an initiatory lesson in American history; the day, or rather yesterday, suggesting it: but, that being Sunday, we presume that the celebration goes on to-day. It was an account of the grand festival in Boston and in all our cities, — the ringing of the bells, and firing of cannon, and the fire-crackers of the boys, and the pretty floral processions in the streets, and the singing of the children of the public schools; the stalls and booths around the Common filled with cakes and pies and all sorts of fruits, and lemonade, which booths are begun to be put up in the middle of the night before, with the noisy sound of the hammer; and the thousands and thousands of people from the country, who come into the city to spend the holiday; and all winding up with the fire-works in the evening. From this beginning, Nannine went on to comprehend very well the origin of the celebration. She has arrived at last to the pleasure of commencing history in this way. She is not yet old enough to study it much from books; but, though fairy stories make her principal reading at present, she is very fond of real knowledge, and is never tired of hearing whatever one will tell her.

. . . .

This summer, Nannine went with me to walk very early in the mornings; often taking our breakfast with us, and going to the Pincio, and sitting upon the fresh grass, and eating it there. It improved Nannine very much, making her look rosy and healthy; for, although she was well, she had begun to look rather pale and delicate during the hot weather. — I have said nothing as yet about the Pincio. This was a lovely place, where we often went to walk. It is a grand promenade, where children go with their nurses, and ladies and gentlemen to walk and drive. It is very beautiful, with trees and flowers; and there are pretty little nooks to go into, — plats or lawns of green grass, hedged round with trees.

But, at the early hour in the morning at which we

went this summer, it was very quiet; and often we met no one but parties of school-boys sitting about, laughing and chatting. These school-boys always look like little *gentlemen*, — they behave so well, and wear *beaver-hats* exactly like men's.

One of the great pleasures of going out so early was meeting the pretty flocks of goats which are brought into the city in the mornings, and driven round from house to house to give milk. The man who keeps them takes the tumbler, or little pail, or dipper, that is given to him, and milks right into it there in the street.

And how often in our various walks have we met great flocks of creatures! — sometimes beautiful lambs, white or black; sometimes they are little pigs, looking so pretty; sometimes turkeys. I suppose there are hundreds of turkeys in a flock.

. . . .

These long summer afternoons, when it was too warm to go out, and our friends were all gone into the country, and we were left quiet to ourselves, how much we enjoyed — we *grown* ones — reading aloud to each other some of the many useful or pleasurable books we had long wanted to read! And the children had their time unmolested in playing dolls. Did ever children have such a happy, uninterrupted play-time? And did they not enjoy it to the full? acting as if

7

their dolls were real live persons and companions!
They were laughable enough, — some of the comical
things they would do and say about them.

Their aunt, little Lulu's mamma, sent each of them
from America, after her return, an elegant China doll,
with little trunks of clothes, all beautifully made;
with every article of dress, even to the little shoes and
stockings, and a pretty mantilla and hat: so that after
this, whenever they went to walk, they depended upon
having their dolls with them.

Once or twice a week, we drove out several miles
upon the Campagna, — often the dolls with us, —
which kept us *all* very healthy and well.

CHAPTER III.

DAILY WALKS.

(THE following diary of nearly a week — as far as Nov. 7 — was originally written in Italian, and is now translated — slightly enlarged, where explanation seemed to be needed — as a specimen of our customary or frequent daily walks.)

October, Saturday. — This morning I proposed to take the children and the maid Lolla to the Piazza Navona to see a collection of wild animals; for none of them had ever seen any. Memie, the dear baby, heard us talking of dressing in order to be ready, and wanted to be dressed to go too. She was so bewitching, so cunning and earnest, that it was not possible to refuse her: so nurse took her, and came with us. We had gone as far as the Spanish Place to take a carriage there, when Josef (our servant) fell in with us, and went also. Thus there we were, almost the whole family, entering the tent of the menagerie!

There was a great ostrich, ugly enough; a young hyena, but looking very savage; a fine wolf, very fat; a

kangaroo, with an appearance so gentle, and color of
a beautiful brown, that it is really a beautiful animal.
The American and African monkeys were numerous,
and did as monkeys always do, delighting to take
whatever one throws at them, and making a spring
sometimes that frightened poor little Memie, and, I
think, her nurse too. The rest of us stood them very
well, and also the enormous snakes, such as the boa-
constrictor, — very easily too ; for they were in a half
torpid state, and could have done us no possible harm.

What astonished us much was the brilliant plumage of several birds of the parrot kind, — *papagalli*,
as they call them in Rome. The splendor and richness
of the coloring, the red, green, yellow, and blue, were
surprising. . . . When the children were sufficiently
amused, we took a turn around the Square to see the
various things spread out; for it is a market-place on
certain days, and this was one. All sorts of cloths
and merchandise are laid on counters set up in the
open street. Then we passed on a little farther, and
stopped at a place where a lottery was being drawn.
Some of our party (the servants) had taken tickets,
and were interested in the drawing, which was going
on at that very moment. And really, true enough,
a pair of ear-rings fell to the share of Lolla's (the
maid's) mother, who is our cook!   .

The drawing of the lottery is a curious sight.

'Those who have charge of it stand in a high balcony, outside the window of a house, where the whole crowd in the street below can look up at them; and a boy turns round and round, by a handle, a cylindrical machine, calling out the numbers at the same time; and then the article is given out. It is so arranged, that I believe almost every one has something, if it is ever so little. In truth, it is much like the scrambling-bags at the fairs in America, and for the same purpose, — to obtain money.

But they are bad, we think, for the poor people, making them spend, little by little, a great deal of money, which, if saved, might come to a nice little sum. But they are willing to risk something for the chance of getting a *great sum*, which falls once in a while, perhaps, to a poor man. . . . Oh! we often think how we should like to see them, instead, laying away their ten-cent pieces and their five cents in a good savings bank, as the Irish Catholics do in America. But no : they seem to be fascinated in seeing what they will get from the lottery. . . . Neither have they such saving institutions here, I suppose, for the poor; and so they have not the encouragement.

Monday. — *My* birthday. Nannine has been frequently asking me to-day if I was " having a pleasant and happy birthday." The dear children tried this morning to make it very pleasant by giving me a little present, — Nannine a pair of sweet little carnelian glove-buttons, and Gianina a pretty little red carnelian hammer to put on the chain of my watch. And their mamma, as a pleasant thing, proposed, instead of a drive, as she had thought of, a walk to the Russian Villa, where we had never been. So she, Nannine, and I, equipped ourselves, and went. It is a charming place; a little woody scene. It is intersected by the grand and beautiful arches of one of the old aqueducts which were built hundreds or almost thousands of years ago, and of which there are so many beautiful ruins on the Campagna. The walls of this one were covered with ivy and rose-bushes and trees. There are quantities and quantities of the acanthus in the villa, — that plant which is so famed for its graceful manner of growth, that it is copied in sculpture. There were bright yellow or yellowish leaves of the oak-tree, and brilliant red leaves of the sumach, which were turned by the autumn air, and of which we brought home a great many.

We called this the "Russian Villa," only because a Russian lady lived there. We had a delightful walk and a *whole* "pleasant" day.

Tuesday. — We went to another beautiful villa near the last, the Altieri Villa, where there is a curious labyrinth winding round and round, made by a hedge of shrubs. In the centre is a pine-tree, splendidly tall

and large. There is a gate at the entrance of the labyrinth; and after you go in, you wind round in a curious
and intricate way until you come to the pine-tree, *if
you can.* But it is the easiest thing in the world
to become perplexed and confused, and not able to
reach the tree, nor to find your way out again if you
did.

But, behold! the gate was locked when we wished to
go in; and so we could have no adventures.

Thursday. — Our walk to-day was in the Villa Torlonia, within the city walls, on the side of the Porta
Pia. The Duke Torlonia, who owns the place, had
often invited the children's mamma to take us all
there to walk; but this was the first time she had
taken advantage of the invitation. We were all ready,
— mamma, the children, and myself, — and were just
coming out of the door, when our good friend from
America, Mr. D., came up. He had come to the house
with the intention of amusing himself with the children, in the garden : and he turned, and went with us.
Arrived at the gate of the villa, we rang the bell.

After a long time, a servant came ; and, mamma's card
being taken in, the gardener showed us all the novel-
ties of the place. It is a very beautiful villa. There
are two long avenues of ilex-trees, which meet overhead, forming a beautiful arch. At the end of these is
a pretty columbarium full of beautiful pigeons.

There are especially many winding paths, and here and there flowers and handsome trees. In one place is a small, round lake, in the centre of which rises an immense water-lily. I had never seen a water-plant so large, with leaves so beautiful and elegant, and of such a size.

In front of the house, the ground is planted in little circles of flowers, which have a pretty effect. There was a palm-tree, graceful at the top; but the stem was wrapped round with straw to protect it from the cold of the coming winter.

We all had a charming time, the children running up and down the long avenues; and Mr. D. enjoyed it as much as any of us. . . .

In this fine splendid weather of October, we go about a great deal among the villas, of which there are so many in Rome, all of them beautiful places. . . .

Nov. 7.— We have had a delightful afternoon on the Campagna, going out of the Via Salara Gate.

The Campagna there is exquisitely beautiful, with soft, lovely views of smooth meadows and elegantly curved or sloping velvety covered little hills, coming here and there into the plains.

Mr. and Mrs. S——w, and their sweet daughters, were with us in another carriage. Leaving the carriages in the road, about five miles from the city, we rambled over the fields and hilly slopes, to the great delight of the children and every one. We stopped a while, in the midst of a great flock of two or three hundred sheep, to look at the pretty white lambs; the shepherd, with his sheep-skin jacket on, and leaning on his crook, laughing very good-naturedly at our enjoyment.

Oh! how many times, in driving out, have we stopped and enjoyed the sight of these pretty creatures, and have seen them driven and gathered into their folds by the shepherds; and the great shepherd-dog so faithful, following round with his master, taking such good care of the flocks! No one dares to encroach upon them if he is near. The great herds, too, of noble, splendid-looking, gray cows and oxen, we never cease to look at with delight, they are so royally grand.

When we get out upon the Campagna, and leave the carriage in the road, and go off to search for or to examine some ruin, or to gather daisies and wild-flowers in the fields, the children and all of us feel just as *rural* as the animals themselves; and we seldom finish without a frolicsome run up and down the sloping banks and little acclivities. The perfect freedom, and the great space all around, and the fine air, make it very inspiring and invigorating; and we draw in such long breaths of health at every step, and every nerve is so filled with this simple, open-air, country pleasure, that it is very delightful, and keeps us well month after month; for we are as well, or even better than some of those who went away from the city in the summer for health.

Saturday, we made a little picnic for the children in the Villa Borghese. Besides our children, there were Mrs. S.'s and Mrs. G.'s; and Mr. and Mrs. S——w joined us afterwards with theirs.

This is a splendid villa, with great parks and avenues; and we had games, — hide-and-seek, puss-in-the-corner, playing ball, and so forth. But what pleased the children very much was seeing the aviaries, — pretty places formed of lattice - work, where were beautiful birds. And some pretty deer too, that were in the parks, or enclosures, interested us very much. There were some lovely fawns, pretty little creatures; but they kept mostly among the trees and hedges, and would not stay very long for us to look at them.

THIRD YEAR.

CHAPTER I.

GOING TO THE OPERA.

Our Christmas festival this year was a dinner-party of ladies and gentlemen. But each lady, to her surprise, found on her plate, beside a bouquet of flowers, a handsome *bonbonnière*. As the day we — their mamma and myself — happened to be out selecting them was the birthday of the little niece in America with the "golden, fairy-like curls," * in hearing about whom the children were much interested, and with whom they had become much acquainted by frequent allusions in letters, &c., from home, their mamma chose for me a pretty one, — a large ball striped with handsome colored velvets, hollow, and filled, of course, with sugar-plums, — that I might send it to her.

A friend of ours in Rome, who went to America last summer on a visit, spent a day at the house where little Anna was (for that was her name; she was

---

* See page 68.

visiting at her grandpapa's then), and very kindly drew a picture of her for me. This she brought with her when she returned to Rome; and at Christmas the children's mamma took it, and had it framed, all secretly for a surprise; and it is very sweet! It is hung up in our room; and Nannine often looks at it, and says, "I like that picture of little Anna, it is such a pretty picture!" She and Gianina take an immense deal of interest and delight in hearing about her.

On New Year's the children had a holiday, which was always a great treat to them; for, although their lessons have not been much mentioned, they studied regularly in the forenoons. Gianina, was now old enough to have lessons. She began when she was four, and was now past five; and Nannine was seven. It was only once in a while that they had a whole long day of play or amusement, or perhaps two or three days, or a week, at Christmas or so; but generally every day, through all the weeks and months, summer as well as winter, they were occupied in the mornings studying, and made good progress. Nannine had got on so well in French, which she began the year before, that if we went to Switzerland the next summer, as was talked of, and where it would be needed, we thought she would be able to use it very well.

When Gianina was five, she began to read Italian; and she learned it very easily, because she already spoke it. It was her first language; therefore she understood it perfectly. She had not learned to speak English until she went to America on a visit, when she was about two years old; but, by the time she was three, she could speak it very well.

She could also now read English very nicely.

.   .   .   .

This year we had no balcony at the Carnival; and, although we were invited to some of our friends' balconies, we seldom went; for it was very rainy weather. I think there was but one pleasant day. But the great event to the children was going to the *opera* on the last day of the Carnival; for they had never been. It was in the daytime, and was given purposely for children.

In the morning, it rained tremendously. Once in a while, there was the least peeping out of the sun; but, nevertheless, it was a stormy time. It made but little difference to us, however, as we were to ride to the opera. So at half-past nine we were off, — the two children, their mamma, and myself; and we called for Mrs. F., the lady who sketched little Anna's picture, to go with us. There had been a great time in getting boxes; for on the last day it is always very crowded: but, through the intervention of an Italian gentleman, a very nice one had been obtained for ourselves, and some for other friends. So, arriving there before the time to commence, there was a great visiting back and forth in the boxes, which happened to be all near together.

The house was entirely filled, and made a brilliant show. There were many children, some in costumes: ours had only pretty wreaths of real roses around their heads, which made them look very lovely. The opera was "Il Trovatore," or "The Troubadour," in which there are many beautiful scenes.

The Troubadour is the son, or supposed son, of a Gypsy mother, who in reality, by mistake, sacrificed her own child, when an infant, instead of this one. But neither he nor any one else knows it; and she clings to him always with great affection. There are some Gypsy scenes which are very picturesque; groups of Gypsies sitting around, and some of them striking a chorus on an anvil.

The Troubadour falls in love with a lady, and she returns it: but, at the same time, another person loves her, — a count; and when the Troubadour and the lady are in their bridal dresses, all ready to be married, the count comes, and prevents the ceremony; and they are separated.

The Gypsy in the mean time is taken prisoner in the belief of her having made depredations on the neighboring estates; and the son, the Troubadour, also is imprisoned. Then there is a beautiful but mournful scene, — monks in their brown gowns and hoods

appear, singing a dirge for the souls that are condemned to death; and Leonora, the lady-love, listens
to them with great distress, knowing that her lover is
one of the condemned ones. Presently, from the tower
in which he is imprisoned, she hears him singing, accompanied by his guitar, an adieu to her. This touching song and her singing were rapturously applauded
and encored. "Bis, bis!" ("Again, again!") were repeated a hundred times; and at last he came down from
the tower, and made his appearance in front of the
stage; but he would not repeat the song. Three or four
armfuls of bouquets were thrown to the lady. She
picked them every one up, but was obliged to go off
the stage three or four times to deposit them.

It was nearly three o'clock when we were ready to
leave; and, coming home, we had a glimpse of the
Carnival people in the Corso. They looked very gay
in their fantastic dresses; but the rain was pouring
down, and they must have had a dismal time of it.
I do not know how the *moccholetti* went on during
the evening; but it may not have rained just at
that hour, otherwise they must have all been put
out, *nolens volens.*

And now began the quiet Lent, when nearly all the
strangers or visitors went away to Naples, and came
back again at Holy Week.

. . . .

On Easter morning, this year, when we came in to breakfast, how bright and beautiful the table looked, strewed all over with flowers, as is the custom of the Italians! The table-cloth was a *carpet of flowers.* Josef, our good servant, was so pleased to see us pleased! for it was his work. Then presently was brought on a great plate of hot cross-buns and eggs and ham, and what not, — a regular Easter breakfast.

After breakfast, we, the family, went to our little quiet English church, and enjoyed the services there, while all the grand ceremonies were going on at St. Peter's.

CHAPTER II.

CHILDREN'S LETTERS.

THIS season the children had received letters from little Anna's grandpapa in America, who was much interested in them, and whom they liked much to hear about, although they had never seen him. When Gianina was quite a little thing, about four years old, she gave me one day a little blue-ribbon bow that she had been playing with, — it was a lady's bow, that she happened to have among her playthings, — and wished me to send it to him. I sent it when there was an opportunity, and this was the description given of Gianina: "The little girl is an interesting little thing, a regular picture-like little face, blue eyes, fair hair and skin, a soft, mellow, peach - like bloom." Grandpapa was very much pleased with the ribbon bow; and, for her little sake, he sometimes wore it in his button-hole. When he had an opportunity, he wrote to both the little girls the letters which are mentioned above, and which pleased them very much. Their father and mother thought it a very "kind" and "gracious" attention on his part; and her mamma said that Gianina should dictate a little answer in return for hers, and she would write it down for her, as Gianina could hardly write much then. But soon she could print, and form words very nicely, and was able to write herself. So one day they both wrote in lesson-time, and the following are the letters: —

MY DEAR MR. W., — I thank you for the little letter you sent me. I hope you will like this little letter that I am just writing to you. We have got a garden all full of flowers; but, in the summer, there used to be a great many more. We are just having school. We have a book-case hung up over Nannine's bureau. We have a blackboard hung by a blue string.

Your little friend

GIANINA.

ROME, ITALY, April 5.

MY DEAR MR. W., — I am very glad to have a little letter from you. I accept it as kindly as if it were written on my birthday. Baby is very fat, and can walk very well; but she cannot talk English. She can only talk Italian, and she speaks very funnily: she says *to-to* for *fuo-co*. When they ask her, "Volete del pane?" * she repeats it right over, "Volete del pane?" She

---

* "Do you want some bread?"

means "Yes, I do want some." She has blue eyes and golden hair. On the 8th of April, she will be two years old. The garden is full of tulips and hyacinths and gilly-flowers and pansies. Toity* is very kind indeed; for she only made me write this letter to-day, besides my French lesson.

The other day I went to walk with Mr. B., the minister; and I had a very nice walk. On Easter Day we went to papa's studio, at the top of the house,† to see the illumination of St. Peter's; but it had been raining, and the shavings had got wet that were in the little pans of grease that were meant to set the wicks on fire with. So they could not illuminate it that night; but they put it off till Tuesday night, and we went in the carriage to see it. First we went to the Pincio to see it change into the golden light; and it was very beautiful. Then we went down to the piazza of St. Peter's, and saw it there; and then we came home.　　　　From your little friend

NANNINE.

"Grandpapa" sent to know the heights of the children, as he wanted to compare them with some little girls at home.

Nannine was just four feet high; Gianina, three feet

* The familiar name by which the children called the writer.
† A private studio.

seven and a quarter inches; little Memie, two feet nine and a quarter inches.

We had a place marked on the wall in our room, where they stood regularly, when each birthday came round, to see how much they had grown since the year before. Sometimes it was quite surprising.

I made a little silk dress to send home to Anna; and we tried it on to Gianina. It was a little too small for her; but little Anna was a year or two younger than Gianina, and it fitted her quite nicely when it arrived, although it was a little large. . . .

May.—The prince and princess and their family are now staying at the villa a few weeks, occupying the rooms and the great hall below us; and they have just sent up to invite us to go this afternoon to another villa of theirs (which is near the Church St. John Lateran), as it is a festa day; and it is a good place there to see the procession in the streets. They themselves are all going. I am sitting with my things on, waiting for the children and nurse to be ready. . . .

We went, but were rather late to see the procession; it being mostly over before we reached there. The children's papa and mamma came afterwards, and then we all walked in the villa; the children, with the little Donna Francesca, the little daughter of the prince, amusing themselves in running among the alleys and around the flower-beds. It is a very pretty place.

The little Francesca is a nice little thing, of Gianina's age, plump and rosy, frank and good-natured. She always wants Gianina to go to their rooms and play with her every afternoon when they come home from driving, and often comes for her. The other day they had a party of children, which they have every week at one of their houses; and this time they had it here in the villa, having the garden to play in. Many children came, and they all played for a while in the great hall; and, as our children had been invited, I took them in. The prince and princess have a little son about as large as Memie. When we went in, he was drawing round a little carriage which belongs to the house, and is, I believe, about as old: it is a little model carriage, and always stands in the great hall. The princess put the little boy behind, and our little Memie at the pole, and took her hand, although she is quite tall, and led them up and down the hall several times. She appeared to be quite in her *element* so, and very charming.

Then all went down into the garden, and there was a fine entertainment of ice-creams and cakes, and then another grand play, running around among the flowers, and in the broad avenues, before it was time to break up.

.   .   .   .

June 1.—It is now quite decided that we shall go to Switzerland this summer. We leave here by stage early on the 4th for Civita Vecchia; and shall go from there in the steamer the next afternoon, arriving at Leghorn in the morning; and, sailing at night, arrive at Genoa the next morning, where we shall stop a day or two.

We are told, by a gentleman who has frequently crossed the Alps, that it is too dangerous to go by the northern passes of the mountains so early in the season, especially as there has been a more than usual quantity of snow the last winter. We shall therefore go by Turin, where we shall stop two or three days; and cross Mount Cenis, which is the lowest pass of the Alps, at least from Italy; then by Chamberry and Geneva, stopping a day or two; then across the Lake of Geneva to one of the points there, and by Friburg and Berne to Interlachen. It is a circuitous route: but the nearer passes after leaving Turin could only be travelled by mules, which would be too tedious for the children; and the luggage, at all events, would have to be sent round. We expect to be between two and three weeks on the road. There is a railroad a part of the way, from Genoa to Turin; and I think that is all. For the rest, we shall go probably by *vetturino.**

* The *vetturino* is a man who supplies and drives a travelling carriage with two or more horses.

CHAPTER III.

JOURNEY TO SWITZERLAND.

JUNE 4. — After eight hours' ride in the stage, — or *diligenza*, as they call it in Italy; in French, *diligence*, — we are stopping over night at the hotel in Civita Vecchia. The children are all asleep in the adjoining room. It is evening, and I commence a little account of our journey.

Their mamma (their papa was too busy to go away this summer), the children, myself, and Mr. R., a friend of the family, who is to accompany us almost all the way, and Josef and Lolla, the two servants, filled the great lumbering coach. Not exactly lumbering, however; as we went along with pretty good speed with four horses, changed every hour, and which the postilion, who rides on the back of one of them, kept always cheering up with the loud snapping of his long whip-lash, and his cheery voice often singing out. A postilion, by the way, is a curious-looking fellow, having always a gay dress of bright colors, and wearing often a cap or hat with a feather in it. He has nothing to do but look after the horses, and sometimes shows off grand airs enough in managing them. There is another person, the guard, who has the care of the carriage and luggage, and looks after all our wants.

How pleasant and beautiful the Campagna was! — for it is all Campagna between Civita Vecchia and Rome. It was dotted all over with gay, scarlet poppies, which grow wild in Italy; and other flowers, blue, purple, and yellow. Nannine and I undertook to count the different kinds of flowers we should see on the way: we numbered eighteen; but I do not think we counted them all.

When we arrived, and stopped at the hotel, how charming it was to feel the fresh air of the sea coming in delightfully, and to see the salt water all spread before us, and hear its rushing sound breaking upon the rocks! The hotel is very near the water, and our windows open upon a long balcony behind the house, which looks directly upon it, and in which the children enjoy very much running up and down.

GENOA. — We left Civita Vecchia on the next afternoon. The weather was fine; but, nevertheless, we had to go through all the uncomfortable process of a sea-voyage. Nannine was not sick at all; but poor Gianina and baby were quite ill. Our good faithful Josef — for the maid, too, was pretty sick — how devotedly he took care of baby, as if she were the most precious thing in the world!—as indeed she was. He would scarcely leave her out of his arms a moment. The boat was perfectly crowded; so that we all—I mean our party, besides a few others—slept on deck all night, some with mattresses, and some only with shawls and cloaks on the seats.

We are now for two or three days in this busy city of Genoa,—at least it seems busy and lively to us, after our more quiet Rome. We spent yesterday in visiting the truly beautiful palaces and churches; but the children passed much of the time at the lovely Villa Doria, a beautiful place. To-day we have all been—all excepting baby and the two servants; for mamma did not want to have baby fatigued too much —to an enchanting villa called Pallavicina, six miles from the city. It is wonderfully beautiful everywhere; . one is always coming to something new; and part of it is almost like Fairyland. There are little beautiful temples here and there, with windows of colored glass, which make it seem inside as if you were in the midst of a rainbow; and pretty little bridges with handsome railings; and caves; and subterranean passages filled with water, on which is a boat, into which you are invited, and a boatman rows you around.

But the most curious of all were some mysterious water-works. Little fountains, or fairy streams of water,—they were so fine and delicate,—in one place .

came spouting up from the ground, all of a sudden, directly under your feet; and you did not know how or whence they came! Nannine was swinging in a beautiful swing among the trees (for it is all pleasantly shaded with trees); and all at once a whole shower came up, and sprinkled her all over! Then Gianina wanted to try it and she, too, got sprinkled. And, if you sat down on one of the pretty seats arranged near, before you knew it the fine spray would come jetting up all about, and make you spring and jump to get away from it, until we discovered that it was a trick on purpose to amuse people! The gardener, who went about with us, showing us around, slyly touched some little spring or machinery out of sight, and put all those magical, fairy showers or fountains in motion!

.   .   .   .

Whether our pleasant time in Genoa caused us to forget that we still had our journey to pursue, and so were a little tardy the next morning, or whether the people at the omnibus-station were over-punctual, we found ourselves just five minutes too late, when we arrived at the station, to take the coach: it was already far out of sight! This was to have carried us a distance of four-hours' ride to the cars in which we were to travel to Turin. What could we do? Lose our passage? No! Quick as thought, another carriage was procured to drive us after the omnibus or stage (which, of course, would travel a great deal faster than a common carriage), and overtake it if possible. It had rained during the night, and the roads were wet; and the horses were driven so fast, you would have laughed, had you not been too *sorry*, at the woful spectacle we presented; particularly those in the front, with hats and coats and faces completely bespattered with mud!

The poor little children, too, inside the close, narrow carriage, going so fast, felt miserable and dizzy enough; and, I suppose, would have been glad, at that moment, to have been anywhere but travelling. The feat was accomplished, however, the omnibus being overtaken; and we were soon transferred to it. (As this was a little mortifying, I would like to say, in a parenthesis, that it was the only misadventure of the kind we had; it being the only time, in all our travels, that we were ever *too late* for the public conveyances.)

After riding for the space of four hours in the omnibus through a pretty country, we came to the railway-station. Soon after entering the rail-cars, we arrived upon the plains of Lombardy, a great level region covered with rich grass, and abounding in the tall poplar-tree, — the Lombardy poplar. This region is highly cultivated, and looks sunny and pleasant. After an hour or two, we had our first sight of the Alps, at first scarcely distinguishable from the white clouds in the horizon, but growing more and more distinct, until, just before reaching Turin, they loomed up grand, and white with snow. Since we have been in Turin (where we now are), we have been to the top of a very high hill, from which there is a splendid view of the great plains of Lombardy on one side, and of the Alps on the other. It is not to be wondered at that the barbarians should wish to pass over that frigid barrier of the mountains into these sunny plains.*

A four-hours' ride in the cars brought us to Turin. We had time for walking out after dinner; and on every side we were reminded somewhat of Paris. It is such a cheerful, busy, pleasant place, with shops full of beautiful jewelry and silk goods! Our hotel is opposite the king's palace, which we visited. It is impossible to describe to you all the splendid rooms, with the gilded walls and ceilings. The apartments of the queen-mother (the mother of Victor Emanuel) were as beautiful and enchanting as those of the " Arabian Nights," with the little boudoirs and dressing-room and sleeping-room ; but all looked home-like too, domestic, and pleasant. I think we were pleased, most of all, with three little common wooden chairs which the queen-mother had purchased for her grandchildren,

* See the companion volume.

and which were standing all together in one of her rooms. She was absent while we were there, and that is the reason we were allowed to go through her apartments; but she was expected back that very night, and perhaps those little chairs were a present she had just sent on before her to her grandchildren! They were so plain and strong-looking, it seemed as if she meant that they should toss them about, and take comfort with them, without being afraid of their getting injured.

CHAPTER IV.

JOURNEY TO SWITZERLAND CONTINUED.

On Monday morning, the 13th, we were ready to leave Turin. So in due time our luggage was packed, and then ourselves, into a *vettura;* that is, a travelling-carriage, of which the driver is the *vetturino.* He carries us each day as far as he thinks we ought to go, and stops at the proper places for meals and for the night. He engaged to take us as far as Geneva in four days and a half. On the first day we arrived at Susa, a town at the foot of Mount Cenis, where we stopped for the night; and it took us all the next day to ascend and descend the mountain. I have already mentioned that this is the lowest pass by which one can go into Switzerland from Italy (at least it was the nearest one for us). Switzerland is so surrounded by the Alps like a great wall, that you can only enter it by such passes; and over this one a splendid road had been made by Napoleon Bonaparte. Nevertheless, ascending the mountain was a very slow process ; and often some of us got out of the carriage, and walked an hour or more at a time; and sometimes we would get ahead of the carriage, and then we would wait in some little garden or on the roadside for it to come up. Once in a while, you meet with a farm-house; and there is also a House of Refuge every little way, such as that upon Mount St. Bernard, where the great St. Bernard dogs were trained to search for and save travellers overcome by the snow. I believe there are not many of these dogs left; but we saw one in Turin, — a great, noble-looking creature, stout and strong as the pictures represent them, and with shaggy hair almost as white as the snow itself.

This was not the season for us to be overtaken in a terrible snow-storm: so we had no such adventure as one of those great dogs coming to track us out under the drifting snow, with a basket of provisions and a bottle of wine hung round his neck for our use! But the good monks who established those houses, and trained the dogs, were the means, no doubt, of saving many lives.

The hill-tops around us were white with snow, as well as that of Mount Cenis itself; and we could have a better view of them than of the one we were travelling over; for, when we got up nearer and nearer its white head, we went straight into the clouds, which hid it all away from us! The mist was so dense, that we could not see any thing distant: we only knew there were patches or fields of snow all around, which we were passing over; and that we were in the very midst of a thunder-storm! The sleet and hail came down heavily; but we rode on regardless, only we had to wrap ourselves closely in our cloaks. Then we began to descend; and before nightfall we had reached the town at the foot of the mountain, on the other side. The next day, we arrived at our stopping-place before sunset. It is the haying season; and we went out into a splendid hay-field, where the children had a grand tumble upon the ricks of new-mown hay. Even little Memie rolled about, and was half buried in it, to her great delight. The sweet scent, and the fresh air, and the rural scene, — how delightful it all was!

On the fourth day, the pretty Swiss cottages began to appear, and the country — Savoy — was very pleasant. In the course of the morning, passing through the town of Chamberry, we got out of the carriage, and visited the handsome cathedral there. A little farther on, where we stopped at twelve o'clock for a late breakfast (we had had an *early* breakfast before), we had time to stroll a while in a garden, and sat upon the grass; and Nannine and Gianina enjoyed rolling down a slope between the winrows of new-cut hay.

At noon, the next day, we arrived at Geneva. . . .

Geneva. — Three years ago, we were at this same place, and spent a week. What a large party we were then!—little Cousin Lulu and her mamma; and Cousin Harry, and his baby sister, and their mamma, with us. And what frolics the children had all together, sometimes shouting at the top of their voices!

It was autumn then; and what quantities of fine purple plums we used to buy in the streets! And what a beautiful little golden canary-bird we went to see at one of the shops, where there were also innumerable beautiful watches; for Geneva is famed for its watches.

The good madame, too, who kept the hotel,—how much notice she took of the children! We are not stopping at the same hotel now; but we have taken Nannine and Gianina there to see her, and she was much pleased. She thought they had grown *so* much!

We are now at the Hotel Bergues, on the opposite side of the river from where we then were. How very beautiful the views are from here!—the "swift" and "blue Rhone" all in front; the boats sailing upon it, with lateen-sails spread out like great wings; and others, looking, in the distance, like fairy-boats, with their little white sails set,—make a charming scene. And far away over the water is Mont Blanc, with his snowy head, which we have tried to rise early enough to see, bright and clear, in the morning; as, during the remainder of the day, he is commonly covered with mist.

Leading from one of the bridges which cross the river, opposite our window, is a little island. It is a tiny place, but large enough to be a pretty play-ground for children, and also a promenade for ladies and gentlemen. It is shady with trees; and there are seats all about, and little tables for coffee and ice. There the children often go. . . .

Three pleasant days in Geneva; and then we sailed in a steamboat, across the lake of the same name, to the beautiful town of Vevay. From there we made some pleasant excursions, stopping two nights; and on Wednesday morning (the 22d) we took the diligence for Friburg, and arrived there in the afternoon. Friburg is famed for containing the largest organ in the world; and in the evening this is played upon for the benefit of strangers. Of course we went. The music was grand and wonderful. It seemed to us as if the whole church were filled with it. Even Gianina, young as she is, and late as it was, was kept wide awake by it; and she asked in a whisper if it was "sung by voices." Sometimes it did sound marvellously like human voices. In the morning, we took a carriage to Berne; and, on the way, what should we meet but another carriage filled with friends, who had been in Rome last winter! It was very pleasant to meet them; and we all alighted, and stood in the road, and talked a while. They had lately parted from our good clergyman, Mr.

B., who was on his way to Geneva, where he expected to meet with us. We were very sorry to have missed him; and we knew he would be disappointed in not seeing us, for he was a dear friend of the family. How fond he always was of taking Nannine and Gianina to walk with him! and how much they enjoyed it too!

We arrived very early at Berne, and had all the afternoon for walking about the town. What we wished to see very much were some bears belonging to the city, which it always keeps; a bear being the emblem of the city of Berne. One of those now taken care of by the city was presented by the Emperor Louis Napoleon. We went two or three times to the place where they are kept, but were not fortunate enough to see them, as they would not come out of their dens for us; and, as we left the city early the next morning, we were obliged to content ourselves with some funny-little wooden bears in imitation of them, which Mr. R., our travelling companion, bought for the children.

At Berne, this good friend, who had come with us so far, and who had contributed greatly to the pleasure of the journey, was now to take leave of us, and go on to Paris. Nevertheless, when the carriage was ready, in the morning, he got in the same as usual, and rode a few miles with us; then bade us good-by, and walked back to Berne. We were sorry that he could not see the pretty place where we were to be all summer: so, after we arrived there, we sent him a package of letters describing it. Nannine and Gianina wrote also, for they were great pets of his; and very soon there came answers, and this nice one for Gianina, telling all about those *bears*, which he had really seen after going back to Berne: —

PARIS, July.

MY DEAR LITTLE GIANINA, — To show you how much I was pleased to receive your nice little letter, I will give you a long account of the bears of Berne, which I saw for you.   Your very true friend,

M. R.

WHAT MARTIN SAW FOR GIANINA.

After leaving the great old clock-tower, where he had seen the wonderful sights for his dear friend Nannine,* he walked on, thinking to himself, "Now I will go and see the bears for my other dear friend, Gianina." When he came to the great pit, he looked over the parapet; and there were the bears on the little mound under the tree, in the part to the right. One was a large grisly bear, which he called "Mother-bear." The other was small and black: this one he called "Baby-bear."

* The author regrets not being able to give that entertaining letter also; but it is not at present accessible.

As soon as Martin looked down to see them, they began to play and romp together. Mother-bear would pet Baby-bear; and Baby-bear would pull Mother-bear's hair with her teeth, and play all sorts of tricks, just as little Memie does sometimes. Some children who were there to see them threw down some bread; and the bears stopped playing, and ran down from under the tree to eat the bread. They must have been hungry; for they ate until all the bread was gone. There were two little brown birds that ate the bread with them, and the bears did not offer to hurt the birds. This was very kind and amiable, and Martin liked the bears for it. When the bread was all eaten, the bears ran back again to the mound.

This time, Baby-bear climbed up the tree, and lay across a branch, just high enough to reach down and touch Mother-bear with her fore-paw. Every time she touched her, Mother-bear would try to catch Baby's paw; but Baby would draw it back so quickly, that she couldn't. By and by, Mother-bear ran up the tree, and caught Baby: then they came down, and hugged each other very lovingly, and rolled down the mound together, just as little Gianina rolled down the new-mown grass at Aix les Bains the other day.*

When they had rolled all the way down, Baby-bear

---

* Page 128.

jumped up on her hind-legs, and stood quite erect. She looked just about as large as little Gianina would dressed in a bear-skin. Presently Mother-bear jumped up on her hind-legs too. Then they walked up to each other, and hugged and kissed; and Baby-bear bunted Mother-bear, just as little Memie knocks her head against her mamma sometimes; and they rolled over, and played together for a long time, until Mother-bear was tired. So she got up, and leaped away towards the bear-house, and stopped outside the door to wait for Baby, who didn't want to come yet. But, after a little while, she got up, and leaped away after her mamma. Then they hugged and kissed and rolled over together once more before they went into their great house.

It was a very pretty sight to see them; and Martin was greatly obliged to them for being so kind and amiable as to show off for him to describe to his little friend Gianina. They were very sorry that they did not know when Gianina made them a visit the day before. If she had only sent in her card, on a piece of bread and butter, they would have come out immediately to receive her and all her party. They hope, that, when Gianina visits Berne again, she will not fail to pay them a visit. She should not forget to send in her card. Her very good friend also hopes she will remember to make his kind compliments to both Madame and Mademoiselle Bear, and tell them how much he was gratified to make their acquaintance.*

* In Mr. Abbott's "Rollo in Switzerland," there is the following interesting account of the origin of bears being kept in Berne: —

"Berne is famous for bears. The bear is, in fact, the emblem of the city, and of the canton, or province, in which Berne is situated. There is a story, that in very ancient times, when Berchtold, the original founder of the city, was beginning to build the walls, a monstrous bear came out of the woods to attack him. Berchtold, with the assistance of the men who were at work with him on the walls, killed the bear. They gloried greatly in this exploit; and they preserved the skin and claws of the bear for a long time as the trophy of their victory. Afterwards they made the bear their emblem. They painted the figure of the animal on their standards. They made images and effigies of him to ornament their streets and squares and fountains and public buildings. They stamped the image of him on their coins; and, to this day, you see figures of the bear everywhere in Berne."

CHAPTER V.

SUMMER IN SWITZERLAND.

BÖNINGEN, NEAR INTERLACHEN.

OUR "Pension" (boarding-house) is the loveliest little place imaginable, — all clustered with vines, and buried in trees, so that we can scarcely see it until we reach the very door. It is a regular little Swiss cottage. The parlor, looking so lovely when we came into it, is almost formed of glass; at least, two sides of it are all of window-panes, which we can just slip aside, — for they are open sidewise, — and let the sweet, fresh air in.

In front, a great lake,* ten miles long, is spread before us with its bright silvery water; and, in the rear of the house, our windows look out upon green fields, where they have been making hay this last week. Beyond these rise great hills, which look as if their tops might be reached in fifteen minutes; but it would take four hours to ascend them. They are also dangerous, being filled with precipices and craggy places. Indeed,

* Lake Brientz.

I suppose they are impassable for any but the hunter: he climbs them sometimes in pursuit of the chamois.

At present, there are only ourselves at the cottage, with the kindest and most pleasing little host and hostess in the world. They would do any thing for us, and would only make us live too luxuriously. Real fresh country milk we have; and butter and cream every morning and night, with delicious bread. And the dinners!—I cannot begin to tell you how nicely they are prepared, and how extravagant, for only so few of us. Some of the meats we could readily dispense with; but the dessert is too tempting,—such nice custards, delicate puddings, strawberry-tarts, &c. We often tell good Mrs. Shoemaker (the landlady)—a funny name!—that she gives us *trop de bonnes choses.* Regularly, for tea, we have a great dish of strawberries, with cream.

Although there are so few of us, four languages are daily spoken. Our servants and little Memie speak only Italian, the rest of us English among ourselves. Mr. and Mrs. Schumacher (their real name) speak Swiss in their family, and French with us.

Occasionally some one stops to take dinner. For instance, two gentlemen, an Englishman and a German, came over yesterday from Interlachen; and to-day they came again, to bathe and fish in the lake. They told us a sad story of a little boy, who a few

days since, in descending one of the Swiss mountains
not far from here, lost his balance, and was thrown
from his mule, and so much injured as to cause his
death. What a painful affliction for the friends who
were with him! and *we* are so happy here! . . .

We did not then know, but soon afterwards learned,
that this was a beautiful little American boy whom I
had known at home. How suddenly cut off from the
fond embrace of his parents! We longed to go to
them; but it was too late: they had already started on
their sad journey home. It made us feel very, very
sorrowful for them.

Thus "in the midst of life we are in death." Were
we always as loving, gentle, and good as we should
be, we need not fear being so suddenly taken from
life; for, should such a fatal accident then happen to
us, we should only be transferred from one scene to
another still more pleasant and happy.

CHAPTER VI.

EXCURSIONS IN SWITZERLAND.

THE climate here seems very much like that of New England; sometimes cloudy or rainy, and sometimes fine. The barometer indicates just now very fine weather; and we are hoping that it may last over to-morrow, the Fourth of July, for which we have planned a pleasant excursion, — an afternoon drive to Lauterbrunnen.

We made an excursion the other day to Giessbach Falls, for which we have to cross the lake in a small row-boat. It is a two-hours' sail. The fall comes pouring and roaring down into the lake with its white foam. After landing, we climbed up the hills by a pathway, sometimes losing sight of the falls; for they are very circuitous, often rushing over deep precipices, and hiding away in a low-valley. Their source is a great way off, up the hills. There are beautiful views all the way; and at length you reach the flat, level top of a hill, where there is a house, — a kind of tavern, — and a shop filled with quantities of the beautiful carved wood-work of which you find so much in Switzerland.   What elegant wooden spoons and forks, with flowers and leaves carved on them ; and plates with acorns or grapes, or some such pretty object, sculptured all round the edge ; and such beautiful toy-cottages of different sizes, and lovely little animals, — graceful deer, chamois-goats, and cows and horses!   We could scarcely tell what to select, all were so beautiful.   But Nannine and Gianina chose, among other things, some funny little Berne bears, in remembrance of those we did *not* see ; and among their mamma's purchases was a pretty little toy-watch, the back of red carnelian, to send to "little Anna" in America : for their dear mamma, when buying things for her own children, often thought of pleasing little Anna, although so far away.   She and I chose models — for we thought them beautiful — of the famous Swiss lion sculptured in stone, which we hope to see when we go to Lucerne.

But we left all these things until we should come back, because the shop was only half-way, and we had to climb up another hill or two before reaching the top of the fall, although from there we could see it before us pouring beautifully down the steep green hillsides. After clambering on, first crossing a lovely green vale, you go up, up an ascent until you come to the top. Then you may walk in behind the cascade ; but you would get pretty wet, sprinkled by the showers of spray. Two pretty rainbows spanned the white foam above and below. All around are many fine trees; and the beautiful grass-covered valley which we crossed is spread out before you, sheltered by the high hills from which the falls precipitate themselves. There they are shut in from all the world beside, and the place seemed to us one of the most charming and beautiful spots we had ever beheld.

From the top, the falls go winding down through the ravines, and over the rocky slopes, many hundred feet, before they reach the lake. How immense they would be could they be seen in one view! but I have already said that they go hiding themselves away here and there.

Returning to the shop, we took the things we had purchased, and descended the hill to the lake, where we found our little boat awaiting us; and we enjoyed the row home, although pretty well fatigued by the excursion.

On the afternoon of the Fourth of July, which proved to be a splendid day, the two elder children, their mamma, and myself, took our drive through the beautiful Valley of Lauterbrunnen.

This valley is almost too lovely for description. It goes from Interlachen (near us) direct to the Jungfrau,* the beautiful "Virgin Mountain," always covered

---

* Pronounced Yūng-vrow

with snow. It is called "Virgin," or "Young Maiden," because it has been always so fresh, with the pure white snow on its top, which no one had been able to reach, I think, until Professor Agassiz, not many years since, with a small party, accomplished it. We can see it from Interlachen; and often, at sunset, it is bathed in a lovely rose-colored light, so like a beautiful rosy blush.

When we set out in the carriage, and drove on over the smooth, pleasant road through the Valley of Lauterbrunnen, the Jungfrau was right before us a great part of the way, with her sister snow-capped mountains, three or four in a group; and it seemed as if we must come close upon them. But we could not really reach them. It needs horses or mules to take one quite there, and it would be an excursion for a whole day. We went only as far as the Staubbach Falls, at the end of the valley, — another very beautiful cascade, but wholly differing from the Giessbach. This falls perpendicularly over a cliff, nine hundred feet, in a fine stream, apparently; but this appearance is owing to its very great height. It is scattered into spray before it reaches the bottom. Oh, how fairy-like and ethereal it looks, this fall! A poet has described it as like a graceful *horse's tail* waving in the air!

From under the spray as it fell, or near it, we gathered some flowers to carry home and press. Nannine was delighted in the gathering; for she has a sort of passion for flowers; and we have a big heavy press, which good Mr. Schumacher gave us. It is excellent for some of the thick-stemmed flowers which we find, — as the Alpine rose. We have also pressed in it some very large pond-lilies, which we got on the other side of the lake, opposite our house. They are larger than the New-England pond-lilies; otherwise they resemble them precisely, excepting that they have not the sweet fragrance of our lilies.

We often take a pleasant row across the lake to some pretty places on the other side, where there are beautiful fields to stroll in, and two or three little hamlets, and the pretty pond filled with those beautiful lilies.

Sometimes we take a pleasant walk over to Interlachen, two miles from us. Nannine, and even Gianina, can walk the distance very well; and sometimes we go in a boat. There is a Swiss lady staying at our Pension a few days, with her son and daughter. They are all very agreeable, and often accompany us. Their language is the Swiss, which is a very droll-sounding language : it does not seem as if one could ever learn it, unless brought up in Switzerland. With us they speak French.

Little Memie does not take any of these excursions with us; but she has a nice donkey, on which she goes

to ride every day with the maid. The young Swiss
gentleman mentioned above has drawn so nice a picture of the maid Lolla, with her broad-rimmed hat,
seated, with Memie in her lap, upon the donkey, and
our funny Josef walking comically by their side, with
a long stick to beat up the donkey! It made us all
laugh to see it, it is so natural and well drawn.

Sometimes baby sits alone on the donkey, with
Lolla or Josef walking by her side; but she does not
like that as well. She takes a tumbler of goat's milk
every night from a little goat that is driven up to the
gate and milked; and she is growing as fat as butter.
The following letter tells more about the goats and
about baby; for we still call her " baby," although she
talks very nicely now. Here they give her a pretty
Swiss name, — " Mimoli."

Switzerland, July 10.

My dear little E——, . . . Shall I tell you something about the great flocks of goats that pass by
our cottage every night? There are as many as fifty,
or seventy, or a hundred, in one flock. In the morning they are driven out to pasture, and in the evening
they all come home. Almost every one has a little
tinkling bell around its neck; and such a tinkling as all
the bells together make! Most of the goats here are
not white, as they are in Italy, but fawn-colored, and

brown, and black. They are very tame; and we sometimes take bread for them in our pockets when we are going out, or pick up some tufts of grass as we meet them in the fields, and let them nibble it out of our hands. A whole dozen of them will come flocking round us at once to get something to eat. They are so pretty, and such gentle little creatures!

Very often the boys who drive them will carry a bunch of flowers or strawberries in their hand. They are always pleased to see us taking notice of their goats; for I think they love them very much: and then they offer us the flowers or strawberries. If we have no pennies to give in return for them, and do not like to take them, they will answer with a pleasant smile, "No matter," and let us have them all the same.

There are many strawberries in the fields about here; and yesterday, when we went out to walk, Nannine was delighted to find and pick some herself: it was the first time in all her life. She had a little wooden drinking-cup, such as they use in Switzerland, hanging round her neck; and she filled it with the berries, and brought them home to her sister, who was not very well.

Little Memie goes every day into the strawberry-field, riding on her little donkey; and she delights in picking and eating them as fast as she can. She says,

"Ecco una fravola!" ("Here is a strawberry!") and, before any one can see it, pop it goes into her little mouth!

To-day, while it was raining hard, she looked out of the window, and said piteously, "Non posso andare nel campo, a cogliere le fravole!" ("I cannot go into the fields to pick strawberries!")

CHAPTER VII.

ANECDOTES AT THE PENSION.

JULY 30. — Just now a party has arrived for an afternoon treat in the portico, in front of the house, and out under the trees. They have charming times there out of doors: there are tables spread for dinner and supper; and the servants wait upon them the same as if they were in the house. Very often such parties come for the day, and make it very lively.

There are now a good many at the Pension, coming and going. Some stay a few days, then others take their places; so that the house is nearly full all the time. Among the boarders, for two or three weeks, is a young and elegant Polish couple on a bridal tour. They seem to enjoy very much going off on a day's excursion all by themselves; and, while they are in the house, they are almost always in their own room, and not to be seen by any one, excepting at meals. But they have a sweet little sister eleven years old, who is a delightful companion for our little girls; and she often comes into our parlor to play with them.

She speaks French with them, and this is an excellent practice for Nannine. For some time after we came, Nannine was very shy about speaking French, which quite disappointed us; for we felt sure she could use it if she would make the attempt, because she had always done her oral exercises* with great facility, turning English into French. But, in about three weeks, she came out with it all at once, and now uses it very readily, and is fast learning to say any thing she wishes to.

It is very amusing to hear our Josef picking up all sorts of phrases. He hears the people in the yard calling out to one another, as they meet, in Swiss or German, " Wie geht's? wie geht's? " (" How do you do? " or, " How goes it? ") He takes this to be the name of the chamber-maid! so he goes about knocking at the doors in search of her, calling out, " Wie-geht's! wie-geht's! " and is very much surprised that he cannot make her hear, or that she *will not answer to her name.* It makes us all laugh very heartily.

He is very good-natured and frolicsome, and likes a good chat: so one evening he came up to the portico, where several gentlemen were sitting, and began to tell a story about a certain individual among the boarders who was deeply in love. Josef acted it all

---

* On the Ollendorff system.

out, — how he sighed, and how his heart was affected (suiting his gestures to his words), and how, at something which had happened, he was so startled and distressed, that the *chevaux* (touching his hair at the same time) "stood up on the top of his head." The gentlemen could restrain themselves no longer, but shouted with laughter; for he had made the ludicrous mistake of saying *chevaux* instead of *cheveux*, — *horses* instead of *hair*. "The horses stood up on the top of his head!"

Our maid Lolla learns French very nicely; and when she speaks it, in her quiet way, she seems like a little French woman, she is so neat and trim and lady-like.

Since we have been here, dear little Gianina has had occasionally the chills and fever, which makes it necessary always to keep her in the house towards evening. This has confined her mother and me a good deal; as, when there have been excursions to the more distant falls and mountains and to the glaciers, where we could not take the children, we have often been obliged to go separately, in order that one of us might remain at home with her.

One of the falls we visited thus was the Reichenbach, a grand cascade; and it was there I saw a real chamois-goat. There are not many of these now among the mountains. This one was in a pen, and was kept by a little girl. It was the brightest, prettiest little creature that ever was : he had such sparkling eyes, and so graceful a form !   There was a small hole high up in the pen, through which the little girl put some grass for him; and he jumped straight up, very high, on a shelf, to reach it.   It was beautiful to see his motions.   There was a high rock also in the pen, on which he could climb.

When we visited the Jungfrau, and other mountains, we were very much interested in the avalanches of snow and rocks, which were frequently falling. They make a rolling noise like thunder; and, for the few minutes that you see them moving, they look like waterfalls pouring down through the ravines of the mountains.

The glaciers are very interesting, — great rough places, prickly, with a sort of icicle jutting out from their surface; but there are among them caves of pure ice, reflecting within them the most beautiful blue color, more deeply blue than the sky.   We should have liked to have the children go to these places; but their mamma thought it would be too fatiguing for them, and that they had better wait until they were older.

We have been waiting for the arrival of an excellent physician, who has been expected for two or three weeks, to see what advice he would give about Gianina.   She is better now, so that we may be able to stay some weeks longer; but we shall probably go away sooner than was at first intended. While I am writing, she and Nannine are both in the yard, playing with two young gentlemen, with whom they enjoy having grand frolics. They were making such a shouting just now, and so much noise, that I was obliged to go to the window two or three times to speak to them, fearing they would disturb the rest of the household. . . . They have had letters lately from little Anna's grandpapa in America, which perfectly delighted them. They frisked round, and clapped hands, and hugged and kissed and thanked, and took the letters to bed with them, or put them close by their bedside. We all received letters by the same mail; so that they were still more pleased, I suppose, feeling that they also were large enough to be treated as the older persons were. . . .

Here my letter was left; and I went down and took Nannine and Gianina,—the two young gentlemen joining us,—and we went out into the pretty fields behind the house, and had a walk and a run down the slopes, to the great amusement of us all. A few days afterwards, one of the gentlemen went away,—it was the one who drew the picture of Lolla and baby on the donkey; and yesterday the other was obliged to go, quite to our regret and his own. He was always at our service to talk with, or walk with, or to row us across the lake, which he seemed to enjoy as much as we; and, besides the pleasure of his society, he always spoke French with us, — for he knew no English, — which was excellent and delightful practice for us.

It is now the 7th of August; and we shall probably go very soon. The doctor came, and said that the best place for Gianina was on the Righi. Poor Gianina! The other day, when she was lying on the bed, not well, her little head seemed to be running upon having a holiday, as she had read of in the "Rollo" books, in grandpapa's orchard. So there was nothing to be done but that her mamma, who was sitting beside her, should come and ask me if I would not write to Anna's grandpapa, and ask him if he would let her and Nannine have a holiday in his garden when we go to America. I promised faithfully to send the message; which I did.

It has been a real pleasure on some of our excursions to see Mr. Abbott's name in the books at the hotels; for he has just preceded us, being at Interlachen when we arrived. The children are so familiar with and so fond of the "Rollo" books, that it seems as if their author were an old friend. Thursday, 11th. — Yesterday, it being our last day, we took a lovely walk along the lake to a charming little waterfall, underneath which were growing many pretty blue harebells. In the afternoon, we went to Interlachen to purchase some of the beautiful views of the scenery to carry away

with us. Then we drove over to a beautiful place
called the "Jungfrau Blick," to have one more view
of the Virgin Mount; but we did not see it, it being
covered with mist, or, as Nannine said, " elle était trop
modeste" to make her appearance. But we sat out
under the trees, and had a cup of coffee and a little
treat there, just as the Swiss do; and could look off
upon the lake, which was tinted with a lovely rose-
colored hue.

We are so sorry to leave our little pretty nest, our
Swiss cottage, where we have had so pleasant a summer; but this afternoon we have to start for our destination on the Righi Mountain. The doctor says it
will be too cold to stay there more than a week; and
then we are to go to Weisbad for a fortnight.

CHAPTER VIII.

LEAVING SWITZERLAND.

WE went in a steamboat across the beautiful Lake of Thun, and stopped at Thun; the good doctor being with us, and carrying us all about; for this was where he lived. Here we had a view again of the grand old snow-white Alps, which we were truly sorry to leave; for they seemed like long-familiar friends. From there we went to Lucerne, and met on the way with a pleasant Polish family, who stopped at the same hotel with us, and who had a little girl, who, after they became acquainted, used to come into our room, and play with our little girls.

At Lucerne we went to see the famous lion, of which we bought the pretty models, carved in wood, at Giessbach Falls. It is a momnuent to the memory of the brave Swiss Guard, who so nobly defended the family of Louis XVI. during the French Revolution. The lion, sculptured in stone, is lying with his fore-paws grasping the shield of France, with a mournful look; and is wounded and dying. Little Memie said, as she

stood with the rest of us looking at it, " È ammalato."*
And, when she was asked what he was sick of, she said
he had *the fever*, "ha la febbre;" which is the only sickness of which she knows any thing, Gianina having
had it so lately. It seemed very cunning for so little
a child to notice the mournful expression of the lion.

We stopped but a day or two then at Lucerne, but
went to a place called Kaltesbad, — a hotel, and not
a town, — on the Righi. This mountain is very near
Lucerne, and is a place where everybody likes to go
to see the sun rise, — which is a very splendid sight,
seeing it from the summit. Some persons stop at Kaltesbad, which is half way up the mountain; and then
rise at two or three o'clock in the morning, and go up
the rest of the way before the sun has risen. But there
is a hotel on the top also; and all who can like to go
there and spend the night, although it is often over-
full.

We went up on horseback to Kaltesbad, two long
hours' ride; and all the way along, going up the rug-
ged steeps on foot, were men with their shoulders
loaded with great packages of things, which they were
carrying up to the hotels; for every thing that is eaten
or used there has to be carried up from the towns
below. We thought they must be *so* tired! We were

* "He is sick."

astonished to find a hundred persons at Kaltesbad when we arrived: we did not suppose there would be so many. The weather was cloudy, and some had been waiting there two or three days for it to be fine enough to see a clear sunrise. But two or three days more passed, and still it was cloudy; for such high mountains are very apt to veil their heads in a misty wreath. In the mean time we walked about, went all over the mountain, even up to the top, but could not see at any great distance. We found a few blue-berries, which Nannine was very fond of picking, and Memie very fond of eating. There were very few flowers; we could scarcely find three or four different kinds: but we liked to ramble about nevertheless.

Our week which we were to spend there was half over, and the weather appeared more cloudy than ever. There had been no clear sun at all; and many persons thought they would wait no longer to see the sun rise, but would go back to Lucerne. The children's mamma, too, thought it was rather too cold for them, and she also decided to go down. So we packed up, and got all ready to set out after dinner. Gianina and baby were put into a *chaise à porteur* (a chair carried on poles by men); and the rest of us all came down on foot,—even Nannine: but she bore it as well as the rest of us; for she is as light on her feet almost as a little wild deer. We could not have ridden, as there were no horses there; and we thought it would be less fatiguing to walk than to go in a chair: so we set out with great enjoyment; but the road was perfectly steep a great part of the way, and it took us two long hours to descend, and we were pretty well tired.

Then we had half an hour's sail across the Lake of Lucerne, which was splendidly bright and glowing, with a golden sunset; for the clouds had all scattered and disappeared. And as we sat at the tea-table at the hotel that evening, and could look out upon the lake and Mount Righi, opposite to us, Nannine exclaimed all at once, "What a great fire on the mountains!" We looked, and, behold! it was the splendid full moon rising. "Oh!" we thought, "what a fine day it will be to-morrow, and what a splendid sunrise! and we shall not be on the top of the Righi to see it!" And very truly the morning was glorious, with not a cloud to be seen, and the head of Mount Righi stood as fair and unveiled as possible; and from it there must have been a magnificent sunrise seen by those who were fortunate enough to remain.

(I will say, *sub rosa*, that their mamma and I afterwards went to the top, and saw a glorious sunrise, with the country all around, and the distant Alps looking magnificent; but the children remained then at the hotel. Probably, at some future time, they also will have the opportunity of seeing the beautiful sight.)

In this very region, at the foot of Mount Righi, and around the Lake of Lucerne, which is the "Lake of the four Cantons," are the places where were performed the romantic and brave deeds of the patriot William Tell, whose name is held in remembrance, not only in Switzerland, but in all countries. It was here that he refused to bow to the hat of the tyrant Gessler, which was placed upon a pole; and, as a punishment for refusing to do so, he was compelled to shoot the apple on the head of his own son. He was so fortunate as to hit the apple exactly in the middle of it; but, for fear that he might kill his child, he had carried another arrow under his cloak, with which he meant to shoot the tyrant, he said, if his son's life had been taken. When he was afterwards being carried a prisoner across the lake, a terrible storm arose; and he was set free to steer the boat, because he was the most skilful boatman of them all. Seizing the opportunity, he drew the boat to land, and then leaped ashore, but set the boat adrift again with the tyrant in it: the latter, nevertheless, escaped the storm, and got safe to land. Tell, meeting him at another time, however, shot him: and this was the beginning of a long war between Switzerland and Austria; for Gessler was an Austrian governor.

Switzerland is now a republic, although not exactly like the Republic of the United States.

CHAPTER IX.

WEISBAD AND ST. GALL.

FROM Lucerne, we went to Zurich in a carriage. It was a very hot day, — the hottest that we had had all summer; and the children really suffered from the heat. But the ride was through a beautiful country: it looked like a bright and cheerful garden all the way, and particularly when we came upon the Lake of Zurich, which was very pleasant and refreshing. At two o'clock, we arrived: but it was so exceedingly warm, that we could not go out until towards evening; and then we went almost all about the town, Nannine and I together, and Gianina and baby with Lolla in another direction, in search of an ice-cream saloon; and at last each party only found one small one. But that gave us all that we wanted, however, and made us quite cool and comfortable.

From Zurich we came to St. Gall, where we staid a day and two nights; and, on the 22d of August, we arrived at Weisbad, in the canton of Appenzell. The hotel is large, with nice grounds and pretty walks, and is full of people. But, as we have our meals at a private table, we do not see much of them in the house, excepting in the evening, when we go into the parlor. There all the ladies and gentlemen are as merry as they can be, playing all sorts of games. One is, forming a procession, and following the leader. This one leads them all over the house, through the passages and halls, and up stairs and down stairs, which makes it all very entertaining.

We take long walks through the delightful green fields, where the hay is still making, and go about the village, or on the country roads, and meet the peasants, often in a pretty costume, — the Appenzell; the women sometimes with a scarlet cap on their head, and the men with a bright scarlet vest.

All the women in the village do the beautiful embroidery-work of muslin or lace, which is sent all over Europe and America. They sit by the windows, with little round frames in their hands, passing the needle up and down so busily. We step up, and speak with them a little; but they keep steadily at their work. What elegant collars they bring round to sell! and they are so cheap! at least, cheaper than elsewhere.

ST. GALL.— We stopped a few days at Weisbad, and now have come back to St. Gall, where we stay also a few days. It is a very pleasant town, surrounded by beautiful hills. To-day there has been a grand festival on one of the hills; a splendid place for 'such a purpose, the top being all a smooth, grassy lawn. It was a holiday for the children of the Protestant schools; and a very beautiful festival it was. We were there nearly all day, before and after dinner.

The scholars went up in procession, the girls all in white, and most of the boys in a simple military dress, — dark frock-coats, and white pants. There was a large company of boys, officered and exercised entirely by themselves. None of them seemed to be over fifteen; and there were little things, who looked not more than six or seven years of age: but they went through all the exercises and manœuvres, firing muskets, cannon, &c., with the precision, regularity, and seriousness of old soldiers. They had gymnastic exercises besides, which were very interesting.

It was an immense place, or field; and the children were divided into parties of a hundred or more, each with its master; the girls all by themselves, and the boys by themselves, carrying on their games. It was such a pretty sight to see those large circles of children, all in white, dancing round like so many butterflies, all in perfect good humor and enjoyment! The games were regulated by the superintendents. Some of the funniest were among the boys. In one called

11

"Jacob, wo bist du?"* two were put within a circle, with a little hollow sort of drum on each of their heads, which covered them down to the shoulders, entirely blinding them, and making them look very comical; and then they called out, "Where are you?" and tried to catch each other.

We went almost into convulsions of laughter sometimes, seeing them run all unconsciously into each other's arms! But I believe the game was not up until they had fairly caught each other by trial. A similar game was played in the evening, in the parlor at Weisbad, only it was a gentleman and lady instead of children; and they were blinded with handkerchiefs, and each had a key, which he or she tapped on the floor once in a while; and by this means one would find where the other was. It was very amusing.

Another game was "Cat and Mouse." One stands within the ring or circle of children, for the mouse; and one is outside, for the cat. If the cat breaks through, and gets within the circle, the mouse must run out, and the cat must not be allowed to go after her if it can be prevented. Or if she gets out, and the mouse gets in again, she must be kept out if possible; and so it goes on, until the cat succeeds in catching the mouse, and then some one else takes the place.

* "Jacob, where art thou?" or, "Where are you?"

There were long tables spread under the trees for lunch, with all things nice upon them; and towards evening, after a splendid day, the children were marched back again, in procession, to the town.

CHAPTER X.

VISIT TO MUNICH.

Munich, September.

FROM St. Gall, we came first by diligence, and then across the Lake of Constance in a steamboat, then by diligence again, and railroad, all in a day and a half, to this very handsome city of Munich. Here the children's papa and mamma have a good friend, Mr. M., who takes us out every morning in his carriage, and shows us all the fine places, until three o'clock, when we return to the hotel for dinner. Yesterday we all dined at his house; and, as his family are in the country, he invited a charming German lady and her daughter to meet us. The daughter is very pretty and amiable, and speaks Italian very well; which was very fortunate for some of us, who could not speak German. Of the regular long German dinner I could not begin to tell you. But there was pastry at the beginning; and in the middle, after two or three courses of meat, there was a pudding; and, after some other courses of meat, there were cakes and pies again. It was all very nice; but I do not know what we should do if we had such every day, with all the beer that goes round and round.

We looked at all the pretty curiosities, gifts, &c., which Mr. M.'s boys had collected, or had had given them from time to time, and which were kept in a glass cabinet that was quite large and well filled; it making a most pretty ornament for the parlor. And what pretty vines growing in vases were drooping from the windows down to the floor! There was one hanging by a cord from the middle of the ceiling, its green leaves and tendrils falling beautifully over our heads.

To-day, good Mr. M. dined with us. He took us all over the bronze foundery; but they art not casting any thing at present. It is an interesting place to visit, and especially so to us, because the children's papa is having much work done there,—great statues, which will look *so* fine !

At another time, when we were with Mr. M., who is inspector to King Lewis, the father of the reigning king, Maximilian, we had a fine opportunity to see his majesty. We had just come out of a studio, and he had just gone into one on the opposite side of the street. His carriage, with six horses, and with liveried postilions and grooms, was waiting: so we stood by the door we had just come out of, and waited too. By and by they came, — the queen-mother and one of their daughters; and then the king, who was assisted into the carriage by the sculptor whom he had visited. The carriage was all open at the sides, and rather queer-looking. The king and queen sat on the back seat, so that his face was towards us; and then he observed Mr. M. looking very pleasantly at him, and gave him a sweet smile. His manner was very affable; smiling upon and nodding very kindly to every one who had gathered round, the poor children of the street, &c. We were very glad to see him: for, when the children's papa was in Munich, King Lewis invited him to his palace, and treated him very kindly and handsomely; for he thinks a great deal of his works.

He is very much interested in every thing about art; and, since he gave up the throne to his son, he spends all his time and money in improving the city, and giving employment to the artists. He expends very little upon himself, being very simple, it seems, in all his habits, — so simple, Mr. M. told us, that there is no show inside of his palace, though it looks very handsome outside. But that, I suppose, is because he wishes the city to look handsome in all its buildings.

We went into the palace of King Max, as he is called; which is very handsome. In the throne-room are two long rows of kings, of colossal size, — larger than life. They seem to be of splendid gold; but they are of bronze, gilded. They stand upon both sides up and down the long room. King Lewis had them arranged there; and his object was, as he told his son, that all his "ancestors" might be witnesses "that nothing should be done, that no action should be committed, in that room, unworthy of a king." In many of the rooms of the palace, the walls are beautifully painted with historical subjects. In one suite of rooms, there is the whole story of Ulysses and Telemachus,—the wanderings of Telemachus in search of his father, his stopping at the Island of Calypso, &c. In these paintings, every figure is as large as, or larger than, life; and the whole of each wall is covered with them, as if they were one great picture hung up. Thus they make a very elegant decoration.

There is so much beautiful art—paintings and sculpture and architecture—all over the city of Munich, that it is a delightful place to visit. There is always a feast for one's eyes; fine public buildings with beautiful marble pillars, like those in ancient Greece; and buildings even covered with paintings *outside;* and the churches with splendid stained glass windows,—all very handsome. And there are great, noble grounds called the English Garden, in the midst of the city, with the River Iser running through it,—

the same river that is mentioned in Campbell's poem
of " Hohen-Linden : " —

> " On Linden, when the sun was low,
>   All bloodless lay the untrodden snow;
>   And dark as winter was the flow
>   Of Iser rolling rapidly."

This garden is a magnificent place of green lawns
and groves and lakes and beautiful walks. It is a delightful place for children; and we went there with
ours to enjoy the fresh air and luxuriant verdure.

I must not forget to mention, in Munich, the shops
filled with the beautiful Bohemian or Bavarian glass :
for this vicinity is its native place; that is, where it was
originally made. Whole shops filled with it, of all
rich and beautiful colors, and in all varieties of beautiful work, — how fascinating it was! We went there
at every opportunity, just to look at the beautiful
things. We would gladly have carried away many of
them; but that was impossible: for, besides being very
expensive, how could we, in travelling, manage to
pack away and carry safe those splendid vases, and
exquisite little cups and plates and pitchers, and all
sorts of fanciful things? Oh, no! we could only look
at them, and say how beautiful they were. Only, for
a memento of the place, we could take some of the
simplest little things. What superb punch-bowls, with

the tiny, exquisite rose-colored glasses all around, and the beautiful green and purple and amber-colored objects! But no one can imagine, without seeing them, how handsome they are, all collected in the shops.

CHAPTER XI.

JOURNEY TO FLORENCE.

MUNICH was our last stopping-place before taking the long journey to Florence, on our way back to Rome. We had expected to go to Milan : but that would be so tedious a journey for the children, that we took the easiest and shortest way that we could possibly go; and that was by Vettura, across the Tyrol, by the cities of Innspruck, Verona, Mantua, Bologna, and Florence.

We left Munich on Tuesday morning, the 13th of September, after having bidden farewell, quite sorrowfully, to our good friend Mr. M. the night before, and put ourselves — four inside — into a very easy-going carriage. The maid, baby, and Josef had a comfortable seat in the little *coupée* in front; and the dear baby was scarcely ever inside, which made it very much easier for us; for she always became very restless inside the carriage. As it was to be so long a journey, — ten days in the *vettura*, day after day, — we had to take great pains not to get too tired in the beginning.

Our regular routine was, to be called up every morning at four o'clock, — good Josef taking upon himself the responsibility of awakening us; and then we got ourselves and the children dressed and equipped for the day. How good the children were, waked out of a sound sleep so early in the morning! — they never made any trouble about it. Then we took breakfast, and at about six were in the carriage, and settled down for two or three hours of quiet napping or so, having risen so early. Then, with books, — Nannine and Gianina with their dolls, — we whiled away the time until towards twelve o'clock. The two girls had had and had used up more than one set of dolls during the summer, and at two or three different places their mamma had gratified an irresistible desire for some charming new one that they saw; and now their pet dolls on the journey were some little German ones, with the heads, arms, and legs to move, which make them look so exactly like real babies, and only *too* natural. For the last few weeks, Nannine had been very impatient to get home to see her "Emmy," whom she left behind, and Gianina to see her "Ellen," — two great dolls which they had had for Christmas presents. When we came away, they had been rolled up in napkins, and packed away in the drawers, being too large to take on a journey.

At twelve, we usually stopped for two hours, had a

warm dinner at a hotel, set off again, and passed the time in an after-dinner nap, reading, looking at the scenery, telling stories, playing little games, &c.; for we had a beautiful little box full of games, such as dominoes and checkers, which their mamma had purchased for the two girls at Munich, expressly for the journey. One of our amusements was making rhymes, — no matter how funny or ridiculous they were: two or three were put down on scraps of paper; and here they are.

We were passing by a sparkling little stream of water, looking so cool; and I exclaimed, "If I could only have some to drink!" Nannine, in a sweet way (and as if it were the easiest thing in the world to do), said, "If I had a cup, I would get you some." Upon that, this impromptu was made:—

> There's a pretty river flowing by,
> With water clear and blue;
> And, if I only had a cup,
> I'd get a drink for you!
>
> Well, Nina, there's a cottage near,
> And you might go and ask;
> And, if we could but get enough,
> We then might fill a cask!

The next was probably a fancy sketch, after the manner of Mother Goose:—

There was a little bird singing on a tree,
And I wished very much that he would come to me;
But he sat there, and sang, " Tweedy-dee-dee,"
And I was very happy to see him in such glee.

But the wind it was high, and the tree it did rock;
And I went and looked at the weather-cock:
When I came back, I had such a shock!
For the poor little bird had fallen down on a rock!

I ran to him quickly, and looked at his wing,
Not thinking that ever again he could sing:
I took him in my hands, the poor little thing!
And then some cherries to him I did bring.

He opened his beak, and ate the sweet fruit;
And it seemed that it did him very well suit;
For he uttered a note as clear as a lute;
And I thought, when I heard it, no one could him shoot!

The following, with the date, "Sept. 15, in the carriage, on the road through the Tyrol," was for Nannine, who petted and cared for her doll as if it were a real child, and was as devoted to it morning and night as a real mamma: no pains could be too great for it: —

My baby-doll is lying sweetly,
Good and quiet, by my side:
Mamma says she'll dress it neatly
When we've finished this long ride.

Then I'll keep it clean and neat;
For it is my darling child;
And I love its face so sweet,
And its gentle eyes so mild.

I'll put it in its little bed
When it wants to go to sleep,
And let it rest its weary head;
And now and then I'll take a peep

At its pretty, smiling face,
And its tiny hands and feet,
The cunning frock all trimmed with lace,
And the little apron neat.

And when it's had its quiet nap,
And is all ready, then, to wake,
I'll make a pleasant sugar-pap,
And get a nice sweet little cake.

And sometimes, when I go to walk,
I'll take my darling dolly dear;
And then we'll have a pretty talk
About the sky that is so clear.

But should there come a cloud, or fall
Of rain, to hurt my little pet,
I'll wrap her in a good warm shawl,
That she may not, sure, get wet.

Oh, how I love my baby-doll!
She gives me pleasure all the time:
I like to sit and rock and loll,
And sing her many a pretty rhyme.

About seven, or half-past, we usually stopped for
the night; but sometimes it was later: and once we
rode until nine, Nannine and Gianina both going to
sleep the last hour. We had an excellent driver and
horses: and often, for hours at a time, we went almost
as swiftly as the wind over the smooth road; for a
great portion of the way was a perfect level. In that
part of the Tyrol which belongs to Bavaria, and
which was a whole day's ride from Munich, there were
no hills at all; but Austrian Tyrol was hilly and picturesque. There, one day, we met, as we were riding
along, one of the prettiest sights, in the way of animals, that we ever saw. It was a deer, — I suppose,
an elk-deer, — harnessed into and drawing a lovely
little light wagon made of wicker-work, — that is, all
the upper portion, — in which a man and woman were
seated, and travelling along very nicely. How
elegantly the deer held up his head, showing to advantage his graceful, branching antlers! It was a beautifully picturesque sight; and we all enjoyed it very
much.

We crossed the Brennen Pass, which is the lowest
one into Italy, and stopped that night — the second —
at Innspruck, just in the corner of Austria; then came
by Mauls (a little town in the Tyrol), Botzen, Trent,
Roveredo; and the sixth day brought us to Verona.
Here we stopped almost all the next day, as we

could go from there to Mantua by railroad; and the carriage went on to the latter place, and waited for us there.

On going out of the hotel at Verona to take a little walk, after we arrived, whom should we see but an old friend of mamma's from America! She knew him by a side-view of his spectacles! He was ever so glad to see her, as she was to see him. He was standing in a doorway, chatting with his little bit of a niece. But, early in the morning, he and his party set off again on their journey; and we remained to see Verona. It is a fine old city, and has the most perfect little amphitheatre that there is remaining from ancient times. It is circular, and like the Coliseum at Rome, only very much smaller; and with the seats all around, rising one behind another, it shows us how fine and beautiful the Coliseum was in its best days. We went all over it, and sat on the seats; but we were glad not to see now such sights as they had in olden times, — the fights of wild beasts and gladiators.

At five o'clock, P.M., we took the railway for Mantua, which was only twenty-six miles distant. In the cars we made a very pleasant acquaintance with a young English gentleman, who had a pretty little dog with him which interested our little girls very much, particularly Gianina, who has a great passion for all young animals and pets. They (the gentleman and his dog) and we were the only occupants of our car; and each party was very curious to find out who the other was, whether English or American, both speaking the same language. We thought we should discover, by some particular word or other, whether he was an American or an Englishman; and he, as he afterwards confessed, was putting us to the same test. But only just before we arrived did we find each other out!

Also just before we arrived at the last way-station, when we were just ready to start again, the pretty dog jumped out of the window; and it was too late to recover him. We were so sorry both for him and his master! but we hoped that he might in some way go on with the train; get into the baggage-car, perhaps. When we arrived at Mantua, however, and descended from the cars, he was nowhere to be seen; and the gentleman sent back word to make inquiries about him. We parted here from our new acquaintance; but we met him again at Bologna and Florence, and he had found his dog. He had remained quietly at the station where he had escaped until sent for; which we thought quite sagacious, or *prudent* at least, in the little animal.

It was almost or quite dark before we reached the hotel in Mantua; so that we had no time to walk out, as we always liked to do in every place where we stopped. We retired early too, that we might be up

12

for an earlier start than usual; for we had heard that there had been banditti lately on the very road we were to travel the next day, — the road to Modena. We wished, therefore, to avoid being late in the evening, lest *we* might be attacked, as the diligence had been; for, a little while after leaving Modena, some banditti had come up, and fatally wounded the conductor of the diligence, taking from a bride and bridegroom, who were the only passengers, every thing they had with them. There are many stories of such banditti, or mountain-robbers, in Italy; but we never thought that *we* should ever fall in with any of them, for we supposed they had almost all disappeared in these days: but now here they were, or had just been, on the very road we were going to travel!

So we were called up at half-past three in the morning, before daylight; so early, that it seemed surprising that good faithful Josef could have been awake to arouse us all: but it seemed as if he scarcely ever slept; he was always so ready for every thing day or night. We took breakfast, and set out at about half-past five, and arrived at Modena before dark, without meeting with a single adventure, except crossing the wide River Po in a ferry (if that may be called one), "no hair-breadth escape" at all, and never once coming in sight of a highway robber.

At Modena, we were driven to an immensely large hotel, which was once, perhaps, a great palace. It may have been the one, or like it, where poor Ginevra was shut down in the oaken chest; for this is the city where that sad event took place, — of the young bride hiding away in an old chest, and being shut in by the spring-lock fastening close upon her.

This is the story as told by the poet Rogers: —

> " Great was the joy: but at the bridal feast,
> When all sat down, the bride was wanting there;
> Nor was she to be found! Her father cried,
> ''Tis but to make a trial of our love,'
> And filled his glass to all; but his hand shook:
> And soon from guest to guest the panic spread.
> 'Twas but that instant she had left Francesco,
> Laughing and looking back and flying still,
> Her ivory tooth imprinted on his finger!
> But now, alas! she was not to be found;
> Nor from that hour could any thing be guessed
> But that she was not.
>
> . . . .
>
> Full fifty years were past, and all forgot,
> When on an idle day, — a day of search, -
> 'Mid the old lumber in the gallery,
> That mouldering chest was noticed; and 'twas said
> By one as young and thoughtless as Ginevra,
> ' Why not remove it from its lurking-place?'
> 'Twas done as soon as said; but on the way
> It burst, it fell; and, lo! a skeleton,
> With here and there a pearl, an emerald-stone,
> A golden clasp clasping a shred of gold.

> All else had perished save a nuptial ring,
> And a small seal, her mother's legacy,
> Engraven with a name, — the name of both, —
> ' Ginevra.' "

Poor Ginevra! We would not like to think that any thing so sad had taken place in the great house where we stopped; but certainly it looked deserted enough. There appeared to be no other travellers there, and we were led about through many circuitous passages, the rooms all empty on either side as it seemed to us; but at last we came to a pleasant suite of rooms, which looked quite cosey and comfortable. In these we were established for the night: but it was not yet quite sunset; so we had time to go out to walk, and see the tall and beautiful Campanile, or bell-tower, in which hangs a bucket, which was once, some hundreds of years ago, the cause of a war between the cities of Modena and Bologna. When we came back to the hotel, as the day had been very warm, we made our supper on nothing but *ice-cream.*

The next day we dined at Bologna, and had such an elegant dinner! How much Nannine, especially, enjoyed the splendid fruit, — the delicious plums, apricots, and pears! She would hardly eat any thing else. We had only time after dinner to go and see the two famous leaning towers. These, and the one we had just seen at Modena, and the Leaning Tower at Pisa, were built during the middle ages, when there were many wars between the different cities; and are quite different from any built in these times. They are very tall, picturesque, and interesting.

After passing through the Tyrol, and before coming to Verona, the great Lombardy Plains had commenced, another part of which we had crossed in going *into* Switzerland; and they continued until we reached Bologna. The country was perfectly level all the way from Verona to Mantua, and from there to Modena, and thence to Bologna. We seemed only to be riding through innumerable fields of corn and grapes. The grape-vines climbed around the trunks of the trees, which were planted in rows between the different fields. But at Bologna, which is situated at the foot of the Apennines, the country became hilly; and, instead of taking the usual road over the mountains, we took another, which brought us to Pistoia, only twenty or tweny-five miles' distance from Florence, where we arrived at four o'clock on the afternoon of the tenth day. But *so* tired and faint! for we had stopped the night before at a poor *osteria ;** and the bread and butter which was given us for supper was so poor, that we could not eat it. We felt so sorry for the poor people who had to live upon it! The butter tasted exactly like mutton-tallow;

* A small tavern.

and the bread — I cannot describe it. We smoothed over as well as we could our *want of appetite,* for we did not wish to hurt the feelings of the poor people; and in the morning we came away without asking for any breakfast, and without the nice bathing which we had had every morning, and which had kept us all so fresh and comfortable. We took a late breakfast somewhere else; and at Pistoia we had a nice dinner in a nice little room, but scarcely time to eat it; for we had to hasten to the cars, which were to carry us the rest of the way to Florence. In about two hours we were there, to our great delight; but so fatigued, that we did nothing after supper but take a famously large bath, each of us, children and all, and retire to bed.

The next day, we scarcely went out of the house. We had got on nicely all through the journey, none of us giving out until the tenth and last day; and that, I suppose, was owing to the poor fare, or *no* fare, of the night before, — no supper and no breakfast. We had had splendid weather all the way: the children had been very good; and little Memie had got so used to travelling, that, all the first day after arriving in Florence, she was asking to go to the "carozza."

CHAPTER XII.

STAY IN FLORENCE.

WEDNESDAY EVENING, Sept. 28.

WE have been a week in Florence, and have seen the principal sights. First the grand Pitti Palace, the residence of the Grand Duke of Tuscany; but the large gallery of beautiful pictures in it is open to the public. Here is the loveliest of all pictures, — Raphael's "Madonna della Sedia." It is the original picture, but as fair and fresh as if just painted, although Raphael lived more than three hundred years ago. He died in 1520, just a hundred years before the Pilgrim Fathers landed in New England. It hangs on the wall with hundreds of other elegant pictures; but there are none that you would think as beautiful, with the sweet, heavenly face of the child, and the gentle but happy woman's look of the mother.

Another beautiful picture to look at in this gallery is one of Titian's, who was, perhaps, the next greatest painter after Raphael. It is the "Marriage of St. Catherine." She has a very sweet countenance, and is holding the infant Saviour in her arms. An elderly woman and a young girl are on one side, caressing the child; and the little John, a beautiful little figure, kneeling, and pointing to the infant, is on the other. How much we liked to look at these and all the other fine paintings!

Florence is famed for its many and beautiful pictures, as Rome is for its many and beautiful sculptures.

There is another splendid gallery of paintings in this city, the Uffizii Palace, in which is one room most enchantingly beautiful. This is called " The Tribune;" and, besides some elegant pictures, it contains the celebrated Venus de Medicis, a very lovely ancient statue.

There is another hall containing ancient sculptures, among which is the celebrated group of Niobe and her children, who were struck by the arrows of Apollo. These figures are not placed together, however, in a group: they are arranged separately around the room. They all have a suffering and terror-stricken look; but I believe that only one of them is represented as actually dying or dead.*

The cathedral of the city is the grand and famous Duomo, which is very peculiar, — quite different from any other building. The interior is fine, with arches and richly-stained windows. The baptistery, where all the baptisms take place, instead of in the church,

* See the companion volume, — Fairies of our Garden: Roman Stories.

is another building close beside it. This building has some very celebrated bronze doors. They are sculptured, or carved, with picture-like scenes. The innumerable figures are small, but beautifully done. By the side of the Duomo and baptistery stands also a tall, beautiful campanile, or bell-tower.

For beautiful walks in Florence, there are the elegant Boboli Gardens, which belong to the Pitti Palace, and the Cascini, — splendid grounds, where everybody goes for a promenade, or to drive in the afternoons. A band often plays there, which makes it very pleasant.

.   .   .   .

To all these pleasant places, and many others, we had been during the week: and at last we were belated in packing for our homeward journey; so that some of us were obliged to sit up until twelve o'clock at night.

Good Josef had become so used to calling us early while travelling, that I suppose he thought we must always be up by half-past three or four in the morning; and he waked us at that early hour. There was no need of it, however; for we did not set out until seven.

We went to Sienna by railway, three hours distant from Florence; and thence we were to travel day and night in the diligence until we reached home, which we hoped to do in twenty-six or twenty-seven hours.

But we found we had to stop at Sienna all that day, and could not take the diligence until evening. This gave us time for going about the city. In the cathedral we were shown some splendidly illuminated copies of the Bible, some hundreds of years old. The large letters at the beginning of the chapters and verses were most richly and beautifully painted. The printing of some of the copies was done elegantly, by hand, before the art of printing from types was invented.

Oh, how industrious and unwearied must the old monks have been, who in their cells and monasteries, day after day, copied, word by word, and letter by letter, the great volume of the Bible! for in such a way only was it multiplied in the beginning. Had it not been for these monks and other learned men copying it from time to time for their own use, or for that of the churches and convents, the sacred volume might have been lost or destroyed in the dark ages, when learning was neglected, and barbarism and ignorance prevailed over almost all Europe, — we might say, over all the world; since Europe was the most enlightened portion of the world at that time, America not having even been discovered. Certainly we owe a debt of gratitude to those useful men, who, in their quiet cells, or retirement, preserved what learning they could, and by their devoted labor and industry were enabled to hand down the holy Bible to other times. Now, since printing was invented (and it is multiplied by millions of copies every year), the Bible will forever remain the seed, the plant, the book, to Christianize, civilize, and enlighten the world.* . . .

At eight o'clock in the evening we were all ready for the diligence, and we set out. The children, of course, soon went to sleep; but at every post, in changing horses, which was about every hour, they regularly awoke. They were perfectly quiet and good, and always dropped off to sleep again. We went very rapidly, — often ten or twelve miles an hour; and during the night, the way being an ascent, we had sometimes seven, eight, and nine horses attached. In the morning, we stopped half an hour at Acquapendente, a town on the Campagna, for breakfast; and there the maid Lolla had an opportunity to make a little call upon an aunt of hers who was living there. We did not stop again during the day; but Josef had provided for a lunch of cold chicken &c., in the stage.

The country here was very different from the rich

---

* Philosophers sometimes discuss the question as to whether " civilization " or " Christianity " should or does naturally come first. But we know that people who have not had a true idea of the Deity have never become thoroughly civilized and enlightened. The Bible, both the Old and New Testament, is the only book from which we obtain a correct knowledge of God: therefore it must be the great source of truly enlightening, civilizing, and Christianizing the world.

green hills and fields of the cooler places in which we had been so long travelling; for the hills were bare and barren, the grass being dried from the heat of the long summer. But as we came in sight of the lake, which was called " Thrasymene " in Hannibal's time, the scene was finer and prettier. It is a large lake, and was a long time in view.

We rode on. Eight, ten o'clock in the evening came; but still no gates of Rome appeared. At eleven we arrived at the city, and found the Porta del Popolo* barred and locked! It was soon opened, however. We found no one awaiting us, as we had expected; but somebody *had been* waiting until about three-quarters of an hour before, when they had given us up, and gone home! So we had no *lascia passare,* as we had hoped, and were obliged to go to the Dogana† instead; and it was twelve o'clock before we were at liberty to go. We then put ourselves into a hack (leaving the luggage), and, arriving on our own piazza, had the satisfaction of seeing, right before our eyes, the last light in the house put out! but there was one awaiting us, as we found, in the *portone.* We aroused the son of the porter, who, after waiting to

* The gate of the city which you enter from the Florence Road.

† The Custom House. A *lascia passare* is a paper, or permit, allowing one to pass without undergoing an examination at the Custom House.

dress himself, came down to let us in; then we crept softly up the long stairs, and tried to find the key under the doorway, where it was always placed at night. But by that time Josef's heavy boots came tramping up the stairway; and we soon heard, called out from the hall inside, "Chi'è, chi'è?" Then mamma and the children set up such a clapping, and shouting "Papa, papa!"

Such was our reception after a four-months' absence from home, — every one abed, doors locked! But we had a delightful welcome, nevertheless: all were so happy to see us! The whole house was soon aroused, — the servants, and the porter's family, — and a supper prepared, of cold chicken, &c. The night before, it had been all ready in fine style; and they sat up until twelve o'clock, expecting us. Papa had gone out in a carriage at *four* o'clock to meet us, and staid until *ten*.

The first thing Nannine and Gianina did, after being so warmly welcomed, — before they could think of going to bed, although it was past midnight, — was to go and take "Emmy" and "Ellen" from the drawers in which they had been snugly packed away, and give them a hearty kiss and embracing.

They have had a whole week of holidays since, and they carry around the two great dolls most faithfully every day.

FOURTH YEAR.

CHAPTER I.

THINGS AT HOME.

OCTOBER.

THIS last week we have done almost nothing but "put things to rights." We have now every thing nicely arranged, and to-morrow we begin lessons again.

However, poor Gianina has again had the chills and fever since returning; and we do not know how she will go on through the winter. But the homœopathic physician says that he can cure her in three days; that he has been enabled to cure the worst forms of the disease. Hers is the *terziana*, which is worse than the daily fever, although it occurs only every three days. We are in hopes that he will succeed in his treatment.

All the children now practise dancing a little every morning after breakfast, their mamma playing for them on the piano. They have never taken dancing-lessons; but they make up for themselves all sorts of pretty figures and attitudes, — even little Memie. It looks very cunning to see her trying to do as her sisters do.

Memie is quite roguish sometimes. To-day, after dinner, she asked for a piece of cheese to give the cat, whose name is Moro. When she found that a nice bit was given her, she said, "Moro didn't want it;" and she put it into her own mouth instead! When she wishes to do something which she has been told she must not do, she asks everybody to "go away, and not look." All this she says in Italian; but she is beginning now to learn English. Her papa thinks she is old enough; so he makes her repeat something after him every day. It seems very strange for a little child only two and a half years old to be learning another language. But she makes out quite well; for she is very ambitious to say every thing that she hears her sisters say in English in their play; and she admires to repeat a good deal that they say, although she does not know what it means. She sounds just like a little foreigner, when she tries to speak in that manner. She has learned enough to know that an English question should have an English answer: so, whatever question may be asked her in English, she always answers "Yes," whether understanding it or not. If she sometimes begins to answer with the Italian *si*, she will correct herself, and say "Yes." It sounds very cunning. To-day I showed her little Anna's daguerrotype, which we have just received from America, and made her pronounce the name, *Anna.* . . . It was a pretty big mouthful for her; but, by speaking slowly, she managed it very well.

This daguerrotype of little Anna is exceedingly funny. She was very unwilling to sit for it; and the artist, to persuade her, had told her to try and see a little kitten in the instrument. So her little hands are all spread before her forehead, to shade her eyes; and her whole little face is drawn up into such a comical yet earnest expression, that it makes us laugh heartily every time we look at it. It amuses the children very much, her trying to see a kitten; and their papa says, "She is looking for one with each end of her five fingers!"

Another daguerrotype that came is of Anna's little baby brother Tommy. He is sucking his chubby fist, which delights Nannine; and she only wishes *she* had a baby brother just like him.

Little Anna was at this time large enough to begin to sew; and she had made some neat little thread bags, which were sent with the daguerrotypes: then the following letter was written in acknowledgment:—

Nov. 29.

DEAREST LITTLE ANNA,—I was very glad to receive the little letter from you, and the sweet little bags. You were very good to make them for me, and you sewed them very nicely. . . .

Nannine and Gianina and baby are quite well. Gianina has gone to-day to take dinner with our good minister, Mr. B., because he is very fond of her, and likes to have her come. Baby goes out to walk every day, and can walk nicely; for she is very fat and strong. She has a pretty little bird in a cage in her room. It has yellow wings and a red head. She likes to see it hanging up in its cage, and sometimes she wants to take it in her hands.

Gianina has a pretty canary-bird in her room. When it first came, it seemed rather lonely; and so her mamma bought a little looking-glass and put it in the cage, and then he appeared quite happy. He hops to the glass, and looks in; and he thinks, I suppose, that he has a little friend and companion with him. He sings very beautifully, and is as lively as he can be.

But he has a real little visitor these few days past, another canary, in a cage close beside him; and they are very happy together. The new bird belongs to little Edith ——. She was taken sick, and others of her family also; so that the poor little bird, for two or three days, was almost forgotten. He had no fresh water,

13

and no seed to eat; and, when the children's mamma went to their house, she found the bird very lonely and sad. She cleaned out his cage, gave him some water, sent to buy some new seed for him, and hung up his cage in the parlor window, in the pleasant sun. When we were walking out the next morning, and passed by the house, we saw him still there: but there was no one in the house to take care of him; for little Edith was taken sick in another house where she was staying, and her papa and mamma had gone there to take care of her. So the children's mamma sent a man to get the cage, and bring it to our house, that Gianina might take care of the little creature with her little bird; and, when Edith gets well, we shall send it home again. . . . Good-by!

A sad event took place this autumn, which made us all very sorry. The account of it is contained in the following letter to a young boy, written a few weeks afterwards : —

ROME, Jan. 2.

DEAR G., — I promised some time ago to send you an account of the balloon ascension that was to take place here; but the end of it was so very sad, that I hardly like to write about it.

When we returned to Rome, on the 1st of October, we found preparations making for the ascension, on the Square, right in front of our house. Thus we should have a fine time, we thought, seeing it; and it was to take place very soon.

In two or three weeks, the day was appointed, and the gas was made, and the balloon was partly filled during the night. When we arose in the morning, we saw it swinging backward and forward, looking very large and fine.

The afternoon came, and many persons were assembled on the Square. The old gentleman who was to go up (he was about sixty) was very busy. The parachute was filled with flowers, which he was to scatter after he should have risen, in the balloon, over the spectators. At length he entered, and some of the ropes which held the balloon were unfastened; but it would not rise more than two or three feet from the platform on which it was placed.

They tried it repeatedly. They threw every thing out; but it would not ascend: there had not been gas enough to fill it completely. So the crowd had to disperse, disappointed.

Several weeks passed, and the old man was feeling very badly; for he was obliged to attempt it a second time, according to his agreement. But there seemed to be no day on which he could be allowed to do it, as there were other shows taking place in the mean time. In this country, they always wish for a festival day for any thing of the kind; because, of course, more spectators will assemble on those days. This man had been engaged by a committee to make two balloon ascensions in October, for the entertainment of the people, as, during that month, they always have public exhibitions of some kind. But October passed, and he had no opportunity to make a second trial. At length a day was again appointed, and the balloon was to be sent up from the same place, — the Square, in front of our house.

The hogsheads in which the gas was made were filled with old rusty iron, — a *cartload*, — that there might be an abundance; and water and sulphuric acid were added. The gas was then conveyed by means of pipes and a hose into the balloon. In the morning, we saw it from our windows again, all fully extended, and moving about very buoyantly.

Three o'clock came, a crowd of spectators also. No flowers were taken this time, and no ballast. After a little preparation, the old gentleman entered, the cords were cut, and the balloon rose beautifully, like a shot; so quickly, that, in less than ten minutes, it had entirely disappeared among the clouds overhead. One of our friends happened to be on Monte Mario, which is two miles from the Square, and saw the balloon pass. He said then that the man would "freeze in those clouds;" that he would "never come down alive." It was too true a prediction.

The balloon fell about twenty miles from Rome, and the poor old gentleman was indeed dead. They tried every means to re-animate him: they took him to the hospital, and put him in a warm bath; but he never recovered.

It is thought that he may have died from the too sudden transition. He had, perhaps, not anticipated ascending so rapidly; and it was probably imprudent to have taken out all the ballast beforehand. It is supposed that he had time to open the valves, and let off the gas; for when he was last seen, through a telescope, as he entered the clouds, he was pulling at the cords of the valve.

It made us all feel very sorrowful to hear of this sad termination of the day's pleasure. You may, perhaps, have read such accounts before; but I had never heard of loss of life in a balloon in consequence of cold.

CHAPTER II.

WINTER AND SPRING.

DURING the latter part of the time that we were in Switzerland the weather had been quite cool, and especially while we were in Munich. There we often had to wear cloaks in driving out; and the children's mamma got some nice warm ones for them to wear on their journey home and all winter. They were very neat and pretty,—gray, with plain blue velvet trimming put simply around. They were all alike for each of the three little girls, and though made warm and substantial, for a cooler climate, they would be very serviceable at home too, we thought; for sometimes the cold tramontana wind blows very keenly in Rome during the winter. Yet, notwithstanding it was so cool when we left Switzerland, we found, when we returned to Rome early in October, that the sun was still excessively hot when we were exposed to it even for a moment. But the winter afterwards was very wet. It rained and rained a great deal; and, during a fortnight in the present month (February), the weather was exceedingly cold. The fountains were ornamented with long, substantial icicles that would do credit to New England; and one night there was a little flurry of snow, so that some patches of the garden-walks were quite white for an hour or more in the morning.

Carnival came in the midst of this cold, windy weather, — for there was a north wind almost all the time, — so that there was no temptation to go into the Corso; and scarcely any of the family went at all.

We were congratulating ourselves in the thought, that, when this cold spell should be over, spring would begin in earnest; for the almond-trees and laurustinus were already in bloom. And now I would like to transfer to you the soft air we have been having to-day (Feb. 25), and the chirping of the birds, of which the hedges and trees are so full, that it sounds as if there were a yard near, filled with young chickens.

The children have had a sort of influenza, which has kept them in the house; but this morning — the first time we have been out for three days — we spent two hours in the garden, really enjoying the spring-like feeling of the air, so fresh and mild. It is very unusual for any of the family to be kept in the house, even by a cold; and we make a point of going out once a day at least. The atmosphere without is generally so inviting, that we should feel almost like prisoners did we stay in the house all day: therefore we always go out in the afternoons, if we have not been out in the morning.

The doctor cured Gianina of the fever, as he had promised to do; but he said we must be very careful of her for forty days. She is now perfectly well, excepting the effects of the influenza which she has just been having. (She never had a recurrence of the fever during all the remaining seasons in Rome.) Being extravagantly fond of young animals, Gianina has this winter a pretty little dog, Frisky, whom it is her delight to pet; and this morning, in the garden, we had a great frolic with him. We discovered a solitary bright-yellow orange under a tree; all the rest having been gathered. Taking it to be one of the bitter oranges, not very good for eating, we picked it up, and threw it along the gravel-walk for Frisky to catch.

He ran in great glee, and took it in his mouth, and, with us after him, raced along the avenues, and round and round the garden, through all the alleys; scampering over the beds and through the openings in the hedges. As he ran faster than we, he would stop and turn round every few paces, with the orange still in his mouth, and with such a roguish look, waiting for us to come up. Sometimes he would drop it, and lie down by the side of it; but, as soon as he should see us quite near, he would catch it up, and scamper off again with all his might. At last, when we were fairly tired out, and had sat down to rest, he dug a hole in the ground, and put the orange in, covering it up entirely, and went away. Afterwards he came back, scented it out, scratched away the earth, took it up again, and we had another race for it. We thought it quite a bit of sagacity in the dog burying the orange, although he did it right before our eyes!

He is a young dog, only a puppy, though a pretty large one; and is so full of sport, that he plays all sorts of mischievous tricks. He will probably have to be sent away. What should he do one day but get mamma's best bonnet, which she had just laid down after coming in from walking, and toss it all about the room before any one knew it and could take it away! He is too troublesome; but it would almost break the children's hearts to have him sent away.

The two girls have been to a children's party at a friend's house, where there was a funny exhibition of a dressed-up dog. He had a regular little suit of clothes, and stood upon his hind-legs, and walked round, and shook hands for "good-evening." Then a night-gown was put upon him, and a grandmamma's cap; and he lay down in bed like anybody! An American lady-artist had trained him to all this.

Another friend of ours has always some little pet-dog,—almost the smallest little creature possible,—

which she trains to be as obedient as a child. It is wonderful to see how perfectly and instantly he obeys her. She is not obliged to raise her voice at all: she addresses him as naturally and quietly as if it were a child she was speaking to. The dog she has now is named Jenny. So she says, "Jenny, get down out of the chair!" "Stay there, Jenny; and do not come after me!" He minds her as perfectly as if he were a human being. And what is most wonderful is, that although he always goes to walk with her on week-days, and seems to depend upon it, so that he is half crazy if she goes without him, he seems to know by instinct when Sunday comes, and that she is going to church; and never makes the least attempt to follow her, but allows her to go, as submissively and obediently as possible! If *children* were always as obedient, how fine it would be!

I must tell you also of our pet Moro, the big black cat for which Memie asked the bit of cheese. He is a splendid creature, very intelligent and gentle, and very playful too. The children make a great pet of him; and their papa is very fond of him, and pets him as if he were a dog. He allows him to come into the room when we are at dinner, and even to climb up on the back of our chairs, and put his soft paws on our shoulders, asking for something to eat. He is never refused, or turned away; so that he has come to be very familiar: but he is so dignified and sensible, and knows so well how to behave, that he does not make himself *de trop*, or come when he is not wanted.

On Valentine's Day, our little girls went to a party at our friend Mrs. C.'s, who has one or two children's parties every year, on birthdays and other occasions; for there are two boys and a little sister, who like very much to collect all their young friends together, and have fine times in games, &c. The boys — how ingenious they are in doing all sorts of things! They cut figures out of paper, without a pattern, exquisitely; and can do all kinds of fancy painting, and get up pretty little figures, and make them act comedy; and among their in-door accomplishments are even knitting and embroidery. They can knit a purse, or embroider a pair of useful slippers, once in a while, for a Christmas present to a friend! But, besides all this, they have their daily tasks of work and study, and are as brave, manly, and stout-hearted as any boys we know.

Their little sister M. often dresses at these parties in an Albanese costume, and looks very sweet indeed. The family usually spend the summer at Albano; and there they became acquainted with the young princesses B., whose summer villa was close by, and who were very friendly with them: now they are generally invited, and attend these little parties. They are very pleasing young ladies. The elder is very tall for her age, — not yet fifteen, — and very graceful; and has the most sweet and unaffected manners, but very dignified. The younger appears very amiable, but is very delicate and shy. They seem to enjoy very much joining in our games. We have all sorts of frolics. I say "we," for the boys always want some help; and *I* usually take hold and assist in getting up their games. We have the "flower game," and "old coach," and "hunt the slipper," and "handkerchief burns," and "hunt the squirrel," and some of the games we saw in Switzerland, and many others: in fact, it is just like a child's party in America.

The C.'s like much also to come to our house, sometimes all three; but more often one or other of the boys comes alone. They have fine times playing with Gianina and Nannine. They have a long piece of twine extended between two chairs, and call it a telegraph; and letters — *real paper* — are sent back and forth upon it very briskly. This is a favorite amusement with them all.

March. — We have been dressing a pretty doll for little M. C., who has been lately dangerously ill. She is better now; and we thought a new, fresh doll would help to amuse her and occupy her while she is confined to her room. Nannine went with me to carry it to-day, and she stopped there all the afternoon.

March 18. — To-day we have been having a regular overturn of affairs. Our sleeping-room has been changed, Nannine's and mine; and our beds have been removed to the blue-room, — a room papered and curtained with blue. The front window looks out upon the Piazza, and the other upon the great ruins of the old baths, and over the green garden-beds of the villa, and upon the Campagna and the Sabine Hills.

The room is very lofty and spacious; and when the large window which looks upon the beautiful views is wide open (for it opens like a door), and the golden sunshine pours in, it seems very airy and splendid.

In the midst of the commotion of moving, we had no lessons; and Nannine and Gianina went with me down street shopping, in pursuit of a silk dress. We took a long walk, passed the Pantheon, and stopped to look at the excavations which are being made around it; for lately they have been tearing down some houses that were adjoining, and which had partly concealed it on one side.

This is an ancient building, and is always an interesting place to visit. It was built even before the time of our Saviour, — twenty-six years; and the name of the builder, Agrippa, is still remaining in an inscription over the entrance.

First comes a fine portico with grand stone columns. When you have passed through this, and enter the building, you find it to be circular and lofty, with a dome, open at the top, through which all the light comes; for there is no other window. It is so fine and interesting to look up, and see the open sky far over your head! But the rain also comes down when it showers, and sometimes the mosaic pavement below is wet with it. This was a temple dedicated to all the gods, as its name, "pan-theon," signifies; and around the walls are rows of niches regularly placed, where the marble statues of the divinities * formerly stood. But these were removed, of course, when Rome became Christian; and it is now a church where mass is daily performed (for all the churches here are Roman-Catholic); and, whenever you enter, you may generally see some one kneeling before one of the various altars.

In this church is the tomb of Raphael; for he was buried in Rome, where he spent the last twelve years of his life. In this city, too, it was that he painted so many wonderful works, — great pictures covering whole walls of rooms in the Pope's palace of the Vatican, and many other beautiful paintings besides, which are now the delight of all travellers.

But we did not stop long at the Pantheon now: we went into the shop of a silk-manufacturer, which is close by. The children's mamma had lately seen a

* For some account of these deities, and the change to Christianity, see Fairies of our Garden: Roman Stories.

dress there which she thought would just suit our purpose; but to our regret it was gone, and there were no others that were quite what we wished for. They make silks dress by dress, as they are ordered; and there was no more of the same kind. I inquired how long it would take to make one. Eight, ten, twelve days, according to the pattern, was the answer.

On our return, we stopped at two other principal shops; but the silks were generally so exceedingly expensive, or so extremely handsome, that they were not what we wanted. In fine, we did not see a single one just right. We were searching for a Marie-Louise blue plaided silk.

Nota bene.—A week afterwards, after another long walk, we found a dress, — exactly what we wished.

When we returned at noon, the moving was through: but bureaus had been changed all round, and every drawer was emptied of its contents; and the afternoon was spent in re-arranging them.

CHAPTER III.

REVIEW OF THE WINTER.

DURING the winter, the lessons of the two girls went on regularly as usual; and they made very good progress in them. Gianina now read Italian as well as English, and was studying French, and learning very well.

Nannine's fine practice in French during the summer in Switzerland was of great advantage to her, as she now read it with facility; although, even before we went to Switzerland, she was in the habit of taking up little French books, and reading them with great pleasure. Her papa, at one time, brought her from Paris the "Arabian Nights," in three large volumes, in French, which, for a long time, were her great delight. She became, however, much excited, *devouring* them day and night almost, though it is true she retired early: but they were placed by her bedside; and, the first thing on waking in the morning, they were in her hands, and were scarcely out of them again at any leisure moment during the day. Her papa and mamma thought all this too much excitement for her, and that she had better give them up for a while: so she brought the great volumes forward, and had them laid away, to come out fresh again some other time.

In our morning walks, after we returned from Switzerland, we formed the habit, Nannine and myself, of speaking French together, instead of English, that we might continue the practice of it until our neighbor Carlotta, the young Italian girl who invited us to the school exhibition, joined us; and then we used Italian with her. She had no companion to go out with so early, and was very glad to go with us to walk. We were very much pleased to have her; and sometimes her sister, who is a young lady, went also. They are very amiable and agreeable. They live very quietly at home, their father scarcely wishing them to go into the street at all; and they never do so unless their mother or some friend goes with them. But they do so enjoy walking out, it is a great pleasure to have them go with us.

It is not the custom in these cities for any lady to go alone in the streets; but, if she has even only a small child for a companion, she can go anywhere. So we go all round about, and find new walks, — sometimes in streets that we have never been before, and to old churches or ruins; or we visit some studio, and see the beautiful works of marble, or the paintings, of which there are so many in Rome.

14

One of our favorite walks is out of the Porta Pia (gate). There is a fine sidewalk a long distance outside the walls of the city, which is clean and nice; and we very often fall in with a great flock of sheep, or beautiful little lambs or goats, driven along, which are always pleasant sights to see; and we stop and look at them as they pass by. Sometimes there is a great drove of beautiful ponies or horses; and then we feel a little startled to be so near, and go out of their reach as far as we can. Frequently we walk as far as two miles, or a mile and three-quarters, and back again; for Nannine and Gianina are fine walkers now, and scarcely think of being fatigued. They frequently take their hoops with them; for they enjoy very much driving them during the walk.

This was the usual walk too, for a long time, of a French lady, with her nurse and young baby, a beautiful little thing. The lady was a pretty creature, a countess, the wife of the French ambassador. Meeting her so often, we had quite a little acquaintance; so far at least as to bow, and wish her good-morning, and make inquiries about the baby: all which she returned by shaking hands with the children, and saying to them very sweetly, with her French accent, "How do you do?" in English. The nurse was a peasant woman from the country, very fine-looking and handsome, with her Italian costume of a red bodice, and embroidered lace kerchief over it, and sparkling gold ear-rings and necklace.

The little baby throve finely: it was about the age of our Memie. We could almost see it growing every day, although it was never *bathed*, as that is contrary to the practice of the French doctors here; that is, I presume, not put *into* the water. Our baby, however, throve just as splendidly, we thought, and was bathed every day, according to the English and American custom.

The French lady has another little infant now, and both are taken to walk together, with two nurses; but we do not meet them so often as we used to, our hours being a little different, although we often see them another part of the day in some other street. . . .

Little Memie, who began to speak English this winter, makes very funny work of it sometimes. She tries *so* hard to talk it as her sisters do! Every day she comes in to the dessert after dinner; and, when she gets to the door of the dining-room, she calls out, "Papa, posso entrare?" So one evening, after she had come in, her mamma sent her back to say it in English, "Can I come in?" She went back to the door very patiently and willingly; and then, in her hurry to speak it out, she hesitated and stammered, and at last she exclaimed, "Papa, *posso come in?*" thinking she had done it very nicely! It sounded very funny, and made us all laugh. She goes all round the table, and kisses every one with such a sweet kiss, before she is put up in her high chair. How she likes cakes and bon-bons! but she is not allowed to eat many of them.

The little girls' pet, Frisky, was obliged, at last, to be sent away. He was so mischievous, that it was impossible to get along with him, — tearing clothes and gnawing slippers to pieces in a most destructive manner. I suppose, if we had lived on the lower floor, where he could have run out into the garden at any time, working off his spirits in that way, he would have done better when he was in the house. But being up so many stairs, so that he could only go out once or twice a day when any one would take him, he had to find all his amusement in the house; and was as full of life and mischief as he could be, no matter what he did or what he spoiled.

A good man, whom Josef knew, took him into the country, where we hope he will be very kindly treated. Poor Gianina was greatly distressed at first in parting with him, and cried as if her heart would break; but at length she became reconciled, and bore it quite well.

April 23. — The spring has been quite backward; but we are now having bright April suns and showers, and the country will all be beautiful after this.

May 22. — It is now quite warm. We have had strawberries and green pease in abundance since the first of the month. Cherries, too, are abundant. The garden, also, is all in bloom, with the rose-bushes literally covered, and lilies, syringas, pinks, sweet-williams, &c., in profusion. The orange-trees are in blossom, with their strong fragrance filling the air. Every thing is full of life; the birds in the trees, and the frogs in the fountains, singing and croaking all day long.

And *we* are very busy, too, making preparations to go away for the summer. We are to go to the Baths of Lucca, and shall set out in a few days. We are anticipating great pleasure, as it is a beautiful country there. All this afternoon we have been busy packing. How much one has to *take out* as well as put in! We have the same number to go that we had last year, — ourselves, Josef, and Lolla; and one or two other servants will come afterwards. We go by post, and take the whole diligence, as we did last year, to Civita Vecchia, and then in the steamer to Leghorn. To-morrow I am going into the kitchen to have made some New-England gingerbread for lunch on the way, as that seems to be the fashion this spring. We have made it two or three times for friends who were going away, they liked it so much.

CHAPTER IV.

JOURNEY TO LUCCA.

BATHS OF LUCCA, June 11.

DEAR . . . You see by my date that we have already arrived at our summer's destination. We reached here Tuesday afternoon, 30th May. . . . I suppose you are quite impatient to hear of our journey and adventures hither from Rome.

To begin, then, in due order. We left there on Wednesday morning, May 24, in a spacious diligence, which drove up to our door, and took in all the luggage. We ourselves went down in a private carriage to the Porta Cavallegeria (the city gate which leads to the Civita-Vecchia Road). This gate is near St. Peter's: so, before the diligence came up, we had time to go in, and walk a while about the church. It was the first time little Memie had been there; and she opened her eyes, "as big as saucers," and gazed around most attentively. We then went out, and were stowed into the stage, which had arrived in the mean time: Nannine and Gianina, their mamma and myself, inside; the two servants, with baby, in the open *coupée* in front.

Here the children's papa, who had come so far with us, bade us all good-by, and left us (for he can only come to the Baths for a little visit, in the middle of summer, his work keeping him so busily at home) ; and then we wheeled out through the Porta Cavallegeria for a seven-hours' ride across the Campagna.

We had a great cake of delicious molasses-ginger-bread to beguile us at lunch-time, as we stopped nowhere to dine. We saw but one field of mown grass, it being ten days earlier than it was last year, when we had haying our whole journey through. At six o'clock we arrived at Civita Vecchia, and had our old rooms that looked out upon the sea. After the children had retired, which was quite early after their long day's ride, their mamma and I walked all the evening upon the balcony, listening to the sea, and taking in the fresh air, which came to us most refreshingly. All was wonderfully quiet about the house: there seemed to be only ourselves there. But the next morning, some American friends, Mrs. D** and her family, left Rome in the five-o'clock diligence, and arrived in the afternoon just in time to take the steamer with us. They also were going to the Baths of Lucca for the summer.

Thus we were all in readiness: but hour after hour

passed; still no boat came; and all had to make up their minds to spend another night at the hotel. The next morning came, clear and beautiful, and with it the French steamer from Naples for which we had been waiting; but it was so crowded, that it was with difficulty that some of the party were allowed to go on board. Nevertheless, all were admitted finally; but as to berths, they were not to be thought of. We were fortunate enough, however, to have procured two for our party. The sea was very smooth; but, notwithstanding, Gianina and Memic and some others were seasick for a few hours. Gianina popped into one of the berths; and poor baby would only sit with the nurse, who was as ill as she. But, before night, all were nicely over it (we had sailed at four o'clock); and when it came bedtime, *such* a searching as there was for places to sleep in! The saloon had been given up to the gentlemen, and many of the ladies had to sleep on mattresses laid on the floor of the passage-way below. You must picture to yourself the various half-toilets making in the morning, with the mattresses being bundled up from the floor!

In due time, every one was ready; and we had arrived at Leghorn, and by eight o'clock were put on shore. We had to be rowed a long distance up to the quay, and it was another long time before the luggage could be got through the custom-house. But at length we were quietly established for the rest of the day and night at the St. Mark Hotel, where we were very promptly and delightfully served. The landlord is an Englishman, who has kept the house many years: it is an excellent hotel. A little shopping whiled away the afternoon; Gianina and Nannine getting, among other things, some pretty colored beads to amuse themselves with, making rings, &c.

The next morning, it rained a little; but, nevertheless, at eleven we started by the railway for Pisa, intending to spend two days there, having expected to find a friend who had long desired a visit from the children's mamma, but who, however, did not prove to be there. The country was luxuriant, and cultivated like a garden all the way. There were innumerable pond-lilies in the creeks by the roadside; and the banks were gayly sprinkled with bright-yellow buttercups and scarlet poppies.

Pisa is a charming little city. We staid there two days. The rain, which continued all the first day, caused the Arno River, which ran past our hotel, to rise several feet; and it rushed along like a mountain-torrent. The noise became almost deafening. It is a peculiarity of the rivers of the north of Italy, that they rise very rapidly.

The next day was fine; and Nannine, Gianina, and myself strolled out in pursuit of the Leaning Tower;

for as yet we had had no glimpse of it. After a few inquiries, and walking about a quarter of a mile through the streets, we came upon it, and the whole group besides, — the cathedral, the baptistery, and the Campo Santo. They are all very imposing and grand edifices. After viewing them all on the outside, we found a guide, who took us into the Campo Santo. This is the old cemetery, and is quite curious, containing many ancient monuments, which have been taken from various places. Within is a small space filled with earth brought from Jerusalem in the time of the crusades, I think, and is smooth, covered with grass. A tall rose-bush was growing in the centre, full of roses, of which the guide gave us each one.

The baptistery is dome-shaped, with a quite beautiful exterior. The interior was filled up with staging, for making repairs; and we could not well see it. It was the custom in old times to make the baptistery, where the christening-font is placed, separate from the church.

The campanile, or tower for the bell, was also separate; and in this place — Pisa — it is the famous Leaning Tower. This is very tall; but there is a very easy stairway of two hundred and ninety-five steps within it, leading up to the top. We went up; and it was scarcely at all fatiguing, as there is a gallery running all round every little way, where you can stop to rest, and look out upon the beautiful views, which, when you reach the top, are still more delightful and beautiful. The city, handsomely varied with green foliage, is spread out before you; and a great plain, cultivated like a garden, extends to a great distance in every direction. On one side is Leghorn and the sea; and on the other are beautiful hills, among which lies Lucca. How much we enjoyed going up into this beautiful tower!

In the cathedral hangs the lamp from which Galileo received his first idea of the motion of the earth; at least, so we understood the guide. I may have been mistaken; for we were in a hurry then (as it had got to be late), and did not pay all the attention we might otherwise have done. It looks much like an orrery, and hangs still in the same place in which Galileo saw it.

In the afternoon, we all drove out to the dairy-farms of the Grand Duke of Tuscany, and saw the camels which are kept there for working. There was quite a drove of them; and they were returning from the fields with their loads. They are great sturdy-looking creatures, holding up their heads in the most dignified manner, and looking contented enough. Probably they are very contented and happy, "feeding on *clover*," as it is to be supposed they do, instead of the scanty fare of a sandy desert.

A great many cows were just turning into the stalls to be milked; and we waited, and saw a part of the process. A droll thing about it was, that the men who milked them had the little three-legged stool tied to them; so that they had nothing to do with it, as they went from cow to cow, but to sit down upon it.

We had a charming afternoon, roaming about, and seeing all these animals, — cows, and young calves, and camels, — with most pleasant green fields and trees all about. From Pisa, we came the next day, by railway, to the city of Lucca; and taking a carriage there, and riding without stopping, two or three hours more brought us to the Baths, or Bagni Caldi, as they are called, we having been one week on the journey after leaving Rome.

CHAPTER V.

THE BATHS OF LUCCA.

Bagni Caldi.

ABOUT what shall I tell you first? There are so many things to write of, that I know not where to begin; but of course I must say that we are established in a very nice house, a "villa" as it is called, in the village of Bagni Caldi (warm baths). We keep house ourselves, having taken a whole house, and engaged a cook. The dining-room, Nannine's and Gianina's, and my room, are all on the first or lower floor. Mamma's room and the parlor are up stairs, or on the second floor, as is also the room of a dear friend of their mamma's, whom the children call "Aunt Katy," and who is to spend the summer with us. She is a charming lady, and her visit is very pleasant and delightful for us all. Her husband, who is in the navy, is on a cruise in the Mediterranean Sea: so that she has come abroad to be able to meet him when he comes into port; and in the autumn she will go where he expects to arrive.

The Baths (mineral baths) are on the side of a hill which is directly behind or close by our house, and which is beautifully laid out in terraces. Delightful winding, shady walks lead up to the Baths. But *we* are not invalids, and therefore do not take a bath, except by way of *experiment*, or for pleasure now and then. The whole family are perfectly well, which we attribute to our simple, regular way of living, — regular meals, and regular exercise, and regular lessons, and so on. This summer, for instance, we live *so* simply! For breakfast we have stale bread; that is, not *hot*, but dry toasted, if we like. There is sometimes pollenta, which is Indian-meal cooked in a kind of porridge; or we have boiled rice, &c. The children and myself drink cold water; their mamma, sometimes cold water, and sometimes tea. At dinner we have meat simply cooked, and vegetables; seldom any pudding, but some kind of fruit. While the cherries lasted, we had them every day; and there are plums and delicious apricots. At night we have strawberries, with bread and butter, and some simple cake for whoever likes; and all drink cold water. We all have our cold sponge bathing every morning: thus we keep very comfortable, even in these hot days.

We find the air delightful; and the scenery is really almost Swiss-like, being composed mostly of hills, with a wild, rocky-bedded river, that winds through the valley. This passes our house with a constant noise like a waterfall. The hills are very green, and richly wooded to their tops; and occasionally one is capped by a village or town, which makes one think of similar ones in the middle ages, when they were built for protection in the frequent wars. We have charming little donkeys here too, which carry us about frequently, when we wish to vary our excursions; and the roads are all so shaded by trees, we enjoy much either riding or walking. We all of us go out as soon as the heat of the afternoon is over; usually mamma and Aunt Katy for a carriage drive, often taking, for company, Mrs. D**, who is close by us at the hotel (whose family came in the boat with us); and sometimes the children and myself go with their mamma. But almost always Gianina and baby go on donkeys, with the maid; and Nannine and I walk, having often for companions Miss Lizzy and Kitty D**: and frequently we get up a donkey excursion.

The D**s are a delightful family, and as yet they are the only Americans here besides ourselves whom we know. Miss Lizzy makes herself very agreeable to every one, large and small; and Kitty is an excellent companion for Nannine: they enjoy each other's society very much.

June 18. — We have had a grand excursion to Pisa to see a wonderful illumination there. I say wonderful; for not only every house and door and window was illuminated, but in many streets the different panes of glass, and the whole fronts of the houses, were perfectly covered with the glittering lamps. It was a complete scene of enchantment. There could be scarcely any thing more beautiful in or out of Fairyland: it was all brilliant and magical.

The streets were as crowded as they could possibly be, with a dense mass of human beings, — for people came from far and near, — so that the carriages could only go on a slow walk as we passed in them through the streets to view the illumination. It took us about an hour and a half to go along the Lung' Arno, — the street on each side of the River Arno, which runs through the city, — gazing all the time at the variety of beautiful forms in which the lights were arranged, and seeing the pretty effect of their reflection in the water, and the boats gliding about, decorated with bright Chinese lanterns. It took us another half-hour or more to go and see our old friend, the Leaning Tower, which is a little way out of the city, and which was standing quite alone in its beauty; but it also was decorated with the golden lamps like so many pretty jewels.

Such a scene of general illumination all over a city we had never seen before: every by-street and narrow lane, even, was illuminated with the sparkling lights. And what would you think all this was for? Not for a Fourth-of-July festival, or king's birthday, or great victory, or any such thing, but in honor of the patron saint of the city; for all Roman-Catholic cities have their patron saints. This celebration takes place every three years; and we were very glad to have had the opportunity of seeing so splendid a show.

We had gone down in two carriages to Pisa, — Mrs. D** and her family in one; Aunt Katy, Nannine, Kitty D**, and myself, in the other. But, returning the next morning, — for we found it so hot, we were glad to come away early, — we took Miss Lizzy with us; and Kitty staid, to come with her mother when it should be cooler.

How much more cool and refreshing we found the air at the Baths than it had been in Pisa!

15

CHAPTER VI.

FRIENDS AT THE VILLA.

ABOUT a mile from the Baths is another village, called " The Villa." There we have been expecting some delightful friends, who have now arrived, and have taken a house for the summer. They all make one family, and we enjoy them very much. There is Mrs. —— e and her daughter, and dear Miss —— r, a charming lady, a little of an invalid, who is with them, and Mr. —— s and his family: little May, his daughter, is a nice little companion for Gianina. She looks like a pretty picture, with her long, handsome curls. We see them very often, going there at any time, as it is one of our principal walks; and we often take tea there also: and they, going out usually on donkeys, often call here. They are all delightful friends, and we enjoy them exceedingly.

Gianina played a very roguish trick one evening after coming from there. She had been spending the day with May, having gone over on a donkey; and on returning, about sunset, one of the ladies accompanied

her as far as our door, and then left her. There was a
boy also, to attend them, on another donkey: and, instead of coming into the house, Gianina asked the donkey-boy if he would not go with her a little farther;
for she is passionately fond of riding, and never feels as
if she had ridden enough. He, of course, readily consented; and they went on a long distance. Mamma and
Aunt Katy were out driving; and what was their surprise to see far out on the road, about two miles from
home, at that late hour, Gianina and the boy, having a
grand gallop on the donkeys! They had been riding
with all their speed. The donkeys here are a great deal
better than any we have seen elsewhere, and can really
go tolerably fast; and Gianina had no idea of the distance they were from home. She looked exceedingly
hot and tired; and her mamma took her into the carriage with her, and brought her home. We thought she
felt very much the next day the long, hard trot she had
had, although she did not like to say much about it!

The family at the Villa and ours have made a delightful excursion, or picnic, to Lugliano, one of the
mountain towns, and which overlooks the village. It
is about an hour's ascent by donkey, on a very, very
zig-zag path up the side of the hill. There were nine
donkeys of us, besides almost each one having an at-
tendant, a boy or man, which was not really necessary; but they always will go. Mrs. ——e went too,

carried in a chair, and, though an elderly-lady, enjoyed it as much as any of us.

We started at five, after the heat was over; and had a most charming time, taking a large basket containing our supper with us, and eating it there, sitting on the grass.

The views from the top over the surrounding hills, which were covered with rich foliage, and down into the valley below, where the river winds and the separate villages are dotted about, were very beautiful. I wish you had some of these delightful hills to roam over! They are quite enchanting. Mr. ——s thinks they would correspond with the Green Mountains of Vermont in size and verdure.

In setting out on our return home, with our long procession of donkeys, men, and boys, one after another, through the narrow, steep, rocky pavements of the town, what should happen but that the donkey of Miss B. (one of the ladies of Mr. ——'s family) — or the mule rather, for it was a mule that she had — should take an obstinate fit, and throw his rider right over his head! As he had done the same thing once before, she resolved that she would not mount him again, but would go down the mountain on foot. I also was walking, having left my donkey for the boy to lead; for I always prefer walking down the very steep hills: so she joined me, and we had a very merry time descending. We could not help laughing at the scrambling steps we had to take over the many rough and craggy places; and could scarcely keep from running a great part of the way, the paths were so steep. We went so quickly down the zig-zag ways, sometimes making a short cut through the bushes, and often catching hold of a branch of a tree, and springing forwards to another, that we should have got down long before the deliberate and careful little donkeys, had we not lingered now and then to enjoy the sight of the great trees, and the pretty picture of the rest of the party, the whole caravan, winding slowly among them, round the paths above us; Nannine and Gianina looking demure enough, to be sure, so quiet there, mounted on the backs of their little animals, but sitting very securely in their box-saddles; for the common donkey-saddle is almost a regular little box, having three sides to it at least.

Thus, before we got to the foot, they had overtaken us; and Miss B. and I mounted our little beasts again —*le bestie*, as the Italians call them—as soon as we reached the level ground, and we all trotted home very quickly.

Here is a simple little dialogue, written about this time,* and called —

* Written as a composition in Italian. It is here translated, as affording a slight sketch of " child-life " abroad.

THE EXCURSION.

Carlo (running to his papa). Will you go on a donkey with us? Mamma has gone already on horseback, and Francesco and I are going alone with the guide.

Papa. Very well, my son: I will go willingly. But where is my donkey? You have not ordered another, have you?

Carlo. No, papa ;· but the stable is very near, and they can bring one soon.

Papa. Very well. Go quickly, and tell the guide to bring me a pony instead of a donkey, if there is one.

Carlo. Yes, papa. (Goes to the stable, and returns.) Yes, there is a beautiful pony! They are combing him now, and then they will bring him.

Papa. It is all right, then. Are your donkeys ready?

Francesco. Yes, papa : they are in the yard. (Goes to look at them.) Let us see if the saddles are firm. Yes : they are all right. But it seems to me that this stirrup is not very strong : it will break soon, I think.

Carlo. Here's the pony!

Papa (to the donkey-boy). Put another saddle on that donkey : the right stirrup is broken.

Boy. Yes, sir. (Goes, and returns soon with a saddle.)

Papa. Now mount, my boys, and let's away! What road shall we take?

Francesco. I like that by the mountains best.

Carlo. But, papa, let us go to the meadow beyond the bridge, because it is a beautiful place to gallop : it is so smooth there! I like so much to gallop on the donkey!

Papa. Well, my son, we will go first up the mountain, descend on the other side, and return by the meadow.

Carlo. Thanks, papa! That will be fine!

.   .   .   .

Papa. This ascent is very steep. I think we shall need a good half-hour for going up. Look at the beautiful views! There is a town on the very top of that high hill.

Francesco. Papa, I can count four towns among the hills!

Carlo. I can count five — six! — Don't you see? — there!

Francesco. Oh, yes! there are two just come in sight.

Papa. Yes: there are many beautiful places all around. . . . Here we are at the top! Let us dismount for a little, and let the poor beasts rest. . . .

Francesco. Here, donkey! now eat some grass if you want to.

.   .   .   .

Carlo. Papa, I should like to go down the hill on foot.

Papa. The path is full of stones, my son: you might hurt yourself much. . . .

Carlo. Yes, indeed! these little stones are very sharp and cutting. Oh! I have hurt my foot so much!

Papa. Then get up on the donkey again.

Carlo (speaking to the animal). Stop, donkey mio! I want to get up.

Francesco. How quickly we go down the mountain! We are already in the plain. Now we can gallop; can we not?

Papa. Who is that coming to meet us?

Carlo. It is mamma on horseback truly!

Papa. We are just in time, then, to return home all together!

(Exeunt horse, pony, and donkeys.)

CHAPTER VII.

SUMMER AT THE BATHS.

THE family of the Grand Duke of Tuscany spends the summers at the Baths of Lucca. They have a villa not far from ours; and they arrived soon after we did. They make the streets quite lively at promenading-time, as their carriages are always out. There are three barouches, each with four horses; but they do not often go all together. When the grand duchess herself is in the carriage, it is always preceded by an *avant-courier,* who rides on horseback a few rods in advance. Then the gentlemen who happen to be on the street all take off their hats as the carriage comes up, and ladies bow.

As we were out walking to-day, Nannine, Gianina, and myself, we received very gracious bows from one of the carriages which we met, in which was the young duke, who has just arrived. He and all the ladies in the carriage bowed; which courtesy or etiquette quite pleased us, inasmuch as they did so before we had attempted to. They appear very simple and affable. There is a little arch-duchess about twelve years of age: she is a chubby little thing, as round as a button. She and the other ladies always alight and walk after they have ridden a little way. There is a baby, too, as fat as fat can be, with his cheeks rolling over, they are so plump.

One of the bands which play before the palace of the grand duke in Florence is also here, and plays very frequently on the Square. There are a great many instruments, and they make beautiful music: we often stop to hear it when we are out, and sometimes go out expressly for that purpose. Afterwards we go in often to a little saloon there is there, and take an ice-cream, or *granita* as they call it in Italy.

Almost everybody collects on the Square to listen to the music. . . .

After having written thus far, my letter was left, as we were going on a donkey-ride. Nannine and myself went with Mrs. D**'s family, and Lieut. C. and his young wife, who are here for a little while on a wedding-tour. She is a pretty little bride, daughter of Commodore ——. They were married at Spezia, the place where American vessels of the navy rendezvous.

The air was perfectly clear and delightful; the weather being neither too warm nor too cold. We ascended a height which rises directly behind our house,

— Croce di Ferro it is called, from an iron cross on the top of it. There is also on the summit a pretty little pavilion, where one can have some refreshment if one chooses. We wished for none, however; and, after stopping a while, we came home by a beautiful winding road, and met Mrs. ——e (the elderly lady who was carried in a chair on the occasion of the picnic at Lugliano) on a donkey!—quite to our surprise, since she has not taken to the donkeys before; though all have thought that the riding would benefit her, as she is quite delicate.

After a pleasant two-hours' ramble, we were back in season to hear the music on the Square; but there was so much talking all around, there was but little enjoyment from it.

July 23.—I wonder if the weather is as warm with you in New England as it is here. The summer is extremely warm; but we manage, by shutting out the outer air during the heat of the day, to keep very comfortable; and the nights are made quite cool by keeping windows and doors open.

Aunt Katy, who rooms at present with me, has just brought Memie down to our room from the parlor. She runs about with her petticoat and little white apron only, looking generally as "cool and fresh as a cucumber," as they say; although even she shows at times some heat.

30th. — I just heard an outcry from Memie up stairs: she was stung on her finger by a wasp! I went up to see, and she was sitting in her papa's lap, — who has now come for a month's visit, — with her finger bound up in oil, and very quiet. She is a dear little thing; and now often at meals, if her mother is not present, sits by me, and is *so* sweet! — *molto carina*, as the Italians say.

August. — A great event has taken place, — a baby brother born! and papa and mamma, and all the children, as you may believe, are extremely pleased with the little masculine individual. He is a fine-looking boy, a noble, healthy little fellow, and, of course, will be the pet of the household. So Baby Memie has her nose broken! but she does not seem to mind it at all: on the contrary, she is very much pleased. (The writer would be glad here to say what a *faithful* little sister she proved through all his baby years.)

Nannine and Gianina happened to be spending the day with me at our friends' at the Villa, when the baby was born; and, when we came home, Nannine was delighted to find her wish fulfilled, — that she had such a little brother as Anna had in the picture which was sent from America.

.   .   .   .

During the month that their papa was at the Baths,

— whose visit made us all very happy, — he took a trip to Florence of two or three days; and, when he was ready to return, Nannine and myself went in the carriage to Lucca to meet him at the cars, and bring him home. It was a ride of two or three hours: so we went early in the morning, taking our friend Miss ———e with us, who was glad of the opportunity to have a good long day to see the fine pictures in the churches, &c. We had a very pleasant time, enjoying them very much; and then we shopped a little, and had a cosey dinner in a cosey little room, and afterwards a nap to recover a little from our fatigue. We then drove in the carriage to the Ramparts, a beautiful promenade all round the city, bordered with elegant trees.

The rest of the city of Lucca looks very old and dingy. This is not a handsome city, excepting that the situation is fine; but it was famous as one of the Italian republics in former times.

At six o'clock, we drove to the railroad and took in papa, and reached home about nine o'clock, having had a very agreeable day.

September. — Our dear mamma and baby are doing nicely. He is a pretty little fellow, and grows large and bright every day. He brought to each of the family (or his mamma *made believe* for him) an elegant present on his birthday, — a handsome brooch or some such article. A princely little fellow! is he not? But his mother says she shall teach him hereafter the strictest economy!

Since baby was born, we have had no lessons; but the three girls have been out with me every morning in the carriage to spend some hours, getting out and walking a while in the woods or wherever we fancied.   This morning we drove out, and accomplished a few errands: then we picked up a little girl, daughter of a German lady in whom Aunt Katy was interested; and, after walking a while in a pretty wood, we brought her home to spend the day with the children.   Last Sunday, only Gianina went with me to church; poor Nannine being laid up with a sore foot, which is quite painful.   Baby and his nurse rode with us in the carriage as far as the Villa, that being the home of the new nurse, who is an English woman by birth.   The church is also at the Villa, and we go there regularly every Sunday; often walking, as it is a pleasant walk of only a mile.

Memie has just come along, saying something in the slow, deliberate way which she has when she speaks English, which sounds very cunning.

Sept. 17. — Little Memie is on the floor by my side, making a house with books. She came in just now, leaving the door open. I said, "Shut the door, Memie." — "No," said she: "you shut her." — "Oh, no!" I replied. "Memie go and shut the door."   In the mean time,

the door closed of itself: so she said, "*She shut herself
—did.*" I give you this as a specimen of her English.
She can now, however, express in very good language
almost all that she wishes to say. But I must give
you more specimens of the kind when she was just
beginning. Her mamma was saying to her one night
playfully, "Now you can't go to bed, what will
you do?" She answered hesitatingly, "I come —
Maria" (one of the servants who came after us from
Rome, and who now takes care of Memie) — "I come
— Maria — for — make — sleep;" meaning she would
call Maria to come and put her to bed, as was her
custom.

Once she had been talking a little English, and her
mother wished her to say something else, which she
repeated for her; but Memie replied, "Dat's all I can
di-re" ("say"). For a long time, she supplied the verbs
in Italian; as, "Will you *tagliare** this?" "I want to
dormire.†" "Let me *bevere.‡*" It was quite touching
to see how conscious she was at first of her inability to
express herself in English. Her mother was once trying to make her repeat some English words. She answered, all in Italian, that she couldn't "say such big
words."

Nannine had a habit of letting the door fly to after
her, which she was often reminded of: "Do not *slam*

<hr>

* "Cut."   † "Sleep."   ‡ "Drink."

the door!" One day, on going out, she did the same, when Memie spoke up, "Mamma, Nina *smelled* the door — did!" She used to say, "I am very drink!" meaning "thirsty;" and, in playing with some one once, she lifted up their chin, saying, "Let me kiss you under your knee!" But in general, now, she makes use of very correct expressions, and has learned quite rapidly this summer. She always had the habit of repeating every thing she heard, whether she understood it or not. Even when she was a little thing, just beginning to talk, when she saw her sisters kneeling down and saying their prayers before going to bed, she would insist immediately upon doing the same, murmuring some sounds, without in the least knowing a word they uttered.

There was one little trick that Memie must have played this summer, which we did not discover until two years afterwards. We had brought from Rome a little book called "Classic Tales." It was in my room, but I had missed it; and, when we came to pack up to go away from the Baths, we could find nothing of it: it was a great mystery what could have become of it. There was also in the room a trunk with a thick linen cover, which had been kept on through all our journeys. Two summers afterwards, when this trunk had travelled round a great deal, and had recrossed the ocean, and gone from New York to Boston, and from Boston to Newport, the cover began to look rather shabby, though still quite strong, and we thought we would have it taken off; when, lo and behold! there appeared in the front side, between it and the trunk, the little book of "Classic Tales" we had searched for at the Baths so long in vain. It was looking a little the worse for its travels, but was not much injured. We concluded that Memie, in playing round the room that summer at Lucca, must have put it there; for we did not see how it could have slipped down of itself, the cover was so tight. It may have done so, however, and little Memie may have been quite innocent of the roguishness; we do not know: though perhaps, when she comes to read these lines, some dim, far-off recollection may inform her that she was truly the little culprit. Not a very guilty one, however, it is readily confessed!

16

CHAPTER VIII.

LAST MONTH AT THE BATHS.

THIS month of September we are here almost all
by ourselves. Aunt Katy has gone to Spezia to meet
her husband, who arrived there the day after she did;
and, of course, they are very happy. She was with us
two months and a half, and we shall miss her very
much: and Mrs. D**'s family are gone; but we shall
meet them again in Florence. The friends at the
Villa will remain, perhaps, as long as we do. During
the splendid mornings of this month, we have — Nannine, Gianina, and myself — each of us a donkey
brought to the door; and we go off on a good ride.
Josef goes with us, and is as full of fun and frolic as
he can be; in all kinds of antic ways, making the donkeys trot and gallop. They are fine little fellows, or
rather *large* ones, — the largest and best we have met
anywhere, — and really quite orderly and manageable,
like their *superior*, the horse. We often go to the
Maddelena Bridge, which is two miles from the house;
and, the road being smooth, we can have a fine trot

most of the way. We often dismount, and loiter for a while, enjoying the delightful air, and the shade of the trees or groves along the roadside. Once we spent a whole long day on a pleasant picnic excursion, of which the following is an account: * —

AN EXCURSION TO PONTE NERO.

How beautiful it was yesterday morning when we set out, Nannine, Gianina, and myself, to go to spend the day in the woods, under the shade of the trees! The sky was perfectly clear, and the air so serene, that it was a pleasure only to breathe.

We mounted our donkeys, and went along the road where the factories † are, which leads to the Ponte Nero. All was so quiet, and the air was so healthful and pleasant, that, after the first mile, we dismounted to go on foot slowly, at our pleasure, almost all the remainder of the way, until we reached the factories. We stopped for some minutes at the small and pretty cascade on the right of the road, from which the falling water forms, at the foot, a little lake.

Arrived at the factories, it was necessary to mount again our little animals; and we proceeded thus until

---

* Written originally in Italian. The writer has preferred to translate it literally, although it sounds a little quaint, as giving more the "atmosphere" of the place.

† "Le Fabbriche." These were nail-factories.

we reached the Ponte Nero. This is a very singular place, where the small River Lima has made a passage for itself through the rocks. The fissure is quite wide, and very long, considering the immense depth; and there, far down at the bottom, the water flows in quiet stillness, but looking so dark, or black, that it has given the name to the little bridge which is built over it.*

Crossing the bridge (Ponte), we came to a little grove, which gave us shade enough to take a luncheon there; for it was then almost noon, and Nannine and Gianina were already quite hungry. Josef, our good servant, who did not, however, come with us, had put up for us in a basket a great provision of bread and butter, cold chicken, &c., beside what was intended for our dinner.

With this we satisfied our appetites; and there was enough left for the two guides, to whom we gave also a bottle of beer which Josef had put up: for we took none of it ourselves, and knew that the men would enjoy it highly.

After this little delay and rest, we continued our way for a mile or more across a chestnut wood, and finally came to a beautiful place on the side of a hill, with shady trees, good fresh air, and a beautiful view in front of us of the mountains, and of the towns Pal-

---

* " Ponte Nero," — Black Bridge.

leggio, Casoli, and Crossiana. Palleggio was situated directly opposite us; and the river was meandering gracefully between us and that village.

After an hour or two, in which we busied ourselves with our books and work, which we had brought with us, we prepared for dinner. The grass, the stones, and our shawls laid down, made seats for us; and napkins spread over our laps and on the stones formed the table. We ate with great relish of the cold pigeons and fruit and biscuits, not forgetting our poor little animals, which had been turned out to graze. We called them up, and fed them with bits of peach and sweet biscuits. How they showed their great big teeth as they took them eagerly from our fingers!

We had time enough after dinner to amuse ourselves with a good game of "hide-and-seek" among the large trunks of the trees, to Nannine's and Gianina's greatest delight. But, when the ominous clock — which we heard from the near village — struck four, we were obliged to pack up all our things, and leave behind every pleasure which the rocks and the trees could afford, and take our way towards home. There, before dark, we happily arrived, with no adventure befalling us: not a limb was broken; no one received any harm whatever, but all returned safe and sound, after a most pleasant day! . . .

On one of the days of this pleasant September, Nannine took some small sheets of paper, and made them into a little blank book. Then, with a pencil, she put a pretty edge all round the cover, and wrote on it, "The Fairy-book." As she was going out, she handed it to me to have a story put into it. "Oh, what a task!" I thought to myself: "how can I do it?" But she went away, apparently with all confidence that the story would be there when she came back. Not so with me, however; for, to tell the truth (*sub rosa*), I had never written a fairy-story in my life. However, as poor Gianina happened to have a bad headache, and could not go out that afternoon, but was lying on the bed, and I also was remaining at home to sit by her, I thought I would try and see if I could gratify Nannine. So, while she was gone, some invisible fingers — invisible to her — filled out all the pages of the little book; and this was the story : —

THE FAIRIES' DANCE.

It was the bright time between the summer and autumn; and the fairy queen thought she must have a merry-making in her bower of sweet ivy and gold and scarlet woodbine. So she spoke to her trumpeter, and told him to blow a blast, long and loud, upon his honeysuckle trumpet, to call all her people together.

Now, the trumpeter — and he was a cunning little fairy-trumpeter, I assure you — was staying in the queen's bower, because she always wanted him by her side to summon her people when they were away; and he used to hang up his horn on the wall of the bower. He was short, and the horn hung pretty high: so he jumped upon a toad-stool which was underneath, and reached it with his tiny hands. Then he placed it to his mouth, and took a long breath, puffing out his cheeks, and blew such a blast, that it almost shivered such a little trumpet all to pieces; for it was nothing but the nectary of a honeysuckle.

However, the sound resounded in the dales and among the hills, until every fairy heard it; and they came from bush and from brake, from their naps or their work, to the bower of the fairy queen.

"Now," said she, "we must have a great feast. I wish you all to go and invite our friends. Some of you go to the fireflies, and tell them they must come with their best lights trimmed; for I want my green ivy and scarlet woodbine to sparkle as with stars. And be sure and fetch some glow-worms; for I must have one for my jewelled crown. And tell the crickets and the grasshoppers not to fail with their clearest notes, for I desire a fine concert; and the frogs must not neglect to bring their bass. You must gather some juice from the honeysuckles, some pollen from the roses and the lilies, and some sap from the maple; for all shall be feasted. And some of you go and beseech the moon to send down her most silvery rays, shining in upon my parlor-floor to polish it for our dancing."

So they all went in their various directions. Those who were the nimblest went after the fireflies; those who could swim best went to summon the frogs; and those who had the most airy wings went upwards to seek the rays of the moon.

In good time, they all came back. Whole leaves full of pollen were brought to spread the table; and cups of maple-juice and honey-dew were gathered bountifully.

Then began to arrive the guests. The fireflies streamed along one by one, and took their places among the green and gold and scarlet leaves of the bower, dotting it all over like so many sparkling gems. The glow-worms meekly took their places lower down, and looked like as many pretty soft lamps arranged around the room. One alone, a beauty, was reserved for the queen's crown. Then came the crickets and their grasshopper neighbors; and they were so excited, that they immediately began to twitter and chirp as they crept in among the leaves in the queen's fine drawing-room.

The big frogs — how they came laboring up with their stout bass-drums! The queen said they must stay outside. They should fare as well as any of them; but she could not have their loud music, indispensable as it was, too near her delicate nerves. It was all the same: if they could beat upon their drums, and have some of the good cheer, it was all they cared for; and so they placed themselves near the hall outside.

Then, last of all, as the moon rose above the mountains, you could see her soft rays coming down straight to the bower; and, entering the door, they stretched across the floor, making it silvery bright!

Then said the queen, "Let the music wake up!" At this hint, the musicians tuned up their throats and their drums; and such a twittering and chirping and croaking began as almost made the bower to tremble to its foundations.

But do nót think that the invited friends had nothing to do but to make music for the rest. Certainly they each had their turn in a waltz or a hop, or a jump or a galop. It was funny enough to see the long slender grasshopper performing a gallopade with some fairy nymph! The crickets were employed in the jump, for they did the jumping-dance to perfection; and, when a partner for the hop was wanted, one was always sought among the frogs!

In the waltz, the fireflies shone most: they could whirl round so rapidly, you would scarcely know if you were on your head or your feet. The queen honored them all in the waltz, the jump, the hop, and the galop. When they had all danced to their hearts' content, with many an up and down, a slip and fall, upon the silvery bright moonlit floor, and which they all took in good part, the queen gave orders that the refreshments should be served. Then they all sat up stately and erect, some of them tearing off bits of green leaves for napkins to spread upon their laps; and tiny cups, with all that was nice, were sent round. When it came to the frogs, you would have laughed to see how elegantly they sipped the sugary maple-juice from the pretty little bluebell cups.

After a time, midnight came; which was the hour for all respectable people to be going home. So, very gracefully, one troop after another took leave, with occasionally a trip-up on the polished floor when a very low bow was attempted, especially among the crickets. The grasshoppers were more limber, and could do it better. As to the frogs, their necks were so short, they did not attempt to do much. Thus, with a kind adieu, and thanks to all, the queen dismissed them, each one hoping there might be some time another merry-making.

CHAPTER IX.

DEPARTURE FOR FLORENCE.

On the road to The Villa, the large leaves of the catalpas, which border the way, are turned as yellow as gold by the September air, and cover the ground almost as thickly as a carpet. They are so handsome, so large and golden, that we can hardly resist stopping to gather heaps of them whenever we pass. Some other leaves also have changed; and although it is still pleasant and bright out of doors, in the house, where the sun does not come, it has got to be cool a good part of the day, and every one seems quite liable to take cold: so we think it is time to be removing. It is the last day but one of September. A portion of our friends at The Villa went to-day, — namely, little May and her papa; and the rest of their family will go on Monday. We are to go to-morrow (Saturday).

Our packing was all finished this morning; and there is nothing more to be done this afternoon, unless it is to get a little walk by and by with the children, and to make an Indian-cake to be cooked hot for supper; for Nannine has been begging for one all summer, and has been promised one for to-day. It being a New-England Johnny-cake, the cook, of course, knows nothing about it: therefore, when we have one, I go into the kitchen and make it. It has been too warm, until now, to have so hearty a supper; and so we have put it off.

.   .   .   .

The walk was taken. We fell in with a little Venetian boy whom we have often met. He and Nannine had become great friends, having taken two or three rides together on donkey-back. He was as lively as he could be, and cut the funniest capers with his donkey, as he walked along by the side of him, for a time. The boy, who is here from Venice with his father and mother, is the prettiest little fellow! — seven or eight years of age. He is slight and graceful, with dark hair and soft eyes, and wears a little velvet suit, with a ruffled collar, and ruffles around the wrists, which makes him look like a beautiful little figure of some of the old Venetian pictures. He also, with his family, is going to Florence in a day or two, where we shall very probably meet him again.

The Johnny-cake was baked, and an excellent supper made of it. We retired early, and the next morning, at half-past seven, we were packed into two carriages;

the baby's good English nurse, Mrs. B., going with us to take care of him during the month that we shall remain in Florence : and thus we rode until towards two o'clock, when we reached Pistoia.

The ride was all the way through cornfields and vineyards; the grape-vines being trained and festooned from tree to tree, which has a very pleasant and beautiful appearance. At Pistoia we took the cars, and were surprised at the beauty of the scenery all the rest of the way. The hillsides were covered with towns and villas, becoming more and more numerous as we drew near the city; and we did not wonder, with all the lovely views, that this should be called "Florence the Beautiful." We reached it at three, or half-past. A merry chime of bells was pealing out as we entered the city, which, altogether, looked most cheerful and delightful after our four months of quiet country life.

We are established in a nice suite of rooms, — the same which we had last year at this hotel, the Isles Brittaniques. The hotel is on the north side of the Lung' Arno, and looks out upon the river and the bridges. When the baby was being brought up stairs, Madam S., the beautiful English singer, who had also been at the Baths of Lucca, was coming up the stairs too, to her rooms in the same hotel. She stopped and admired baby, and almost "envied" mamma, she said, "such a noble boy!" She has only one child, a little girl, who looked very pretty and graceful, as we often saw her at the Baths, riding on her donkey. Their house was at the Villa.

That same afternoon, after dinner, Nannine and Gianina went out with me to buy a few cakes of soap, &c. We went round by the Jewellers' Bridge, taking a peep at the beautiful things. This is actually a bridge of jewellers' shops, being lined with them on both sides nearly the whole way up and down. What handsome sets of garnet and of the lovely blue turquoise we saw !

One of the first things we met in our walk was the *avant-courier*, followed by carriages of the Grand Duke; all which seemed quite natural, as we met them so often at the Baths. Hearing the band play sounds very natural, too, and is very pleasant; for they had left the Baths some time before we did, and we had quite missed them.

The next afternoon we went to the Cascini, and drove all around them. How beautiful these gardens, or grounds, are! They are very extensive, and are laid out in handsome walks and drives, with elegant shrubbery and tall trees very richly twined with ivy; for ivy grows abundantly all over Italy, and everywhere adorns the trees, climbing up into them, and spreading its rich foliage all about. Often a band of music plays at the entrance of the gardens; and innumerable people in carriages stop, and collect there to hear it, filling the great space all around. Then the flower-girls — girls dressed in costume, with a jaunty little straw hat on the head — come round with quantities of beautiful flowers, and toss a bouquet into your carriage. They often go away without any pay for it; but they come afterwards to the hotel to get it: so they are quite sure, in that way, of disposing of their flowers, whether you wish to take them or not!

The 1st of October happened to be a grand festival day; and, in returning from the Cascini, we met a long and quite splendid procession in the street. There was a figure of the Madonna carried in front, as large as life, and dressed in an elegant white silk, with a canopy of yellow silk and lace over her head. In her arms she held the child Jesus. How strange it would seem in our Protestant towns or cities to see an image of the Virgin Mary carried about in such a way, and treated with so much reverence and worship! for many went and knelt before it. But Italy has always had in all her cities and towns such shows and processions; and we think they have been handed down from the earliest times, in imitation of the old customs of the country before Christianity was introduced. There are many festival days, and on every festival there is some religious procession of the kind;

but most frequently it is the crucifix * which is carried. This is followed by priests with their church vestments, and monks in their brown or white gowns, — as the different orders of monks have different dresses, — and choristers, who chant the psalms as they go along; and often, even in the daytime, they carry lighted torches. These shows belong only to Roman-Catholic churches and countries.

* A cross, with a figure of the Saviour upon it.

CHAPTER X.

STAY IN FLORENCE.

FLORENCE, October.

FLORENCE is a place for straw-work. All kinds of fancy straw-plaiting are done here, besides the bonnet or hat manufactures. You meet women in the streets plaiting as they go along, just as, in Rome, they knit as they are walking leisurely through the streets; for the peasants in all these countries seem to be very industrious, keeping always busily at work when they have it to do. The straw-work shops are fascinating; and you can but stop and gaze in at the windows filled with all sorts of beautiful straw bags and slippers, and little babies' shoes, and baskets and vases and salvers, and all varieties of pretty things. We have really wanted to buy so many! There is a great deal also of the exquisite white alabaster-work; and here we could not resist taking, for a souvenir, a pretty model of the beautiful Leaning Tower of Pisa, to send to a friend, but which, however, before reaching its destination, was completely crushed, it was so delicate. . . .

17

The little Venetian boy has been two or three times to dine with Nannine and Gianina, and spend long afternoons with them; but, as he does not seem to understand so well playing in-door games as he does playing tricks with his donkey out of doors, they had at first to make quite an exertion to get up some entertainment for him. He enjoys almost any thing, however, in the way of amusement, and is soon pleased. The two girls were invited to spend a day at his house; and they had a very pleasant time. But his family are not to remain long in Florence: they go about the middle of this month back to Venice. Gianina goes often, too, to visit her little friend May, who is delightfully situated in a pretty house with a garden around it, with the lady who has the charge of her; for her father has gone away for some time. Nannine also has enjoyed meeting again her dear friend Kitty; and Miss Lizzy, who makes a pet of Memie, comes very often to get her; and one day she brought and put upon her finger the cunningest little turquoise ring. Memie, too, is very fond of her, and runs to climb up in her lap whenever she comes in. Baby is taken out by his nurse to walk every day, grows finely, and is a darling little fellow. He was vaccinated, which made him almost ill for a week.

Since we have been in Florence, a package has arrived from friends in America, containing little me-

mentoes; and with what pleasure we unfolded them
one by one! Among them was a lovely ringlet of little
Anna's hair. So her locks have all been cut off! and
what were once golden are now a beautiful auburn.
We all admire and treasure it much. Accompanying
it was another beautiful little daguerrotype of Anna,
not *trying to see a kitten*, as before, but standing very
proper and nice, and showing her long curls before
they were cut off.

Oct. 29.—Our sight-seeing for the last fortnight—
for, of course, we have been again to the churches,
galleries of pictures, &c., as we did when we were here
before—has been much interrupted by all the children
having had the most severe influenza, such as they
had never had, with cough, and sick headache. If
they had not had the whooping-cough (they had it
comparatively light in Rome), we should certainly have
thought for a time they were having it, they coughed
so badly. Even the baby also coughed. But they are
all recovered from it now, after having been confined
to their rooms for several days. The weather has
been changeable and fall-like, and quite trying a portion of the time; which was the cause, probably, of the
children's bad colds. They are rejoiced to be out
again, as we all are.

During this stay in Florence, we had a new amusement, which really became quite exciting all round. It

was a new kind of charade, in acrostics; and was given to us by an English gentleman, an old friend of the family, who formerly lived in Rome.

The method is to select two words that bear some relation to each other, and which contain the same number of letters; as air, sky; water, earth. These two words are written down lengthwise, and the corresponding letters of each make the beginning and end of some other word which you may select, in this way: —

W	av	E
A	lm	A
T	owe	R
E	mme	T
R	ic	H

Then the definitions only of these words are given, from which you may discover the original words, thus: —

1. A watery element.
2. A battle in the Crimean War.
3. Picturesque in a landscape.
4. Something very small in our eyes.
5. What many wish to be.

From these definitions, you are to find out the elements given, water and earth; or they might have been reversed, *earth* coming first, and *water* last; and any other words made of them, like this: —

<pre>
E   uta   W
A   nn   A
R   io   T
T   rad   E
H   ono   R
</pre>

But the prettiest acrostic charades are made from proper nouns, as Homer and Ilion (another name for Troy), being a poet, and what he has written about; Odyssey and Ulysses, a poem and its hero.

The following is an example: —

<pre>
1. Part of a tree.   P it   H
2. A " goat with wreathed horns."   A ntelop   E
3. A quick mode by which to travel   R ai   L
4. A winter ornament of New-England houses.   I cicl   E
5. Desirable when cold, unpleasant when hot.   S u   N
</pre>

These two acrostics are a *lover* and his *beloved.*

We and our friends the D**s were very much interested in these new charades; and for some time they passed very briskly back and forth between the two families, each trying to get up new ones with which to puzzle the other.

Mr. B., the English gentleman, gave us the following splendid one, which I believe was original with him;

but it required gentlemen's heads, we thought, to solve it. At least, it seemed to us more than enough for ours, — mamma's and mine, — and we sent it over to Gen. and Mr. D** (the father and elder brother) to unravel. In the course of the evening, a note was returned by Mr. D**, announcing that the "united genius" of his father and himself had "succeeded in solving" it; and he gave the words and answers all beautifully written out. Of course, it looked *very easy* when we saw it all plain before our eyes; and we thought we were very dull not to have discovered it before! It is true, we did *suspect* what the answers might be; but we could not make out all the definitions. The "head of a rustic ghost," for instance, we puzzled ourselves over that for a long time.

These were the definitions given: —

(1.)   1. The eagle-tamer.
     2. The latest victory.
     3. The head of a rustic ghost.
     4. The Muse of love.
     5. Something known to bakers and drummers.
     6. Troublesome to fish and columns (of troops).
     7. A South-American river.
     8. "Knowledge in the making."

The two words to be found signify
The fall of the eagle, and the eagle.

In case any of our very young readers should attempt to solve the above, we will tell them, that, in place of "the latest victory," "an eastern quarter of the world" will do as well, and that "the head of a rustic ghost" is — a *turnip!* Also that "knowledge in the making" is *opinion.*

Mr. D** sent also in return this original one, "just made," he said, "on the spur of the moment," — at a time when it was particularly rainy, cold, and uncomfortable; and it will do for our friends who are abroad, when the weather is in the same condition : —

(2.) 1. A confused medley.
      2. Lacking a full supply of wits.
      3. What goes up faster than a balloon?
      4. A stop put to trade.
      5. A stuck-up Oriental.
      6. An apostolic parent.
      7. The opposite to truth.

The two words signify

> The foreign name of a favorite city, and
> An unpleasant time of the year there.

The following is also an original one by Gen. D.: —

(3.) 1. The Legacy of Curius Dentatus, the Censor'
        to posterity.
      2. Of the earth.
      3. The finest ornament of the tree.

4. A starting-point in history.
5. John Bull's delight.
6. A word hard to be spoken.
7. A vain imagination.
8. A primitive dwelling.
9. The parent of habit.
10. Man's last companion.

A hero of antiquity,
Proved a man.

This, too, was sent to us by him :—

(4.) 1. A diminutive fiend.
2. A devotee of Flora who could not see.
3. The family name of a Scotch chieftain.
4. A part of the foot hard to fit well.
5. More than one silly bird.
6. The official title of a man who is getting thrashed.
7. An Italian town.
8. A general who saved ancient Rome.
9. A perfect balance.

A bad state for a man to be reduced to, and
The same thing carried to an extreme.

The two preceding will do to puzzle the boys who may read this book, or any girls who like hard work.

They were so hard, that neither mamma nor I found them out for a long time. I do not know how easy such might not be now, if we should try! Of course, Nannine and Gianina did not trouble themselves at that time about any of these, as they were quite beyond their efforts at their age then.

The following will be found very easy: —

(5.) 1. The name of a British queen.
     2. Produced in cold climates, used in hot.
     3. What time makes picturesque.
     4. Name of some of the English kings.
     5. An initial which is a word.
     6. An English title of nobility.

     A poet and his work.

(6.) 1. The two first syllables of a word meaning truth.
     2. A French participle of two letters.
     3. A pleasant thing after dinner.
     4. Two letters that sound like words.
     5. Useful on the seashore and to cleanly house-wives.

     A mother and her offspring.*

---

* See Appendix.

Here also are some puzzles and conundrums which amused us at the time : —

> You o my o but I o thee
> O o no o but o o me
> Then let my o thy o be
> And give o o for thee and for me.

> Captain **B B B B**
> Has sent his **C C C C**
> To the **E A S T**

Which runs faster, heat or cold?

Ans.   Heat; because you can *catch cold.*

Why is a hen as economical an animal as farmers keep?

Ans.   Because for every grain she gives a *peck.*

.   .   .   .

At this time, in Florence, Nannine wrote a pretty little verse which came into her mind as she was lying awake in the night; and in the morning she wrote it down.   This is it : —

A GOOD-NIGHT.

Good-night, good-night!
  The moon is bright;
The stars shine out with golden light:
  It is a very pretty sight

> To see them shining over land and sea;
> They also light my room for me!

She had written her *first* little piece in July, while we were at the Baths: she had often made *rhymes* before; but this was quite real little poetry. Yet, although the lines rhymed nicely in repeating it, she wrote them all straight along as if it were prose, and asked me to copy them for her, and put them all right. The following is a copy:—

THE FAIRY SONG.

> Come early in the morning,
> Before the dew is gone,
> Before the sun has poured
> His hot rays on the lawn,
>
> And you will see us all there,
> Fairies great and small:
> Our queen sits in the middle,
> And around her we sit all;
> And to her we run so quickly
> When we hear her merry call!
>
> So come early in the morning,
> Before the dew is gone,
> Before the sun has poured
> His hot rays on the lawn.

After these beginnings, Nannine occasionally came out with other little pieces of poetry. She was always rather shy about them, however, and did not like to have them much talked about.

CHAPTER XI.

TOUR BY PERUGIA.

DURING the month in Florence, the children's mamma was looking out for a good woman to take back with her to Rome for the baby's nurse; and several persons made application.

Two or three times, Nannine, Gianina, and I, while walking in the Boboli Gardens, had noticed a nice-looking English maid with two pretty little English children dressed exactly alike, and who looked like little twins. One afternoon in particular, as we were going up and down the long, beautiful avenues, we saw the same cunning little creatures. They were so small, they looked almost fairy-like; and we could not help going up and speaking to them, and asking the maid all about them. The maid was a fine, healthy-looking young woman, and appeared exceedingly well; but we did not know who she was, and she knew nothing about us. But, that very evening, who should come to inquire about the place of nurse for the baby, and offer her services, but this very English maid! We recognized her at once; and mamma liked her looks so well, and her recommendations, that she soon engaged her. Thus Mary, which was her name, was established as nurse to the little boy.

In the latter part of the month, a dear aunt of the children's mamma arrived in Florence with her son and daughter, a young lady and gentleman, to go on with us to Rome: therefore it was necessary to have two large carriages to accommodate the whole party; and the journey was to be by the way of Perugia, and would take a long week, as we should not travel on Sunday.

We left Florence at eight o'clock on Wednesday morning, on the first day of November, snugly packed in our carriages, and had splendid weather all the way; it raining only one afternoon. We had a most pleasant time, some of us changing frequently from one carriage to the other. The aunt, and Cousin Hatty, and Cousin M., were very lively and delightful; and we had a great deal of enjoyment. We stopped the first night at Arezzo, the town where Petrarch, one of the great poets of Italy, was born; and in the morning we walked out to see his house, which is still standing. The next night we came to Lake Thrasymene, which is large and beautiful; and I suppose that the very plain over which we passed, on the border of it, must have been the battle-ground of the Romans and Carthaginians two thousand years ago, when Hannibal conquered, and then went on to Capua. This was one of the few *defeats*, history says, that the ancient Romans ever suffered; and it startled them very much, — making them fear that that great conqueror might be coming on immediately to Rome.

The next day brought us to Perugia, where we wished to stop some time; for it is a fine old city, situated grandly on the summit of a high hill. It was one of the "twelve" ancient cities of Etruria. The ascent is so long and steep, that it was quite necessary to put oxen to the carriages to aid the horses in drawing them up the hill; and, on some other long hills of the journey, there were additional horses or oxen attached.

These long, slow ascents gave us sometimes an opportunity to get out and walk, which we enjoyed very much; the autumn sun was so golden, the air so fresh and invigorating, and the views so extensive and fine, taking in whole panoramas of rolling hills and vales, looking literally like "mountain-waves."

But we must not forget Perugia. It was a fair-time, and the city was exceedingly crowded. There was such a dense throng in the streets, like our Fourth-of-July celebrations at home, that we could scarcely, for a while, get about from one place to another; and at night we had to sleep upon mattresses made up for us upon the parlor floor of the hotel!

Our great object was to see some beautiful pictures of Raphael, and his master Perugino, which are in this city; for here Perugino lived, and Raphael, when a young man, studied with him, and had looked and gazed with delight upon those very pictures of his master which we now saw, and which are really beautiful. There is a tender grace and loveliness in Perugino's works, — in his Madonnas with the Child; for that was the great subject which occupied all the artists of that time: they were never weary of painting her and the infant Saviour in every variety of beautiful attitude and expression. In this city, too, is the earliest picture of Raphael's that is known to be existing. It is the loveliest little picture of the little John and the child Jesus embracing each other. They are represented as little children, two or three years of age, sitting together on a bench. There is nothing else in the picture: it is very sweet and interesting. . . .

Here at Perugia, what splendid roasted chestnuts we found on the Square! we bought many handfuls of them. This was nothing new in Italy; for, in every town and city, there are roasted and boiled chestnuts at the corners of almost every street: but these were uncommonly large and fine, and we thought them delicious, especially the cousins, who were just coming into Italy; and they bought them in quantities.

A few miles out of Perugia is the town of Assisi, where there is a grand old church to the memory of St. Francis, who was a devoted monk, who spent his life in poverty and in doing good, and who is deeply revered by the Roman Catholics. It is a beautiful excursion to make, the church and town stand so picturesquely on a hillside as you approach it. But it was too difficult to go round that way with the carriages and luggage, and all did not care about going: therefore, very early the next morning, before the others started, Cousin Hatty and her brother, and Nannine and myself, took a post-chaise and went there, intending to get back and meet them on the road by the time they should arrive. It was but six o'clock when we set out, scarcely daylight at this time of the year, and very cool; but we were well wrapped up. The postilion in his gay costume, with hat and feathers, and his long boots which came far above the knee, seated astride the forward horse, dashed on in great style and flourish; and we enjoyed exceedingly our rapid drive in the fresh morning air. Soon the sun began to rise, throwing his golden light over the vast panorama of hills and valleys; and whole little lakes of mist, rising and nestling among them here and there, added much to the beauty of the scene. When we approached the church, standing so noble and lofty upon an acclivity, the view was exceedingly beautiful.

The church is very old, and contains paintings by the oldest masters, Cimabue and Giotto, who were living at the time it was built. They were the very first painters who painted at all in the modern style of art, and were called the revivers of painting; for pictures before their time were strange-looking figures, with neither grace nor beauty. And even theirs are very different from any that are painted now, although they were considered quite beautiful in their day; but they are at present so faded and worn, that many of them can scarcely be seen.

After stopping as long as we had time to spare, we jumped again into our post-chaise, and with our dashing postilion, who would sometimes almost startle us with his fast driving down the hills, we soon returned. In half an hour or little more, we were again upon the high road, and were very glad to find that we had not kept the rest of the party waiting with the carriages; for they had not yet come up.

They came soon, however; and we were all packed in again, and by noon had reached Foligno, where we dined. It was for this town that Raphael painted one of his most celebrated pictures,—the Coronation of the Virgin, which is now in Rome, in the Vatican Palace.

The next place of interest was the Falls of Terni,

the most famed waterfalls of Italy. They, too, are off the direct road; and we were driven out in a carryall. The falls are very beautiful; but in going about to see them in all their different views, which took us an hour, we were beset by whole troops of beggars, men, women, and children. They thronged around us at every step, until our stout guide succeeded in sending them off only by throwing a whole handful of coppers among them, which the children's mamma commissioned him to do; and then they left us in peace to enjoy the view of the falls during the remainder of the time.

The last day of our journey, when we came upon the great Campagna which surrounds Rome, how natural it all looked! And now, on Wednesday evening, the 8th of November, after a seven-days' journey, we are at length at home again; and all looks *so* beautiful after nearly six months' absence! indeed, it seems too much time to have spent away from so beautiful a place. The reason we have been away so long is because the cholera has prevailed very much this season, and it was very bad in Rome; and the children's papa was not willing that the family should return until the sickness was over. It is now very much diminished, although there are still many cases of it.

The evening we arrived, baby sat erect in the nurse's arms, and fixed his little eyes on every thing most observingly in his new home, as if he, too, thought it beautiful. In a few months, he was large enough for his dear papa to take and carry about the room to see the pictures, which he did every evening after the work of the day was over, and which the little fellow seemed to enjoy very much.

FIFTH YEAR.

CHAPTER I.

CHRISTMAS GAMES, TOYS, AND RHYMES.

Rome, Christmas.

My dear L. . . . . I wonder what kind of a day you are having for Christmas. Here it is most lovely; the sky without a cloud, and as soft and serene as possible. It is so clear, that we see on the distant Apennines the white snow stretched all along their summits. The nearer mountains, the Sabine and Alban Hills, are rarely covered with snow: only two or three times in the course of the winter there may be a little fall of the white and feathery drapery, which lasts two or three days. . . .

We are going to have a chicken-pie for dinner, after our New-England fashion; for we all voted we should like to have one. Only a few family friends, with the aunt and cousins who came with us from Florence, will dine with us; but, in the evening, there will be quite a little party of Americans, and we are going to play games, — "Magic Music," "Clap in and Clap out," "Blind-man's Buff," &c. All the Americans like to be invited here; for the children's papa and mamma always make it very pleasant and social for visitors. The parlor is large, and looks very beautiful, too, in the evening, when it is well lighted.

The children are having a most happy time with their gift-dolls, toys, and books. Instead of a tree, they had stockings hung up this year; and they were quite running over. One of Nannine's presents was "Robinson Crusoe," which she had never read, but had long been desiring to possess. She is highly delighted with it; for she is a great reader, and "devours" all the books she can get. This was my present to her; and I had from her a ring set with beautiful garnets, which was purchased all secretly in Florence while we were there!

Their papa has had made for Nannine and Gianina a beautiful baby-house. It has a roof and little chimneys, and windows and doors painted on the outside, making it look like a real house. It is quite large, with parlor, bed-room, dining-room, and kitchen; and they have beautiful little sets of furniture for each room, — chairs and a sofa covered with red satin for the parlor; for the sleeping apartment, a lovely toilet-stand and wardrobe, and bed with pretty lace curtains; and in the kitchen, which I think they enjoy as much as any part, is a whole cooking-range, supplied with every article of convenience. All these things have been presents from different persons, but not all this year: they had had them from time to time, and had kept them nice until now. The kitchen-set of iron-ware was furnished anew by their mamma. We saw it when we were out one day shopping. It was so complete, with every part so perfectly made, she thought the two girls would be highly delighted with it; and they are. They are extremely fond of getting bits of dough and paste from the kitchen, and making it up into little cakes to put into the little spiders, and so forth.

They have the baby-house now in their own room; for, since we returned home, Nannine and Gianina have been promoted to a room by themselves 'for the first time, excepting while we were at the Baths of Lucca. I was truly sorry to part with them, who had been with me nights as well as days for so long a time; for Gianina had also roomed with us the last year. But it was thought it would be better for them — make them feel more responsible — to have only the maid to look after them. They have now a new maid, a French woman. This keeps up their practice in French very well.

.   .   .   .

The servants were changed almost all round in the

course of this year.   The good nurse Pina had become
very much out of health.   She had had the care of the
children, Gianina particularly, for a long time; and was
getting to be almost too old to do so much, for she
never would spare herself.   She made the greatest pet
of Gianina, and indulged her so much, that her papa
and mamma were afraid she would be spoiled.   When
Gianina was a little thing, but quite able to walk, she
would often carry her in her arms when they were out
walking, when her papa and mamma thought it not at
all necessary; but she would do it, notwithstanding all
they could say.   She was now so much of an invalid,
it seemed best that she should be relieved.   It was
very hard for her to leave, and very hard for the children to part with her; but at length she consented, and
went to an uncle's, living near Naples, where her old
home was, and where she would be well taken care of.
Marguerite, the French woman, is now in her place.

The cook, who was Lolla's mother, has also gone
away; and there is a good man-servant in her place.
And our trim little Lolla, too, has gone.   She is married, and gone to housekeeping.   She looks very gen-
teel and nice by her husband's side, who is footman to
some prince or other.   Instead of her, we have Theresa, the wife of Josef, who was married many months
ago; but she did not then come here to live.   She is an
excellent woman, very capable and obliging.   Josef is

the only one of the old servants remaining, excepting Maria, who was at the Baths of Lucca with us, and who comes every day to take Memie out to walk, or to help carry the baby. Mary, the English girl, proves to be such a good, faithful nurse, that we all consider it a very fortunate choice. She is *so* strict about the baby! she will have him taken care of only just so and so. But he grows finely under her care.

.   .   .   .

January. — Letters came from America, giving an account of a pretty tree dressed with presents for little Anna's birthday, which occurred a day or two before Christmas. Her mamma wrote, " We made ornaments of tissue-paper; and every thing was very pretty and tasteful after the tree was all arranged. The children invited came at four, and had games by themselves until nearly five. Then they were taken into the room where the tree was lighted; and all of them, with the grown people present, joined hands, and danced two or three times round the tree. Then a piece of poetry was read about it, and they played again until supper-time; after which, the presents were distributed. The mottoes attached to them were very pretty indeed. Tommy (Anna's baby brother, who was sucking his little fist in the daguerrotype, and who was now between two and three years of age) was perfectly delighted with his little boy. He was almost crazy to touch it while on

the tree, and to play with it; and wanted some one to
'unbutton its jacket.' Anna was much pleased with a
handsome little cake and some cunning little doll's
shoes which were sent to her."

Her dear grandpapa, who loved Anna very much,
wrote for her these few lines: —

> "I am six years old to-day,
> As dear papa and mamma say.
> How kind and good they are to me!
> And good and kind to them I'll be.
>
> In all I say and do and tell,
> I'll ever try to please them well;
> Then God will bless me from above,
> And I shall ever share HIS love."

The "little boy" that was sent to Tommy, and
whose "jacket" he wanted to "unbutton," was the
cunningest little fellow, the letter said, that ever was:
he had on his left arm a hoop, and in his right hand a
stick. Grandpapa named him *George Gingerbread*,
for he was made of gingerbread; and he sent with him
these odd little lines to Tommy: —

"Halloo, Tommy! I'm the boy for you! Come on
with your hoop, and let us have a drive.

> " Christmas is coming,
> And we'll not be *dumming;*
> For soon Santa Claus will be here.
> He's a jolly old fellow,
> Always jovial and mellow:

> And, before he is knocking,
> We'll put up the stocking;
> For he brings bundles of *laff* (laugh),
> And of frolic, not chaff,
> And a rare lot of goodies,
> For those who've well done
> Their lessons at school
> And their duties at home.
> Then hurrah for Santa Claus!
> Let us mind all his laws;
> For he comes once a year,
> And expects to find here
> All the good and the true:
> May he find me and you! "

Anna packed up a box of tiny things from the tree to send to her grandmamma and aunts, — little bags made of nut-shells and pretty silk; a little mite of a basket, about large enough to hold a very small needle-book, spool, and thimble; little *bon-bons*, pin-cushions, etc., all on the *small* scale, "looking as cunning as the little girl herself." For grandmamma, there was a sweet little pin-cushion worked with worsted on canvas, — Anna's own work.

The same package of letters contained also an account of a fine Christmas-cake that was made for the children at grandpapa's (for Anna's tree was at her own house) : —

"In the centre of the table was a nice plum-cake, with a gold ring in it. It was decorated with tasteful

little streamers of paper, on which were written these
mottoes : —

> 1. Who chooses aright a slice of cake
>   From among the plums a ring will take.
>
> 2. Some will look high, some will look low;
>   Yet both may pass the golden glow.
>
> 3. A golden ring, a golden ring!
>   If Eliza should find it, she'd dance, and sing,
>   " A golden ring, a golden ring! "
>
> 4. Fanny must try; for she may win
>   The slice of cake with the golden ring.
>
> 5. Closer, George; look deeper in;
>   For the ore is richer than copper or tin.
>
> 6. Carrie, with sparkling eye so bright,
>   Will seek the prize with wild delight.
>
> 7. Heigh-ho! Horace will try,
>   If he can, the ring to spy.
>
> 8. Molly the witch, and Molly the sprite,
>   Will get, if she can, the ring to-night.
>
> 9. Johnnie may try, though but four years old,
>   In this nice plum-cake, for the ring of gold.

" After the children had taken their slices, and every
one else had been helped to a piece, no ring appeared.
A good deal of the cake still remained, and they were
thinking of searching for it, when it was proclaimed

that Eliza had found it in her slice.   All were exceedingly glad that it fell to her; for she had not been well
for a day or two, and was not able to enter into the
merry Christmas proceedings so wildly as the rest
were doing."

CHAPTER II.

BIRTHDAY AND VALENTINE PARTIES.

DURING this month (January), *we* had a cake with a ring in it also. I must give you an account, from the beginning, of the beautiful and successful time we had. It was on Nannine's birthday. The children had never seen any little play: so we thought we would have the acting of Miss Edgeworth's "Old Poz" for their gratification; and not only theirs, but there was quite an assemblage of ladies and gentlemen also to witness it. In the first place, the parlor was very bright and beautiful; and the play was performed at one end of it, there being a side-door to pass through.

Then Mrs. Bustle the landlady, and Old Poz, and the old man, and Lucy, and the servant (which part was acted by a young gentleman from New York, who turned the character into a black servant, and made it very comical), were all ready, and the blackbird in the cage, and the old man's money in a box.

When the screen was drawn aside, Lucy was the first to appear, with a watering-pot in her hand, watering flowers. She was dressed in a pink frock, with a little silk apron. Then the old man with a cane and a long gray beard appeared upon the stage, telling the pitiful story of his losing his money, which he thought was stolen. Then old Poz was seen eating his breakfast, with Lucy trying *so* hard to tell him about the poor old man; and the landlady coming and talking about the goose-pie; and at last Lucy bringing in the blackbird that had carried off the money! It all seemed quite real, and was very entertaining, and very much enjoyed and applauded.

There were a few charades acted afterwards, and then the birthday cake was brought in. Besides the ring, it was also announced there was a bean in the cake; and any lady in the company who should get the bean was expected to give it to any gentleman she pleased; and, if a gentleman should get the ring, he was to give it to any lady he preferred.

As the cake was in honor of Naunine's birthday, she was expected to cut the first slice; but, being too shy before so many persons, she did not wish to do this, and the few other children who were there were helped before her. But when she cut finally, and the slice was in her hand, lo and behold, there was the ring also! quite to the astonishment of all, that, in a party of more than sixty persons, it should have fallen to her for whom the party was given.

Some of the guests thought it must have been so designed; but it was entirely accidental, the ring having been put into the cake at the confectioner's, and no one having seen it until it was in her hand. As to the bean, it never was forthcoming! The excitement or curiosity was kept up to the last slice, and then it was supposed to have been *swallowed.* But the truth is, the confectioner, by mistake or from some misunderstanding, *did not put it in.*

February. — We *grown* ones have had another amusing time in a Valentine party, which the children's aunt and cousins had. Each lady and gentleman wrote a Valentine for a name that had been drawn beforehand, and which was sealed up when drawn. Then, when the evening of the party came, the Valentines were all thrown together and drawn again, — those of the ladies by the gentlemen, and the gentlemen's by the ladies; and each gentleman presented to the lady who received his a bouquet, and each lady fastened a ribbon bow on the shoulder of the gentleman who received hers. The two funny Valentines which follow were written for the two gentlemen's names which came to our share.

The first gentleman, a little while before, had personated the character of a lady in a little play; and he

went also by the sobriquet of the "Modern Raphael,"
which explains the allusion in the verses: —

<blockquote>

1. " Boggs ! " — What a name !
    Yet 'tis all the same
    In poetry or verse;
    And I truly rejoice
    That I had no choice,
    Or perchance it might have been worse.

2. In the nick of time,
    I have found a rhyme
    To couple with my Boggs;
    And I would have him believe,
    On St. Valentine's Eve,
    That my Muse is chorused by frogs !

3. My Boggs, alas !
    Has an alias,
    And passes for Julia Standwell;
    But the name I prefer
    Both for him and for her
    Is the *mud*-ern Raphael.

4. But sweet Valentine,
    I am ever thine,
    Let the name be what it may;
    And I venture to hope
    That your fair eyes may ope
    On many returns of this day.

</blockquote>

The other gentleman had acted in the same play
the part of a widow, Mrs. Juniper.

1.　Dear Mrs. Juniper, I hope you may not prefer
　　　Any other damsel to me;
　　But, if it is so, I'll not give you my bow,
　　　However disappointed you be.

2.　A widow like you, I know should be true
　　　To her long-lost Juniper-berry;
　　But in Carnival-time it would not be a crime
　　　To join me in making so merry.

3.　And oh! hear me declare, — with thy raven hair,
　　　And thy cheeks as red as a poppy,
　　If thou wilt but be mine for this one Valentine
　　　I'll never again be un-HOPPY!

The aunt and cousins had a very lively time at the Carnival this year: it was the first time they had seen it, and they thought it delightful. They had a large balcony which would hold twenty persons, and we all of us went several times. Nannine and Gianina particularly enjoyed it very much. As they are larger, they can do more and more every year, being able to throw the *confetti* now, or toss a bouquet very nicely.

CHAPTER III.

ACTING OF MONKEYS AND DOGS.

I MUST tell you of an exhibition of monkeys and dogs which we went to see one evening. It was a very comical affair.

The first scene showed half a dozen monkeys all dressed, and seated at a table, eating their dinner. They were big fellows, most of them, and of a species we never had seen before. Their heads were extraordinarily large, more like the head of an ox than any thing else. There was a pretty wee one, that did errands, bringing bottles of wine and so forth for the master, and always taking a sip when she could get a chance!

In another scene were two conscript-soldiers. The monkeys were dressed in uniform, with swords; and they went through various evolutions, sheathing and drawing their swords, and fencing, in a very droll way. Then there was circus-riding, the monkeys performing the feats of horsemanship that are usually performed in a circus, such as springing over banners, jumping through hoops, et cetera.

There was one cunning little monkey that did all these things beautifully. She looked like the tiniest little girl, and rode sweetly on the pony.

There is no saying what the dogs did not do. They waltzed and spun round in a marvellous manner; fired off pistols; and one, personating a deserter, was shot at, and acted *dead* admirably: two others coming along with a little cart, he was picked up and put into it, and carried off by them.

There was a beautiful, fat, snow-white goat, trained to walk on her knees, and to do other things very intelligently.

The animals were all wonderfully trained.

The last scene was the storming of a town. There was a patrol of monkeys, mounted on horses, and wearing long white cloaks like those that the mounted guard in Rome always wear on evening occasions. They looked droll enough.

The soldiers were represented by a troop of dogs that scaled the walls, rushing into the thickest of the fight, with muskets flashing all around, and the fire glaring on all sides. They really showed great courage and daring, vying with the troops at Sebastopol, we thought!

.   .   .   .

I read once a curious story of a dog and a doctor, which may help to show the way in which such animals are trained.* It was about a small dog that was very much injured by the indulgence of his mistress.

This little creature belonged to a rich lady, who, with all her riches and her fine living, did not possess the soundest sense in the world. She loved her little dog, and gave him all possible attention. He had to eat the richest of food, bread and butter, sweetmeats, and meat most deliciously cooked; and, for drink, he had coffee and tea, with milk and sugar, and also beer and wine. He slept always upon a soft and beautiful cushion of silk. Almost the whole day long he was eating or drinking, or was sitting in the arms of his mistress, or sleeping upon his cushion. He grew so fat, that, in a short time, he was not able to take any exercise at all. This made him peevish and irritable; and then he gave up entirely his play, refused to eat, and, in short, became truly ill.

The injudicious but kind-hearted mistress took the dog to a doctor, and begged him to cure him. The doctor replied that he could do so; but it would be necessary, he said, to keep the dog at his own house a while. It was not a pleasant idea to the lady to leave her favorite in the hands of another; but the doctor would not undertake the cure on any other conditions. Therefore, finally, she left him, and went away, with

* This story, after being read, was put into Italian; and this is a translation from that version.

the expectation of returning in a few days to take him again, as the doctor said she would be able to do.

When the lady was gone, the doctor commenced his remedy. He took a long whip that was in a little closet in the room, and snapped it loudly. The dog heard it, but did not move: he only snarled and growled a little. Then the doctor gave him a touch with the whip; when he immediately sprang, and ran, as well as he was able, round the room. He was quickly tired out. However, this little exercise was good for him, and was what the doctor wished. He then placed a piece of dry bread and some water before him; but the little creature would not taste any of it: so the doctor went away, and carried the food with him. When night came, there was nothing for the little dog to sleep upon but the hard pavement, or floor. The next morning the doctor returned, and took the whip from the little closet. It was only necessary to snap it: the dog immediately began to run as before, and went round and round the room. After thinking he had sufficient exercise for that time, the doctor placed the bread and water before him, and left him alone. This time he ate with a good appetite after his fasting, and slept well.

In the evening, the moment the doctor entered and took the whip as usual, even without his snapping it, the little creature began to run, and did not stop until he was ordered to! Then he was very hungry, and ate extremely well the simple food which was given to him, and at night he slept profoundly. The next morning there was no more need of the whip, since he was perfectly well, and ran and played and frolicked with the doctor. Soon the lady came to receive him. She was extremely pleased on seeing him so well recovered, and thanked and paid the doctor, and carried the little dog home with her.

CHAPTER IV.

SCENES AND ANTIQUITIES IN ROME.

MARCH 6. — The spring is coming on beautifully. The weather, in general, has been perfect of late. The soft blossoms of the almond-trees are scattered over all the gardens and villas. Several flowers are in bloom in our garden, — anemones, hyacinths, tulips, laurustinus, etc.; and the children, as usual, have a daily delight in picking them, especially the violets, which they are never tired of tying up in sweet bunches.

We had a charming drive yesterday — Nannine and myself, with a lady friend — to the Aventine Hill and around the Palatine. These hills are on the edge, or one side, of the city. From the Aventine, the views are very lovely. The Tiber on one side, very yellow indeed, runs along its base; and on either bank of it are the buildings of the city. On the other side of the hill, the country stretches far out with picturesque walls and buildings, and Monte Testacceo, as green as an emerald. This latter is a mound-like hill, perfectly bare of trees, but covered with grass. It has been formed by a collection of broken pottery and other rubbish which was thrown there in former times.

From the Aventine, we rode round the Palatine, which is rendered picturesque by the noble ruins of the Palace of the Cæsars. Here the emperors of old times lived, and Nero built the "Golden House;" so called because it was so very magnificent. In those days, the palaces covered nearly the whole hill. We got out of the carriage, and rambled around among the ruins, and visited some other antiquities. One was the Cloaca Maxima, which is the great sewer of the city of Rome now, as it was when it was first built, twenty-five hundred years ago; but we could see only a very small part of it. We went to the pretty circular Temple of Vesta, which is as old as the time of the Emperor Vespasian,—the same emperor, who, with his son Titus, besieged and took the city of Jerusalem about thirty years after the death of our Saviour. It was they also who built the Coliseum, which was quite completed about ten years after Jerusalem was captured. The marble columns of the little Temple of Vesta are very pretty and graceful; but the temple itself, inside, is now all filled up with hay or straw and rubbish. This was one of the temples built for the worship of the heathen deities, and is therefore interesting, as there are but few of such ruins now remaining.

Near this is the Ponte Rotto, which stands on the

foundations of the very first stone bridge, as is supposed, which was built in Rome, in the time of Scipio
Africanus, who carried the war against Carthage into
Africa, and defeated Hannibal there.* He was one of
the magistrates of the city when that stone bridge was
finished; and he therefore, very probably, had something to do about it.

8th. — To-day, Nannine, Gianina, and I dined at the
Coliseum ; that is, we took our cold lunch with us, and
had a picnic there. The girls enjoyed it highly. It
is but twenty minutes' walk from our house, and we
often go in the same manner. We rambled about, up
and down the steps, along the corridors, and among
the broken walls and seats, picking up little fragments
of pretty stones which belonged to the ancient mate-
rials and ornaments, and gathering the few flowers
that we could reach. The Coliseum is now very lovely,
with soft green verdure here and there, and bright-
yellow wall-flowers sprinkled over it like stars. But
these flowers are generally very high up, among the
crevices of the arches, and cornices of the walls, which
makes it difficult for us to get them. It needs some
man or boy to climb up to those perilous- places, and
reach them; for they are often on the very topmost
edge of the high ruin. Sometimes, when we have had
some one with us, they have got for us handfuls of the

* See the companion volume.

bright-yellow flowers, and, once in a while, a sprig of the beautiful purple lady's-slipper.

I have told you yet nothing of the Coliseum; but every one knows that it is one of the grandest old ruins in the world. It was finished and dedicated in the year 79 or 80; so that it is about eighteen hundred years old. It was large enough to hold between eighty and ninety thousand persons. It was of an oval form; and the seats inside, tier above tier, went all around it. It was the grand amphitheatre where all the great public games went on, on which occasions they had shows of gladiators and wild-beast fights. Thousands and thousands of wild beasts were brought there for this purpose. They were kept in vaults below, and were drawn up in their cages through traps in the floor of the arena, which occupied all the centre of the edifice. The doors of the cages were made to fall open of themselves when drawn up, and the animal would leap out; and then the cage was lowered down again. They were fearful shows, such as we see and know nothing of now; but the most painful part of it is, that, when the persecutions of the Christians took place in those early times, some of them also were cruelly placed here to be put to death, and the wild beasts were let loose upon them. The good bishop, St. Ignatius, a disciple and friend of the Apostle John, thus died in the

Coliseum, killed by lions. We take the following interesting account of the event from history,* for our larger readers : —

"It is certain that Ignatius had been intimately acquainted with the apostles; that he had been educated and brought up amongst them, and was chosen by them to be Bishop of Antioch. For forty years he had retained this charge. They were stormy years, full of anxiety and danger. By prayer and fasting and preaching, Ignatius had kept his people together, and supported them under the terrors of persecution. For himself he had one longing, — to be a martyr in his Master's cause.

"He was now, however, an old man. It may have appeared likely that the aged bishop would be allowed to depart in peace; but the tempest was at hand. Trajan, the Roman emperor, entered Antioch: he passed through the city with all the pomp and solemnity of a Roman triumphal procession. . . . But there was one man to whom the emperor's arrival was the signal of death. The shouts of the multitude, as they followed their sovereign through the splendid street, were the prelude to the shouts which were soon to accompany the dying agonies of Ignatius. . . . The Christians were called upon to join in paying honors to their monarch, which their faith forbade. . . .

* Miss Sewall's History of the Early Church.

The citizens of Antioch were in a state of excitement when they found that the Christians did not unite with them. . . . Ignatius also became aware of the danger to which he and his brethren were exposed, and, without waiting to be accused, hastened to the presence of Trajan, and declared himself a Christian. . . . He was then examined and questioned; and the emperor decreed that he should 'be carried in bonds by soldiers to the great Rome, there to be thrown to the beasts for the gratification of the people.' . . . He joyfully suffered his bonds to be put upon him. The journey of Ignatius was long and very fatiguing, . . . the soldiers also being very impatient, . . . as it was feared he might otherwise arrive at Rome too late for the public shows in the amphitheatre, in which he was to suffer. . . . As they approached Rome, many of the Christians, being prepared for his arrival, went out to meet him, some rejoicing in the opportunity afforded them of beholding a man so venerated for his wisdom and piety; others only anxious for his safety, and desirous of taking measures to calm the people, that they might not desire his death. Ignatius, however, soon put a stop to any such intentions. . . . He persuaded them not to hinder him 'who was hastening to the Lord.' . . .

"The thirteenth of the calends of January, according to the Roman reckoning, . . . a day of peculiar solemnity, . . . had now arrived. The people were gathered in crowds, and the games were nearly over: no further delay, therefore, was allowed. Ignatius was hurried to the amphitheatre: the wild beasts were let loose upon him, and death soon followed."

The Coliseum is now consecrated to the memory of those noble Christian heroes and martyrs, who never shrank or turned away from the fearful trials thus placed before them. Every little while, the Roman priests and monks have preaching and prayers there. And we had rather see it as it is, a ruin, because the scenes and times are now so changed, than to have seen it in all the pride and glory of its former days. It is quiet, but grand and beautiful, and a delightful place to visit.

There are often troops of boys there, playing and shouting, running in and out, which makes it the more pleasant and cheerful.

After our lunch at the Coliseum, we went through the sculpture-gallery at the Capitol, which is not far from the Coliseum, — the Forum lying between them. It stands on the very spot where the Capitol stood in ancient times, when the Gauls climbed up by night to get into the fortress as it was then, and the geese cackled. The hill has been gradually dug away since those times, and now a long flight of steps leads up to the entrance.

It used to be a place for offices, but is now occupied as a gallery of art. Here is the famous statue of the Dying Gladiator, which is so celebrated. It is a very grand but mournful figure. It looks *so* melancholy! as he is sitting upon the ground, perhaps upon the battle-field, ready to die, far away from his home and his children. He is supposed to have been a soldier, not a Roman, but a Gaul (one of the *barbarians*, as the Romans used to call them), although it goes by the name of " Gladiator." Gladiators were those who fought with each other in the Coliseum and other places, for exhibition at public games, or entertainments for the people.

In this gallery, or museum, is a room filled with busts of the distinguished men of the times of the Republic and of the Empire of Rome. There are the Scipios and the Catos, and Cicero and Pompey, and Julius Cæsar and Marcus Brutus, and the many emperors who came afterwards.

And there are also busts of philosophers and poets, and other famed men, — Socrates, Plato, and Aristotle, Homer and Virgil, Sophocles, Demosthenes, Herodotus, Seneca, &c. Although many of these men were Greeks, their statues and busts were as common in Rome as those of the Romans themselves.

It seems very strange to see all these busts of the men of ancient times around you; and it enables one to see how much the art of sculpture was employed in those days. Indeed, it was employed an immense deal; for, besides living men, the deities were represented in innumerable statues. There are gods and goddesses in every variety of figure; Jupiters and Apollos and Mercurys and Venuses and Minervas and Dianas and others. Probably, all those who could afford it in ancient times were ambitious to have some of these figures in their houses; and all the palaces, and country villas, and public buildings, were beautifully adorned with them. Niches, or places in the walls, both inside and outside, were made expressly for them.

The Vatican Museum in Rome is another great and splendid gallery of art, the largest and most beautiful in the world.*

March 12. — The children, baby and all, with their maid and the nurse, were going to be sent to the Villa Doria, to run about and pick wild-flowers, as they have frequently done; and I jumped into the carriage with them, it was so bright a day. We took our lunch with us, and had a picnic under the trees. The grounds are very large, and are beautiful with groves of lofty pine-trees, and lawns covered with green grass, which is sprinkled now with anemones and daisies. It is much like an English park, I fancy. Though fine, the air was

* See page 342.

unusually cool to-day; so there was not quite as much enjoyment as there might otherwise have been. We had, however, a very nice time, walking about to look at the beautiful fountains, and filling our baskets with flowers. The children are never so happy, I believe, as when picking flowers; but, when there is such an abundance of them, they become very fastidious, and will empty out a basketful ever so many times to fill it with those that seem still fresher and finer. Nannine is almost wild about flowers. She began to study a little book of botany last summer at the Baths of Lucca; and, being so very fond of them, it interested her very much.

April, Tuesday after Easter.— After dinner yesterday (we dine now at half-past two), Nannine went out with me, stopping at aunty's. She was to stay, and accompany her aunt— who had the opportunity of going to a private room in the American minister's house — to see the fireworks in the evening. Our minister is himself absent, and his rooms are not open as they usually are on such occasions; and the Americans have all been obliged to accommodate themselves wherever they could. He left permission, however, to open one or two rooms for certain invalids, and aunty had also the privilege of going there. I went with some friends, we all of us expecting to stand in the Square: but in a short time we all had the opportunity of going into the same rooms with aunty and Nannine, quite to our satisfaction; for there we could see the fireworks beautifully, and were not exposed to the crowd. They were magnificent. I cannot describe any thing half so splendid and beautiful. Some of the most beautiful were flowing cascades of golden sands, as it were. The grand escapade of rockets at the end was like a whole firmament of falling stars, and had a magnificent effect.

The aunt and cousins are going shortly to Naples; and Nannine and myself are going with them to stay a few weeks. Nannine has not been very well of late; and it is thought that the sea-air of Naples, and perhaps the salt-bathing, may do her good.

CHAPTER V.

VISIT TO NAPLES. — VESUVIUS. — POMPEII.

EARLY in May, we made the journey to Naples by *vettura*, — five of us. Cousin Hatty and Cousin M. were always in the *coupée* in front; aunty, Nannine, and myself had all the inside of the carriage, with the exception of one corner being taken up with shawls, cloaks, baskets, and a huge cake of gingerbread, which we had provided for lunch. It was a four-days' journey. Soon we were out upon the broad Campagna. When we reached Albano, we stopped there long enough to visit again the lovely Villa Cesarini: and in the pond in the garden the same beautiful white swans were sailing, and pluming their wings, as when we were there before; but they had grown immensely, we thought.

On the journey, we passed the Appii Forum, the place so interesting from the incident of St. Paul's stopping there when he was brought a prisoner to Rome, and where the Christian friends from Rome came to meet him. We crossed the famous Pontine Marshes, which *he*, too, then crossed.   They are said to make one very sleepy; but we did not perceive that they had any such effect upon us.   There were herds of buffaloes moving about in the marshes.   We passed the Promontory of Circe, where, as the story relates, Ulysses but just escaped falling into the snares of the enchantress.   It looked almost like an island, it rose up so bold and lofty on the coast.   And at Terracina, where we stopped one night, we came upon a whole village of Gypsies, as they appeared to us.   They were living in huts, and looked just like the pictures and descriptions that we have seen of Gypsies; such little weird places their small rooms were, with a fire in the centre, and a kettle hanging over it, and they cooking their dinner, the women with short red gowns on, and kerchiefs on their necks.

As soon as we came upon the borders of the kingdom of Naples, the children in the streets, whenever the carriage stopped, flocked around us, and made the most comical signs and gestures with their hands and mouths to signify that they wanted us to give them something to eat.   Their black eyes were so sparkling and shrewd, and they acted every thing out in such a droll way, we could not help laughing in their faces. This is the famous pantomime of Naples.   *I* believe they are too lazy to talk; and so they make signs in this way.

Before arriving at Naples, we heard that Mount Vesuvius was on fire. "Oh, that is grand!" we exclaimed, although it startled us a little at first; and dear aunty wanted to turn right back to Rome. She thought it would be terrible to be so near if there should be an eruption. But we all persuaded her that it would be the finest thing in the world to see, and what we should enjoy above all things. I do not suppose it occurred to any of us that the city would really be overwhelmed, — it was so many hundred years since such an event had happened, — or we might have felt more terrified about it than we did.

When we entered the city the next evening, we were anxious to see how Vesuvius looked; but we could see nothing of the mountain until we nearly reached the hotel; and, as the melted lava was flowing down the side of it farthest from us, we did not see a great deal of the eruption then: it only looked like a large fire on the top of the mountain.

In a day or two after we were settled in our boarding-house, one of the first things we did was to ascend Mount Vesuvius, and see the eruption. Thousands of persons went out every day, or rather night; for it was necessary to go by night in order to see it distinctly; for, of course, the fire would not show very much in the daytime. So, an hour or two before dark, we took a carriage, and were driven out, — it is six miles from the city, — and rode up as far as the Hermitage, — a house about half-way up the mountain. We could go no farther in a carriage, and there we had to take mules or horses. Some of us preferred to walk; but two pretty white ponies were brought up for aunty and Nannine, and we set out on our "winding way." But aunty soon dismounted, not enjoying the rather perilous journey; and Cousin Hatty took her place. Then we went on. The path was sometimes very craggy indeed, and the night was dark; but the guides had torches, and in the distance the whole sky was lighted by the streams of red lava which were flowing on miles and miles along the mountain. The red vapor, or smoke, that rose from it, looked as if it came from a city on fire. The lava melts and burns all that comes in its way as it flows on like a river; and it had reached some towns or villages on the mountain-side, and the inhabitants had been obliged to leave them. We went on two miles, and then reached the new crater which had been opened, and from which the lava was pouring; for the eruption did not proceed from the old crater, which is on the top of the mountain, but from a new one a little below. We went near enough to see the red-hot stones and sparks and flames thrown up in jets, as we see them in pictures; and the stream of lava, precisely like a golden river, or a river of red-hot melted iron, pouring out of the side of the crater; and to hear the terrible noise of thumping, hammering, and thundering underneath, as if all the giants of old time were assembled there, and were having a grand carousal. Or it was more like the old heathen deities, and Vulcan himself at his forge; and we did not wonder that people in those days had so many stories about their mysterious doings underground: it seemed to us that we could imagine how such stories originated, and how they believed there were living beings in the earth who were making all this commotion; for Vesuvius has always been in such a state; and every few years, from time immemorial, there has been an eruption.

We stood and looked over into the fiery stream that was running down; but the cooled-off lava that was under our feet was still hot, so that we could stop but a little while. It hardens in a day or two, and becomes perfectly black. It cools even more quickly than that when it is taken out from the melted mass; for men were there with long poles having little ladles on the end, dipping up the lava, and putting it into small moulds while it was hot, sometimes dropping a coin or medal into it. We took one or two that were done while we were there, and which immediately became hard and black.

Another night we went and saw the stream of fire rushing down over some rocks like a waterfall; and, in one place, men were cutting a channel for it to run in to divert its course, that it might not destroy a bridge and town that were right in its way. We thought it all a very grand and sublime sight; and aunty was so fascinated, she couldn't bear to leave it: we could scarcely get her to go home, notwithstanding all her fears beforehand! It was late enough when we returned, — long past midnight.

Another excursion that we made — but this was in the daytime — was to see Pompeii, the city that was destroyed by an eruption of Vesuvius about eighteen hundred years ago. It is a long way from the mountain; but a tremendous cloud or shower of ashes and rain came from there, and spread all around, reaching even as far as that rich and luxuriant city, completely covering and burying it. Most of the inhabitants, probably, had time to escape; but one family took shelter in a cellar, and the marks are still left — though very dim — where they pressed up against the wall. For many hundred years, this city lay buried in the ground; for the ashes had entirely filled it, and grass had grown over the top. But the earth has now been dug away in parts, and we see the streets and houses with their walls still standing just as they were built, but with no roofs over them. I suppose the roofs were burnt, or broken in by the load of ashes. It is pleasant, but strange, — there being no persons in them, — to walk through the streets, just as they were laid out and paved in ancient times, with the rows of buildings all along. The little court-yards still remain, with fountains in them; but there is no water. There are pretty ornaments, such as small marble rabbits and dogs, ducks, geese, and lambs, in some of them; but most of the things that were found have been taken away, and placed in the large museum at Naples, where it is interesting to go and see them. All sorts of things are seen there; even a loaf of bread as it came out of the baker's oven, only black, to be sure. It is round, marked in pie-pieces on the top, like some loaves that we have now. There is a jar of olives, sealed tight; but you can see through the glass how real they are. There are ladies' netting-needles, and instruments for extracting teeth, and utensils for cooking, and stoves, etc. It would be impossible to name all the articles to be seen.

One day, we made a long, delightful excursion to Baiæ, and the places on the way, — places where the wealthy Romans and others had summer villas. In one of these, Scipio Africanus died; and his daughter Cornelia,* the mother of the "jewels," lived there a part of the time. Here the young Augustus stopped, on his way home from Greece, where he had been studying at an academy, which he left after his uncle,

* See the companion volume.

the great Julius Cæsar, was assassinated; and came on
to Rome, where after a few years he became emperor,
— the first emperor of Rome.

One of the places on the way to Baiæ was the
Sibyls' Cave. Oh, what a strange place it was! It
seemed like going down into the regions of Pluto.
It was into such a place as this that he might have
carried the beautiful Proserpine when he seized upon
her as she was gathering flowers. Only, I believe,
he had a chariot and black horses; and no chariot
and horses could have passed down this place. There
is a long, narrow passage, as dark as midnight;
it goes winding down, down: you can only see just
before you by the light of torches; and the floor, or
bottom, is covered with water. You could not go on
foot; and we were suddenly seized by the guides, and
carried along, fearing and trembling; and, when we
came to the end, there was a dark cave, where in
old times the Sibyls dwelt. There is nothing in it
now but a bed of *stone* and a bath: the Sibyls disappeared long ages ago.

One of the loveliest excursions we made was on
the Mediterranean. We sailed in a little row-boat
from the beautiful shores of Amalfi to the Blue
Grotto. The day was lovely, and the sea sunny and
smooth. The men — the rowers — were so merry,
singing songs and calling out to animate each other,

that it was very amusing. "Macaroni! Macaroni! Buono macaroni! Macaroni a pranzo! Coraggio! Coraggio! Molto macaroni questa sera! quattro libri di macaroni!" They seemed to think that this was the greatest treat in the world. Macaroni for dinner, and macaroni for supper, was all they desired; and yet I suppose they eat and live on macaroni half the time! When we arrived at the Island of Capri, where we staid all night, an entertainment was made for our amusement by the boatmen and the people of the house, in which *macaroni* performed a very conspicuous part. It was the Neapolitan dance, the Tarantella: yet each man and woman had a plate of macaroni which they held up over their heads as they danced; and every little while they would throw back the head, and swallow a long string of the macaroni which they put into their mouth with the left hand while they were in motion. I suppose the object was to show how skilfully they could do this; but they let fall a great part of it on the floor, which to us was not at all agreeable: on the contrary, we thought it very disagreeable; for they went on dancing all the same, right over it, which they did not seem to mind in the least!

While we were at Capri, we went to the top of the hill, — for the island rises in the form of a hill, — where were the ruins of an imperial villa. Nannine had a horse to ride: the rest of us thought we would walk;

but we were astonished to find what a long way it was. I believe it was two miles; and we were very, very much fatigued; for it was ascending all the way. It did not seem as if seeing the place where the wicked, tyrannical Emperor Tiberius had lived — for this was his villa — could be a reward for so much fatigue: but we thought more about those poor people, whom, for punishment, he threw down the cliffs; and beholding the exact places where things occurred in ancient times, however sad and melancholy they were, has a sort of fascination when one is travelling. There is an interest in seeing places that are mentioned in history, where people before our time have lived, and in knowing how they lived. The view, however, was beautiful, and well repaid us for our toil. The broad, blue Mediterranean, and the *giant* Mount Vesuvius, — for so it looked, rising so lofty, only it was soft and smooth in the distance, — were all before us. How grand are these works of Nature! and how beautiful with them God has made the earth!

The Blue Grotto too, which we went to visit, I must not forget, and which was *very* blue, — of the beautiful turquoise color. A man who plunged into it for us to see looked like some strange animal dyed blue, — an enormous frog, or some such object; and was not very beautiful, I must say! But the cave was exquisitely so, with its liquid floor of blue reflected from the roof in lovely blue shadows. This grotto is on one side of the Island of Capri.

Nor must I forget the small ships and boats which we passed, fishing for coral. They had nets thrown out as in common fishing; and they drew up one while we were close by them, with a fine piece of coral in it, which aunty bought. It was a lovely scene; the sea was so smooth and bright, and the little vessels lay so quietly with their white sails set, or moved but slowly and gracefully about.

One of our pleasures when we first arrived at Naples was having an abundance of oranges, — large, splendid oranges, which we found plentiful everywhere in the streets. Cousin Hatty and her brother were exceedingly fond of them; and they bought quantities of them wherever we were going to take with us. But, after a few days, we ceased to eat them; we had really had as many as we wanted; and Nannine could scarcely be induced to take one again all the rest of the time that we remained. We found, too, that eating a few of them made our lips very tender. It was a beautiful sight to see the boat-loads of oranges that were brought up to the shore every morning, looking so golden and fresh, with the green leaves still on them!

The water — the sea — was right in front of our boarding-house; for we were on the Chiaja, a principal street running along the shore. Between it and the water, however, is the Villa Reale, which is a pretty promenade. There we sometimes saw very handsome costumes, in all bright colors, of the peasants, and of the Italian nurses carrying little children.

The shops that we liked most to go into were those of the lava and coral work; for this is *the* place where that work is manufactured, whole shops being filled with nothing but beautiful lava and coral pins, bracelets, and rings, which were very rich and handsome. . . .

We had a charming donkey-ride through a beautiful woody road, to visit a convent, or rather monastery; as it belonged to monks. Upon that account, we could not go inside to see the splendid views from the windows; for the monks allow no women to visit their domiciles: only Cousin M., being a gentleman, could go. But we had a fine view from the garden outside; and again the sunny Mediterranean was spread out before us, and the city, and the beautiful Vesuvius, rising like an immense cone on the opposite side, the light smoke curling out of the crater high up into the air.

At a little distance from our boarding-house was the tomb of Virgil, in a little wild nook, although quite within the borders of the city. It seems a singular place for a tomb: but it is pleasant to think of it in the neighborhood of people, inasmuch as his name is almost a household word; for not only in Europe, but in far-off America, the boys, and even the girls, at school, con over the pages of his great poem, the "Æneid." And yet Virgil lived before the Christian era. He died about twenty years before the birth of our Saviour. How wonderful that the work and influence of a common man should be so extensive and lasting! But Virgil was not a common man: he was a great and beautiful poet, as this shows; and in his character he is said to have been "amiable, modest, and gentle."

Virgil had lived much in Naples. Some writers say that he spent seven years and wrote the "Georgics" there. He was much attached to that city, and desired to be buried there. He was intimate with the Emperor Augustus; and there is an interesting story of his once reading to the emperor and his sister Octavia, who was a very beautiful and virtuous lady, some verses of his on the death of her young son Marcellus. Augustus had adopted this favorite nephew for his heir, and had hoped that he would live to succeed him on the throne; but he died quite young, and was mourned by all. While Virgil was reading his verses to Octavia and Augustus, they were both much affected; and, at one part, the mother fainted away. This incident took place in one of those villas at the seaside which we passed in going to Baiæ; or rather we passed the ruins of them, since nothing but the smallest remains and foundations of those places are now left.

. . . To come down from ancient to modern people, from a former royal family to the present one.* We were much interested one day in Naples in seeing the royal family pass in the street. They were in a very simple carriage without any top; and we were quite diverted to see them sitting quite crowded, three upon a seat, like any other mortals! There was a little child in front, between the king and queen; and on the back seat were three other children, boys. When we met them, they were just passing the barracks, where a band was playing; and one of the young princes (the eldest, I presume) took off his cap to the soldiers, and kept it off until they had quite passed; which looked very courteous and pretty, we thought, though probably it was etiquette also.

. . . .

We tried the salt-water bathing for Nannine,—not in the sea, but with baths in the house: but they did not suit her well, exciting her nerves too much; so we discontinued them.

We were at Sorrento a few days, and left aunt and cousins there, as they were not going to return with us to Rome. Only Cousin M. came back with us to

* Now *late* royal family, since the Revolution of 1861.

Naples, to see us off, — to get our passport for us, and put us on board the steamer; for we were to return home by that way.

We had a great time getting our passport, and almost lost our passage on account of it. It was at the public offices, having been taken by the police when we first arrived in Naples, as is the custom; and Mr. M. had to go back and forth from one place to another nearly the whole forenoon, without being able to obtain it. At length, almost the last half-hour had come, and still it had not been received. We were feeling very anxious and uneasy; for Nannine and I did not at all like the idea of staying alone in Naples, with her dear aunt and cousins gone, waiting several days for another boat. There was scarcely time left to reach the steamer, when, to our great relief, the passport arrived! We were obliged to drive very quickly to the wharf; and a rain came on at the same time, by which poor Mr. M. became wet. This, with the fatigue and hurry he had had in going about the city so much in the morning, not having been very well before, helped to bring on an illness after he went back to Sorrento; and he was very seriously ill for some time, greatly to our sorrow, after all his kindness to us.

We arrived home in safety without any further adventures, and were happily welcomed after our month's absence.

21

CHAPTER VI.

SUMMER AT HOME.

JUNE 12.—The rest of this summer we remain at home, and are too glad not to have to pack and unpack any more, and to be moving about from place to place! But Gianina and her papa and mamma are going to have their turn a little while. They have gone to Assili, taking the baby with them (for he is not yet weaned), to spend a week with the prince and princess, who have many times before invited them; but they have never yet been. The prince and his family have been spending some weeks at this villa this season, and are now going to Assili to stay a little while at the country house which they have among the mountains. Gianina goes for company to the little Donna Francesca, who enjoys her companionship very much. . . .

While they were gone, little Memie was as charming as she could be: she was so docile and affectionate, that it was a pleasure to have the care of her. For her little sake, and for Nannine's, that they might be out

in the fresh open air as much as possible, we planned
a little picnic one afternoon, inviting some young lady
friends to go with us; and went to the Villa Malini,
which is near St. Peter's.

It is so pleasant there! shady with trees; and
there is a beautiful view of the city. We picked
flowers, and made wreaths, and laughed and chatted,
and spread our supper out on the grass, and enjoyed it
all so much!

July. — Since we have all come home (for the party
returned from the mountains after a pleasant visit), and
have begun lessons again, little Memie has commenced
school for the first time; for she is now four years old,
and quite large enough to begin. She will make a fine
little scholar, but cannot do much yet, and stays only
a part of the time. Lately she has received her first
little letter all to herself, which Anna's grandpapa
wrote to her from America, and with which she was
very much pleased. We went to the Villa Borghese
to spend the afternoon the day it came, and she kept
it in her little hand all the way.

I must tell a little incident of Memie which occurred
this summer, and which, in so young a child, appeared
to us very thoughtful and interesting. I had received
letters from home containing information of the loss of
a dear relative, and was reading them to the children's
mamma, who came into my room with little Memie. *She,*

however, seemed to be playing about, and we did not suppose she was paying any attention to the letters we were reading; but, when her mamma went away, Memie would not go. She wished to stay; and as I was going to lie down a little while, feeling quite indisposed, she came and lay down by me in the most sympathizing little manner, and asked if she should tell me some stories. Then she began, and went on in her little child-like way, — precisely as if she were a grown person, — trying to divert me, and to dissipate my sad thoughts! It seemed to me quite surprising that so small a child should comprehend and know so well what to do, when we had not thought she was observing at all what we were talking about. It shows how early children may begin to be kind and thoughtful for others. . . .

This summer, Nannine, Gianina, and Memie all went with me every morning early to the beautiful Villa Medici, adjoining the Pincio, where we spent a couple of hours, and returned home before the shade had gone from the street. Mrs T. brought her children there too, — Cora and Eddie and Hubert; and we had very pleasant times, — they playing, she and I walking up and down, and chatting. The villa is composed of shady avenues, and was a very cool and lovely place. The T.'s were the only American family then remaining in the city besides ourselves; so that we would have *had* to enjoy each other's society, even if we did not fall in so pleasantly together! They came very often to our house, and we went there; and the children were admirable companions. Cora sometimes studied with Nannine and Gianina.

About five o'clock, we went into the garden and spent an hour or two, walked about the villa, or went up through the vineyards to Monticello, a favorite hill, or mound, in the villa, from which there was a lovely view. It was planted on the top with a circle of cypresses and pines, making within a pretty little retreat: in the centre of it was a colossal sitting statue of marble, which several years ago was found buried in the ground somewhere in the vicinity, and was placed here. This hill was always a favorite walk of the nurse Pina with the children.* The children spent a great deal of their time now in the garden in picking flowers. They gathered, in abundance, roses and other flowers, and carried them — their aprons or frocks full — up stairs, and got the good Theresa to make them into wreaths for them. She made such elegant wreaths! Then they put them on, and wore them till bedtime; and they really looked very beautiful. Even Memie had to have her wreath too, and it came to be quite an *institution.*

---

* We are sorry to say, that by the recent encroachments of a *rail-road*, the first in Rome, this lovely spot has become quite despoiled.

July 16. — We enjoy these long summer days very much.

There has never been so much time before for the girls' lessons. They commence now at nine, and study till half-past one: and we are in hopes they will be able to continue this all through next winter, for they have many things to attend to; otherwise some of them would get crowded out. Having the languages to keep up, in reading at least, besides other lessons that children usually learn, arithmetic, history, geography, etc., takes a great deal of time. Nannine commenced German last winter, learning to read and pronounce it, which makes her fourth language; and Gianina has her three to attend to. It is true, these are comparatively easy to them, and do not require of them the same amount of time that they would from children differently situated, as they have them in constant use.

In the afternoon I read a while to them, and they sew. They are each making a shirt, which they will give to the poor old man in the Quattro Fontane. The book which we have taken up for the hot weather, thinking it would be *cooling*, is Dr. Kane's "Visit to the Arctic Regions." Of course, all the statistics and very hard parts are omitted; those would be rather too tedious for them: but I read all the narrative portions, and they are much interested. We had before read a part of Capt. Ross's "Voyages to the North Pole."

Another book, which was enjoyed very much this summer, particularly by Gianina, was the "Little Duke," a story by Miss Sewall, founded on an historical fact. Gianina was perfectly fascinated with it, and wished it read aloud two or three times; and then she read it over several times herself. Nannine's pet book at this time, which she read by herself, was the " Wide, Wide World." . . .

Since the weather has become very hot, we have given up going to the Pincio or to the Villa Medici in the mornings, and, instead, go down into the garden before breakfast. Except driving once a week or so to some villa, we stay now mostly in our own villa: for there have been several cases of scarlet-fever in the city; and their papa and mamma are unwilling to have the children go abroad much to become exposed to it. . . .

Nothing especial happened out of the usual course this summer but some dancing-lessons. The two girls had never taken any; and their mamma procured a young lady to come to the house twice a week and teach them. The next winter, there was a larger class which met at the lady's house, when they were taught all kinds of pretty figures.

I have forgotten to mention that Memie had her portrait taken the last spring. Either her mamma or I went always with her to sit for it: and we had to contrive all sorts of ways to keep her sufficiently quiet; sometimes reading to her; sometimes telling her stories, or showing her pictures, etc. But we succeeded quite well, and she made a pretty little picture. In the course of the next fall and spring, her sisters had theirs taken; and they, of course, sat as proper as could be, — for they were really quite large then, — one of us reading to them during the time, however, to while away the hour.

Sept. 18. — We have passed through the summer without the illness of any one, excepting poor little Memie, who for the last fortnight has had the *tertiana* very severely, and the more so for its being double, — two distinct fevers, each coming in its turn every other day, making an attack of fever every day. She had always been a very healthy child. A little attack of sickness which she had about a week before was almost her first complaint of any kind, and that may only have been a premonitory symptom. But the fever is diminishing daily, and we hope it may soon disappear. . . .

In October, we went to Civita Vecchia for the sea air on Memie's account, thinking it would do her good after her attack of fever. The others were all very well; but their papa thought we had better all go, and so he sent off the whole family! We enjoyed the sea air greatly: it was delightful. We often went to the shore and picked up shells, and spent almost all the time out in the open air. We had no books with us, no lessons; only Gianina and Nannine practised their music an hour every morning. The English consul was very polite, and offered them the use of his piano. He had no family: so we could go into his parlor, and they could practise without disturbing any one. They were at this time learning a little duet, which they soon played very nicely. It was their first together, though they had been practising music some time. Each began when she was six years old, and played regularly every day: they were both quite fond of music. . . .

At the end of ten days, the sea air not seeming to improve Memie's health very much, we returned to Rome; and, as soon as the cold weather came on, she became quite well again.

SIXTH YEAR.

CHAPTER I.

BIRTHDAY PARTY.

WEDNESDAY, November.

YESTERDAY was Gianina's birthday, and we had a fine frolic. There were a dozen children invited to play in the afternoon; and we had games, — "Hunt the Squirrel," "Handkerchief burns," and "Cat and Mouse." In the midst of them, Cousin *Wilhelm* came in; a very tall young gentleman, who had come to spend the winter in Rome. He was here the other evening; and I had engaged to go to walk with him on Tuesday, entirely forgetting there was to be a birthday party. I had sent him a note in the mean time, but which, however, he did not receive: so when he came according to agreement, instead of the walk, he joined us in our plays. It was very funny to see him with his long limbs diving down under the hands, and plunging across the circle in and out, in hot pursuit of some child or other, or closely pursued by one! We had a very merry time of it.*

After the games came ice-creams and the birthday cake with a ring. The ring was found by a little English boy in his slice of cake. The cake was frosted over, and had on the top the little girl's name and age written in letters of sugar, and looking very handsome. Around the cake were eight little wax candles lighted, according to the German custom; a candle for every year of the child's age. They looked very pretty lighted around the cake, being fastened to the plate each by a bit of clay. They took the children's fancy more than any thing else; and they were allowed to burn after the cake was eaten, until they were consumed. . . .

After the preceding letter was written, this note was added: "I have given the account of the party for little Anna, thinking she would like to hear it. Dear little girl! how I should like to see her!" *Little* girl! no longer *very* little, as the following anecdote would seem to show. At the last birthday accounts, she was six; but, in this anecdote I am going to copy, she was

---

* It is hoped that the "cousin," although now arrived to the dignity of a professor, in looking back upon this bit of *abandon,* will enjoy the remembrance of it as much as it added to our pleasure at the time; it giving the greatest zest to the children's plays to have this *tall gentleman* taking part in them.

six and a half years old. The incident had taken place in the summer, when she and Tommy were visiting at their grandpapa's; Tommy being then but little more than three years of age. Their aunt wrote, "I went one night, in their mother's absence, to put them to bed. After Anna had said her little hymns, we fell into a conversation about the birds, &c.; Tommy wishing to know, if he were a bird, would he have feathers? and adding, 'If I was a turkey, wouldn't I gobble?' Then we talked of who made the birds, and who made themselves; Tommy asserting quite boldly that God did not make him. Anna said, 'Tommy is changed very much from what he used to be. If you asked him who made him, he would answer, "God;" who made mother and father, he would answer, "God," so lovingly and affectionately! but now, if you ask him, he says God didn't make him!'

"Tommy quite held his own; till finally I left them, and sat down by the window, telling them to go to sleep. Tommy kept on talking to himself; till at last he made this declaration, very quietly, — 'The birds made me, and — God helped 'em.'" A curious way, truly, of getting out of his difficulty! But he was such a little fellow then!

Their mamma wrote me at the same time, "Anna pulled out her letter-drawer the other day to pick out her letters from Rome, and enjoyed reading them again as much as if they had been new ones; especially Nannine's, which is so nicely printed. And the little sylph, too, she got out to show to Tommy."

The letter of Nannine here alluded to was one of her first ones; for, of course, she could now write running-hand very well. The little sylph was a very small paper-doll, which Nannine had drawn on thin paper, and cut out herself, and sent to Anna in a letter. Anna had sent back word that she was very much pleased with it.

One of Nannine's pet occupations at this time was the drawing and cutting of paper-dolls. She had passed through the doll's phase, when dolls were all in all; then the fairy phase, when every thing, — all her leisure time, — from morning to night, was fairies. They were amusing, — the secrets she and her sister had together about the fairies: they could not even whisper so and so, — "the fairies wouldn't like it!" They spoke, thought, dreamed, and lived fairies. Then came on the "Chinese" phase. Nannine had a most absurd taste for acting "Chinese," as she called it. What it meant one could scarcely tell, and probably she knew not herself; but it was as much as any thing like the droll little Chinese figures that are shaken into all sorts of attitudes. This amusement worked itself off after a while, and then she took to making paper-dolls. She had always been very fond of drawing, and now she drew and cut out dolls very nicely. A year or two later, she cut and painted really very beautiful ones.

The spring after Nannine was seven years old, she had quite a fit of philosophizing: she used to say very odd things; and one little conversation that I took down at the time (I thought it *so* peculiar!) comes in quite appropriately here.

"It seems to me," she said in a musing tone, "we are all dreaming: we are not real persons; there are no real things. It must be a dream: it can't be real."

"It seems to *me*," I said, "that we are very real persons, with real flesh and bones."

"Yes; but, in our dreams, we dream also of real flesh and blood. I think, that, when we wake up from *this* dream, we shall find it was all nothing."

"But," said I, "I do not suppose we should dream in our dreams of real flesh and blood if we did not have such really."

"Oh! it must be so: we can't be any thing. When that great change comes, we shall see that there was not any thing; that it was all nothing. We are only cut out of paper, — flexible paper. The animals are earth, and we are paper.

"How silly I am!" she said, looking up and smiling; "but I do think we are all dreaming, and in the end we shall find it so."

People "cut out of paper!" — like paper-dolls! — with this difference, however, — a very grand one too, — that *we* have life, which is not bestowed upon "only" paper-dolls!

CHAPTER II.

WINTER OCCUPATIONS.

DEC. 14. — We have had in the parlor this evening a great wood-fire, making splendid hot coals. It was a fire good enough for a New-England winter's evening. Although the day was cold, it was very fine, and the too girls and I took a very long walk out of the Porta San Giovanni; or rather Gianina and I walked together, and Nannine was on a donkey, which she rides of late, on account of some little weakness in her ankles. She cantered on far before us with her donkey-man. We stopped at the Church of St. John Lateran, which is one of the largest and handsomest in Rome. It was most beautifully illuminated inside with thousands of candles in chandeliers and other pretty forms. There has been a great festa held in the church for the whole week past. . . .

All this winter, Nannine generally rode instead of walking. Her ankles had become quite weakened, partly from her growing fast; and it was concluded by her parents, that if we went to Paris in the spring, on our way to America, as was now talked of, we should stop there long enough to have them attended to by a good surgeon.

Mamma wished to have the Christmas festival this year quite handsome: so a great many persons were invited, and we were busy gilding nuts, and oranges, &c., to hang upon the tree, and in making streamers, and putting on the candles, — two hundred candles.

The presents for each person were to be drawn by numbers.

Many beautiful *bonbonnières* were sent in for presents, to be placed on the tree. There were some really lovely things. But those that were drawn were mostly very simple (for it was a very large party to provide for), although they were all very cunning. I should like to carry home a whole trunkful of these pretty things, such as they have at Carnival-time, etc.

The evening passed off very pleasantly. Memie had a present of a very big doll, almost as large as herself; and it was about as much as she could do to carry it round. She was now large enough to enjoy the occasion as well as her sisters; and dear baby — quite a large one now, but still in his little white frocks — was brought in for a little while, to be *looked at.* He of course, in his turn, looked about, and saw all that he could or wished.

Nannine has just had her tenth birthday. Last year she had quite an idea of celebrating *Rollo's* birthday, which she found, by his books, came just the day before her own.

On the seventeenth day of this month occurs one of the prettiest of the Roman festivals, that of St. Agnes. The church of that name is prettily trimmed with gay-colored hangings. After mass is over, two of the loveliest little snow-white lambs are brought forward. They are very young, round, and fat; in fact, just of the prettiest age: and, having always been taken care of from their birth, their little soft wool is as clean as possible, and as white as down. They are decorated with a pretty ribbon around the neck, and are placed on a red silk cushion. Lying down on it, with their little innocent — *lamb-like,* as we say — expression, they do look very cunning and beautiful. In this way they are carried to the altar, and there they are conse-crated.

They are afterwards carefully kept until they are sufficiently old to be shorn, and out of their fleece is made the cloth for a particular part of the vestments of the cardinals.

The church where this ceremony is held is named for the martyr St. Agnes.

During this season, I read aloud to Nannine and

Gianina a book which interested them deeply. It was
when the evenings had become longer; and, if we had
not time before tea, we would read an hour or so afterwards. They were never willing to retire until they
had had this reading; for it became extremely interesting. It was a story of the times of the early Christians in Rome, when most of the people were still
followers of the old religion of the country, — that of
gods and goddesses. The principal heroine was such;
and although her intimate friends, the young, lovely
Agnes and Cecilia, became Christian, she made no approach to it. Even her lover, the noble St. Sebastian,
who was afterwards martyred, pierced with many arrows, could not persuade her to leave their old philos-
ophy and dreams. Sebastian was an officer in the
household of the emperor, whose palace was on the
Palatine Hill, near the Coliseum; but the emperor
himself was still of the heathen religion. The windows of Sebastian's chamber looked directly upon the
Coliseum; and he could often hear the roar of the wild
animals which were confined there, to be let loose
upon the victims that were to be martyred. He, like
all the other Christians, had to keep his belief very quietly to himself; but, by his pure and holy faith, he was
always preparing his mind to be ready to meet the
time when he, too, should be called upon to confess
himself, and perhaps to give up his life. That time

came; and so it did to the sweet Agnes and Cecilia; and they all very faithfully and beautifully died in testimony to our divine religion. Only at length when these friends had all been taken from her, and her brother even had become Christian, did that heathen lady, the heroine, become so too. Even the children in those days had to live, as it were, between life and death. There was a little boy who had to struggle manfully against the boys in the street. He was sent to carry the bread of the holy sacrament to the house of a sick person, because it was thought that he, a child, would not be suspected or molested for being a Christian: so it was fastened on his breast, and his jacket buttoned over it. When he had gone a little way in the street, the boys, however, began to follow, and soon attacked him. He resisted most bravely, knowing the precious secret he had within, and kept his hands tightly over his chest to preserve the bread from being lost or touched. He was a noble little hero, and his faithfulness was rewarded by his being able to escape safely with his trust.*   After Nannine and Gianina began to study history, in coming across any new people of whom they had not heard before,

---

* Although the book above referred to was in its composition a fiction, it is presumed that the historical incidents on which it was founded are correct; at least, no doubt, similar ones were constantly occurring.

their first question always was, "Were they Christians?"

This last year, the two girls attended the catechising which the minister of the English Church where we attended held in the vestry on Saturday afternoons. Every Sunday also, after the morning service, they studied the catechism with their mamma. Then, before tea, they all walked up and down the long avenues in the garden, repeating the hymns they had learned during the day, and other of their favorite hymns. This was one of the pleasantest hours of the week, they thought, they all enjoyed it so much!

A dear aunt had given to each of the two girls a prayer-book and Bible of a convenient size to carry to church, which they valued very much; and on Sunday mornings they came out of their room, already dressed, fresh and neat, for church, with their little Bible in their hands, and busied themselves with it until breakfast-time. The house was at some distance from the church; and we had to go soon after breakfast was over, if we walked: sometimes we rode. After they had their own books, Nannine and Gianina learned to find the different places themselves, and were able to join in the responses. Gianina's voice was usually heard, quietly joining with her mamma's in the chants. Both the sisters sang some hymns very nicely.

CHAPTER III.

LAST VISITS.

IT was at length decided that the family should go home on a visit; it being now nearly six years since they had last been in America. Therefore a part of the remaining time was spent in going over old places; and making last visits to the picture-galleries, and to the Vatican, with its hundreds and hundreds of beautiful statues arranged in noble halls. There is the most beautiful of all statues, — the Apollo Belvidere; and there, too, is the famous Laocoön, the father with his two sons being strangled by a serpent. The many statues in the Vatican Gallery are a whole world by themselves.

We visited also the fine old ruins of temples and baths, which are very numerous, and make the city of Rome deeply interesting, because they show us what it was in ancient times. We visited the Capitol and the Via Sacra, along which passed triumphal processions, — conquerors with their chariots and milk-white steeds, drawing after them the captives taken in battle; and the terrible prison on the way, where prisoners were immured, — the same in which the poor African Prince Jugurtha died.*

This prison still remains, and we went into it. It is low in the ground, dark and chilly. In it also St. Paul, it is believed, was imprisoned, and perhaps St. Peter.

Close beside it is the Forum, where noble speeches were made; where Cicero and Brutus perhaps often spoke, and roused the people to patriotism, and love of liberty. These were the virtues which were famed in Rome in its early days, in the times of the republic, before bad emperors and tyrants had sway, and before the city became spoiled by luxury, and love of dominion; for then ambitious men sprang up, who themselves wished to rule, and who often desolated the country with civil war. Civil war! brothers fighting against brothers; citizens of the same city or country fighting against each other! What a dreary thought! How could the world bear it, unless some good was to come of it in the end? There would be, it is to be hoped, this good at least, — people would experience how sad and sorrowful such suffering was, and so turn from it, and desire never to pass through it again. If war is necessary, we must be brave-hearted and courageous enough to endure it at all events, let come what will; but may we try to avoid it whenever it is possible!

* See the companion volume.

Oh, how far I have wandered from my subject! But these remarks seemed applicable to the present moment, when we also in America have been suffering from "civil war." . . .

Feb. 13. — We had a long, pleasant ramble this afternoon, Gianina and myself, to the Baths of Titus, afterwards to the Coliseum. They are near each other. These ruins of the Baths of Titus are very extensive, consisting of many rooms. Some are small and square, resembling those of Pompeii; only the ceilings are arched. There are some with niches in them, where statues were placed; and when these baths were first opened, some years ago, — for most of these ruins were for many years buried under ground, — statues were still found there, which have been placed in the Vatican Gallery.

In these ruins there are many long passages and noble halls. I suppose all the walls of these were originally beautifully painted; for some of the fresco painting still remains, of a rich red color, and shows how handsome these rooms of the baths must have been in their day. Now they have nothing but the bare ground for a floor, and the open sky for a roof; yet they are so picturesquely decorated here and there, with green shrubbery and trailing plants, that they are exceedingly beautiful, and interesting places to visit.

CHAPTER IV.

CARNIVAL.

CARNIVAL was a very merry season to us this year. We had a large balcony, and occupied it almost constantly. There was a good deal of company besides, including two young gentlemen, relatives of the family, who had been spending the winter with us. They thought the Carnival very fine; and they made our balcony very gay and lively. There was a lady in the balcony opposite, in whom these young gentlemen were very much interested. She was throwing flowers and *confetti* with all her might upon the passers-by in the street: and *they* threw some splendid bouquets across to her; at least, they tried to do so; but, being so large and heavy, the bouquets *would* drop into the street. At last a *railway* was contrived, which was very successful. From one balcony to the other were stretched cords, which could be slipped along, and on these was placed a basket filled with articles; then the bouquets and other things passed back and forth very briskly.

One gentleman of our acquaintance acted a very funny character. He was in the street below, and was dressed in bright costume, very round in appearance,— Falstaff-like, — to represent a *rooster.* He stood under our balcony, and crowed, stretching up his neck, and looking exactly like a rooster. The crowing was to be his signal to attract our attention; otherwise we never should have known him, he looked so ludicrously strange. It was very amusing to see him come looking up, crowing to us, and then throwing up bouquets, and catching some which were thrown to him! One of the things he tossed up was the prettiest little muff, made of plush, just large enough for a doll, and filled, of course, with sugar-plums.

March. — The time is now set for our leaving. We shall go to Paris in a fortnight, which will be about the 1st of April. . . .

During this fortnight, we drove round to various places for one more visit. One afternoon, a day or two before we came away, Nannine went with me to the Campagna, taking a basket with us to get once more some daisies, Marguerites, which she was very fond of gathering. We went to Mons Sacer, — a green mound, which, in the spring, is covered with daisies, like all the rest of the Campagna. This was the Sacred Mount, so famous in ancient times for the Secession of the Plebeians, as it was called; when after various attempts and controversies, and being deprived of their rights by the aristocracy, — the ruling power then, — the people deliberately moved out of the city, and took up their abode at this place, about three miles distant. It must have been like a swarm of bees going out of their hive, and settling on some place or other in a great black mass! only this was a more serious matter: and the senate, or ruling power, felt quite alarmed when they saw the people going off in this manner. They appointed commissioners to go out to Mons Sacer, and try to bring them back. But no one succeeded, until Menenius Agrippa, who had himself been a plebeian, but was now a great and honored man, beloved by both the people and the senators, attempted to speak to them. He told them the fable, which is celebrated on that account, and with which all are familiar, — of the members of the body wishing to set up for themselves, and to have nothing more to do for the stomach, for which only they had been working, as they fancied. Menenius showed them plainly how impossible this was; that when the members forsook the digestive organ, and gave it no food or nourishment, it began to pine, but they also pined with it; the feet became languid, the hands nerveless, the teeth unable to chew; in fact, every thing was out of joint, and lifeless. For the stomach supplies life to the limbs and members, as well as the limbs

and members provide food for it: thus all are mingled together, one as good as another; all are equally
necessary and useful; and each must do its part and its
own work, and then all will go on harmoniously and
well.

The plebeians were persuaded and convinced by this
reasoning and fable of Menenius Agrippa, and they
concluded to return to the city. The senators also
made some concessions, and granted them officers
called "tribunes of the people," who should look particularly after their affairs, and allow them their rightful
demands.

We might take this same lesson to heart in modern
times, and in our own countries: namely, that all should
live peaceably together, no one portion rebelling or
striving against another, but each being kindly consid-
erate and just, the people to each other and to their
rulers, and the rulers also to the people; then all
would go on harmoniously, happily, and well.

CHAPTER V.

STORY OF THE OLD MAN.

ONE morning in the last summer, while Nannine and I were walking in the villa, we noticed an old man among the hedges, picking leaves. We rather wondered how he came there, but did not say any thing to him. A morning or two afterwards, we saw him again. Then we went up and spoke to him, and found that he could not use his right arm much; for it had been a little paralyzed. He could hold but a light bundle in that hand; and with his left he was gathering ivy-leaves, and putting them into his handkerchief. It seems that the ivy-leaves were used in some manufacture; and he had had permission to come into the villa and pick them, for he was very poor. His clothing was very ragged: his jacket, in tatters, hung over his shoulders. We soon made acquaintance with him, and found that he was all alone, his wife and daughter being dead, and his two sons far away; his clothes also being so poor, he could not or did not go to church. This was early in the week. We told him to come in a day or two, and we would have something ready to make him more comfortable, and enable him to go to church on Sunday. There happened to be a piece of merino cloth in the house, which would make a very nice vest: so we took one belonging to the children's papa for a pattern, and went to work, and had it completed before he came. It fitted him nicely, and he looked quite respectable in it.

The next week he was to come again. Mamma and I, in the mean time, had made two strong shirts, which were all ready; and we took them into the garden, expecting to see him; but he was not there. The days passed, and he did not come; weeks went on, but we saw him no more, and gave up all expectation of ever seeing him again.

One day, Mary, the baby's nurse, was giving an account of a miserable old man whom she had seen sitting on a stone in the villa, a few days before, when she was drawing the baby in his little carriage. He looked so poor and comfortless, she said, that she pitied him very much, and had thought of him a great deal since. Then we asked her more particularly about him; and, as she described him, Nannine and I exclaimed, "Why, that is our old man that we have been looking for so long!" We asked her why she had not brought him to the house; and begged her, if she should see him again, to have him stop. Before a great while, she saw him; and he told her that he had been sick, and had been taken to the hospital; which was the reason that he had not come, as we had expected him to do, to get the things we had prepared for him. Then Mary appointed a day for him to come again.

In the mean time, as we had given away the shirts we had made, we went to work and made some more, and some other garments also; and the children's mamma sent to a tailor's, and had a good stout suit of clothes made for him (for it was coming winter), and she had some socks and shoes for him that were their papa's. His vest was still looking tidy, and he got somewhere for himself a sugar-loaf hat such as the peasants wear; and, when he was dressed up, you would not have known him to be the same man! He looked bright and spirited, and fully ten years younger; for he was not very old, — only he had looked so in his poverty and lameness. Neither was he very lame: he only limped a little, or rather dragged his right foot a little; for that, as well as his arm, was affected with the paralysis.

He was very careful of these new clothes, and kept them for Sundays and holidays, and when he wished to go into the street looking particularly well. But generally he came to his work in the mornings in his old suit: his new under-garments, however, we made him wear all the time, and change them every week, that they might be clean and nice. He had very little to eat at home: so we told him to come every Saturday morning and get a good breakfast. He came and sat down on a stone in the villa, and we carried it out to him, — a bowl of hot chocolate, or tea, or coffee, as it happened to be, with milk, and well sweetened with sugar; and some slices of bread and butter, and ham perhaps, or other cold meat, to eat with it. All winter, he came and had his breakfast every Saturday morning. Nannine and I were always on hand to have it there ready for him. Then we gave him a loaf of bread, or a bag of pease or beans to take home for the week, or a paul * or two to help him to buy what he needed.

With what a relish he swallowed that bowlful of coffee or tea! He was as eager to take it as a child to take its drink; and he was such a grateful creature, he never could seem to utter thanks enough. " *Mille grazie! mille grazie! grazia tanto!* " he would say again and again.

We would sometimes meet him in the street, or standing in a shop-door, with his best clothes on, and looking very respectable. Then he would bow very politely, and look very smiling and happy.

It was, of course, a sad thing to this old man that we were going away so soon; and we felt so sorry for him! He would do very well now, because the sum-

---

* A paul is a ten-cent piece.

mer was coming on; but we wondered what he would do another winter, and if he would find any one to look after him. We could only trust that a good Providence would raise up somebody to take care of him.

The morning that we came away, although we set out very early, he was at the door to bid us good-by. He had said he must see the " Contessa " again, as he always called the children's mamma. When the carriage drove off, the tears rolled down his cheeks like rain, and he wept like a child.

Poor old man, how we pitied him! . . .

The family now bade adieu to Rome for a time. They spent a month in Paris, Nannine having the advice that was necessary, and eventually becoming strong again.

We sailed in the steamer from Havre, and arrived in New York the latter part of May.

23

APPENDIX.

ACROSTIC CHARADES.

THE game of charades, which has been given in this volume, becomes a very entertaining one when two or three or more persons are seated around to compose a charade together, or to discover the answers to one. In either case, the search for the words and for definitions is often very amusing. But the author has thought that the following list of charades already formed might be acceptable to many who have become interested in the game.

The key to these, and to those in the preceding part of this work, is given in the companion volume, "Fairies of our Garden: Roman Stories."

7.

1. An article of apparel for ladies and babies, boys and men.
2. A river of Italy.
3. Beautiful on the ocean.
4. Appanage of a bashaw.
5. Two vowels.
6. Latin word for a monarch.

> Two famous horsemen,
> Now in the heavens.

8.

1. Singular, eccentric.
2. A delicious fruit of September.
3. The whole.
4. Something always on the tea-table.
5. What we do when we are very much amused.
6. The origin of yawns.

> Magic words, and
> The place of their delivery.

9.

1. A serpent or snake of the sea.
2. A syllable doubled, forming a pretty diminutive.
3. A part of a book and of a tree.
4. An organ of sense.
5. A favorite opera.

> A heroine and a hound; " they were
> such playmates."

10.

1. A playful domestic animal.
2. The wandering lady of a poetic legend.
3. Indispensable to the wood-yard.
4. Intimately connected with the thread of *the Fates.*

> A domestic animal, and
> Its supporters.

11.

1. A gun extensively manufactured.
2. A formidable sound in a forest.

3. A river in South America.
4. White and feathery.
5. The "father's hope."

> The second, the reward of the first:
> The one not without the other.

12.

1. "A city of palm-trees."
2. A transatlantic mountain range.
3. A small English coin.
4. A religion.
5. A boy's toy.
6. A French participle.
7. A distinguished Western general.

> A famous ancient ruler and his abode.

13.

1. A tall forest-tree.
2. A negative.
3. A verb of two letters.
4. Uncivil in company.
5. Troublesome to rulers.
6. Refreshing in summer.
7. A geographical division.
8. *New* in an ancient language.

> A shepherd and a visitor.

14.

1. A child's first lisping.
2. A noise of a dog.

3. A small number.
4. A place of meeting.
5. A bird of the night.
6. A negative.

A foe and its infant conqueror.

15.

1. Used by painters.
2. A passion of the human heart.
3. A French adverb of place.
4. An ancient race of Northern Europe.
5. " The long-drawn *aisle* and fretted vault."
6. Consummation of hope.
7. A conjunction, both Latin and French.
8. A production of forests and of gardens.
9. A style of verse.

A famed queen and a courtier.

16.

1. The " *wheel* of Fortune."
2. A city of the West Indies.
3. A place of accommodation in travelling.
4. An important European race.
5. An early British queen.
6. One kind of puzzle.
7. Name of a beverage.
8. An English dramatist.
9. An ecclesiastical order in the times of the apostles.

An emblem, and a British royal family.

17.

1. A title, abbreviated in writing.
2. A bird with bright plumage.
3. A part of the United-States forces.
4. Two vowels.
5. A simple weapon used in ancient warfare.
6. A town of the Society Islands.
7. One of the Eastern continents.
8. A Scottish chieftain.
9. A French word in the plural for one of the most important organs of sense.

> A religious institution, and
> The French name of its occupants.

18.

1. A conjunction.
2. An animal of the Andes.
3. A portion of time.
4. Native place of the lion.
5. One of the fine arts.
6. A fashionable young lady.
7. Good for cisterns.
8. A species of tapestry.

> A palace and its founders.

19.

1. A sudden knock.
2. A quarter of the world.
3. Half of pies.
4. A domestic fowl.

5. A preposition of two letters.
6. Signifying to be eaten.
7. A king with three daughters,

       An artist and his profession.

20.

1. A well-known Greek letter.
2. Valuable in a storm at sea.
3. A parent.
4. Part of a wheel.
5. A term used in law often.
6. A carriage used in Russia.
7. One of Walter Scott's heroines.
8. Famous in Dutch painting.

       Useful in European languages, and
       Its originators.

21.

1. A bird's home.
2. " To *err* is human ; to forgive, divine."
3. A medley.
4. To guard, to muse.
5. What we should live for.
6. A woman frequent in Roman-Catholic countries.
7. One of the cardinal points of the compass.

       A lord of the sea, and
       The insignia of his power.

22.

1. An English king.
2. An old city of Europe.

3. A preposition of two letters.

'4. A small French coin.

5. A small tool.

6. A style of writing.

7. One of the planets.

8. One of Cooper's novels.

9. Something used in schools and in house-building.

A class of warriors, and their object.

23.

1. A city of Palestine.

2. Name of mountains in Asia.

3. A heathen deity.

4. Refreshing in summer.

5. Sorrow's relief.

6. Two first letters of a character in one of Longfellow's poem's.

7. A heroine in the Waverley novels.

A famous ancient king, and

A product from his brain.

24.

1. A German pianist of celebrity.

2. The name of a series of books for children.

3. Meaning the whole.

4. Empty.

5. Part of the roof of a house.

6. Moderately warm.

7. A French personal pronoun.

8. What the teeth do.

9. An early favorite of Queen Elizabeth.

A poem and its author.

25.

1. To commit a dishonest act; also the first half of a boy's name.
2. To be indisposed.
3. A very common abbreviation of two letters.
4. A domestic fowl.
5. Assistance.
6. A measuring instrument.
7. A little girl's toy.

> A prisoner, and a friend
> In need.

26.

1. What mariners love to see in nearing port.
2. Where Pluto picked up his wife.
3. Common in some countries after dinner.
4. Famed for curiosity.
5. What every lad likes to have.
6. A verb that shouldn't be used with *had*.
7. Name of a female novelist.
8. What a brave soldier never shuns.

> An ancient queen and her work.

27.

1. Used in sorcery.
2. What Osceola was taken in.
3. A lion's relation.
4. A Trojan princess; or, the " Young Peri of the West."
5. Name of an American poet.
6. A pastoral poem.
7. A Hebrew prophetess.

> The two names of a well-known Roman matron.

28.

The following is very ingenious:—

The word is a vegetable production of certain islands in the
Pacific Ocean.

In an acrostic from the first line will be the name.

The second line, an important State in the Union.

The third line, an important European race.

The fourth line, a celebrated lake in the United States.

The fifth line will be the name spelt backwards.

The name forms the boundary on all sides; descending, ascending, forwards and backwards.

NOTE TO PAGE 187.

Since this little work was in type, the author has been much impressed with a striking illustration of the effect of the Bible upon civilization in the case of English history, as was introduced in a course of lectures on English literature from the earliest times (Parlor Lectures, delivered by Mrs. M. T. Richards, to the high character of whose writings the writer is happy thus to testify).

Literature, in general, had been beyond the mass of the people, even after the invention of printing, until the translation of the Bible into the genuine, simple Anglo-Saxon tongue (the language of the common people), without admixture of foreign or abstruse elements, gave something which could penetrate to every individual heart and fireside, yielding a new impulse to thought and feeling, — an impetus even in learning to read itself; since there was now that which the humblest as well as the learned could embrace and comprehend.

There seemed to be needed a volume, simple, and of universal application, which would thus come home to all, to bring the art of printing, which had then existed for a hundred years, into a living reality, as it were, — an art of every-day use. The Bible was that book, and it had such direct effect upon mental cultivation; so that, from the era of its translation into the common tongue, the way was opened for other learning and acquisitions by the common people, and a spring and stimulus given to all progress, and hence to the rapid development of both civil and intellectual liberty.

Its influence has thus been, upon individuals and upon nations, not only religiously, but in other ways, to civilize and enlighten.

365

9 783337 420062